THE BENT BOX

A Novel By Mike Cranny

National Library of Canada Cataloguing In Publication Data

Cranny, Michael
    The Bent Box

    ISBN 978-0-9920349-2-4

    I. Title

A Cranberry Ridge Communications Publication:

Michael Cranny
mcranny@shaw.ca

CHAPTER 1

Eight o'clock on an unseasonably chill west coast May morning. Archie Stevens, shaking off the effects of yet another bad night, parked his old 4Runner near the station's half-hidden back entrance. He got out, back-kicked the cab door shut, tried in vain not to spill the remains of an extra large black coffee and strode across the parking lot to the door, which is where Cal Fricke, the police chief and Archie's boss, intercepted him. Archie guessed he must have scowled, but if he did, Fricke didn't seem to notice. He shot Archie a *"what the hell happened to you"* look and jammed an opened envelope containing a single folded sheet of notepaper into his hand.

"This is addressed to you," Fricke said. "Read it."

Archie grunted, unfolded the note and read: *I put her bones in a bent box. It's now in the smallpox burial cave on Velasquez Island. Go get her, Archie. The sooner the better.*

He studied the paper—small, precise writing, good, thick stationary. Quality stuff. The cheap envelope with his name and the cop shop address typed on it came from a standard greeting card so nothing there. Archie thought the note a hoax and said so. Said a Detective Sergeant had better things to do. The fact the writer named him probably meant nothing, a name drawn from a hat.

"Who writes in fountain pen these days, Archie?" Fricke said.

"Some people. Not your average person, though," Archie said, wanting Fricke to be gone. "Not many people even write letters anymore."

"Well, there you go. You got a clue. You got a starting point."

"This is a prank. It's bullshit pure and simple, Cal, and I'm busy."

But Fricke insisted. Archie knew he wanted him out of the station anyway, wanted him solving crimes instead of stewing in his office, obsessing and, in Fricke's words, "drifting towards your goddam dark side." This repeated more than once since Archie's recent return to duty. He dropped his coffee cup into a garbage can and turned to go.

"I got work," he said.

"Take somebody with you, Archie," Fricke said. "Ease back on the lone wolf stuff. There may be something to this, so treat it official."

"I don't intend to waste time and money, Cal."

"Do what you're told for once."

Fricke started to give him the talk, but Archie cut him off.

"I'm not paying for another detective out of my budget, not for this bullshit."

Fricke sighed.

"Have things your own way, Archie. Go alone and check things out and come back for a team if it's necessary."

So, okay, he was following orders and surprisingly happy to be alone on the water. The sixteen-foot aluminum boat he'd borrowed from Walter George was adequate but embarrassing, a metal-patched wreck painted in Walter's favorite colors, the Seattle Seahawks' blue-and-green. Archie motored the runabout into rougher water, passing pretty boats whose occupants stopped what they were doing to watch him fight the chop. An attractive woman waved at him from a luxury cruiser and yelled that he should come aboard to join her. He forced a smile, lifted a hand and carried on.

Once across the channel, he pointed the battered bow towards the bay closest to the place he thought the cave ought to be, crossed into calmer water and finally ran the metal keel up the narrow beach. He secured the painter to an overhanging branch near the water's edge, got out, pissed on the sea lettuce and gathered his gear. Then he found the trail he wanted and started upwards, checking his GPS. Half an hour later, he arrived at the cliff face, close to the burial cave.

His shaman Uncle Tony said the bones were from victims of a nineteenth-century smallpox epidemic that wiped out thousands of their people, too many to bury properly, and their internment had been hurried and incomplete, leaving the dead unhappy and confused. Tony offered to go along, to help. Archie had laughed at the very idea of confused spirits and evil things from the other world and said he didn't need a babysitter.

Now, at the cave mouth, Archie's first emotion was irritation. Someone had stuck a weathered skull on a broken sapling and the disrespect bothered him. Not the worst act of vandalism he'd seen, but close enough. The skull seemed old and not what he was looking for so he passed it by, ducked under a ledge of limestone and stepped into the darkness of the cavern.

Inside, the air reeked of earth and mice and old bone. The saltpeter-stained walls glowed like phosphorus. Archie pulled a mini-flashlight out of his pocket and flicked the switch, got a dimmed beam and remembered he had not charged the device. The yellow light picked out skulls on outcrops and sandstone ledges.

He edged deeper into the main chamber where the roof hung more than five feet over his head — a welcome expansion of space to a marginal claustrophobic. His beam illuminated natural alcoves in the fissured rock and, in them, femurs and ribs stacked like firewood. Some of the coffin boxes were little more than cedar dust, and miscellaneous small bones lay around the perimeter of the cave, light as air, green with age, crumbling away into the dirt. The dead abided there by the dozen. Archie remembered Tony's warning that he might trail other spirits out of the darkness, which meant little to Archie. The nature of his work involved trailing spirits after him — the ghosts of suicides and the murdered always followed him. He told Tony he was used to ghosts.

"Not like what I'm taking about, Archie."

"I'll be careful."

"Only one way for you to learn, and I hope the lesson isn't too painful."

"I got to go, Tony."

"I guess you do. Good luck."

At which point Tony turned away to face the sea, returning to the task of mending his nets in preparation for the upcoming salmon season.

Just as his claustrophobia started to get to him, Archie found what he was searching for—a traditional bent box in perfect condition lying longwise on a low rock shelf, its sides beautifully carved and painted. He knew from courses he'd taken at the university that the work was of the highest quality. Although it came from the north and not from his own people, Archie could read some of the symbols—frog clan, a chief's possession. He bumped the edge of the fitted top with the heel of his hand to loosen it.

Inside, the vault of a skull gleamed like fine porcelain in the amber glow. It nestled in an old Chilkat blanket, which, by itself, was undoubtedly worth a small fortune. He lingered a moment, intrigued by the richness and rarity of both blanket and box. But he didn't have a lot of time to think; his batteries were weak and failing. Worse, the mass of the stone above his head seemed ready to close in on him.

He considered his options. Moving the remains would violate good police procedure, plus custom and by law forbade taking anything from a sacred site. He reached in, his hands on either side of the cranium, fingertips on the smooth parietal bones, and flipped it face up. A small, rimmed, round hole above the eye made homicide a certainty. He sneezed and shook his head against a powerful miasma of must and death.

Archie let the skull settle back into its nest, slapped his light with the palm of his hand to shift the batteries but got only a brief flare. The darkness deepened and his head started to ache. Within seconds, he squeezed his right eye shut against the pain.

He replaced the lid and stood away to take one last look at the container. The faint illumination picked out an upside-down face resembling Mickey Mouse. Archie exhaled sharply. The "mouse" was the carved trademark of the famous nineteenth-century Haida master, Charlie Edenshaw. Archie slanted the beam to exaggerate the relief. If the box was an Edenshaw, then the situation became far more complicated than he ever supposed, like finding the body of a murder victim wrapped in an original Renoir.

His beam failed, flickered on weaker than before, and his borderline claustrophobia kicked in accompanied by a fierce headache. He pinched the bridge of his nose hard to try to stem the pain and stumbled outdoors. Once free of the cavern, he stopped, put his hands on his knees and waited for the migraine to pass. As he straightened, he noticed movement above him; something crossing the cliff top, displacing a shower of small stones that pattered into the thick Salal below—likely a deer or a cougar, Archie thought—but when he turned away a hard-thrown rock bounced off his shoulder and stung him, so the lurker was not an animal. Archie called out, identifying himself as a police officer, but this only resulted in him having to dodge a volley of rocks, some of which hit him. He reversed himself and shifted position while his attacker kept to the higher ground and did not show himself.

Archie moved his SIG Sauer pistol to his hoodie pocket and scanned the ground for his pack with his phone in it, but failed to locate it. And now, he heard a new sound, a droning, baritone cicada buzz vibrating the still air.

"Come out and talk," he said. "I'm not in the mood for games."

He figured the prankster might be a kid, or one of the crazy hippies who occasionally lived on the island, and he half-expected laughter, the joke over and now getting boring. When he called out again, another missile sang through the air. Instinctively, he twisted his body and threw himself sideways, but the object, thrown hard, grazed his forehead and made him stagger, and hot blood welled out from the bruised skin above his left eye. Off-balance and half-stunned, he jerked the

SIG out of his pocket and slammed the slide back. But the space around him was empty and silent.

He glanced down at the smooth, egg-shaped stone lying in the duff and realized, with a shock, that his attacker used a sling. Somebody good with such a weapon could easily kill him, so he eased back into the trees and out of the most likely line of fire to assess the damage. He touched the goose egg starting, felt the wet blood and the abrasion close to the eye.

The cicada hum returned, loud and low at first but rising to a shrill whistle, the sling gathering momentum and energy. Archie didn't hear or see the stone that knocked him down, but suddenly he was on his knees, in pain, losing consciousness.

When he opened his eyes, the sun had moved perceptibly. He checked his watch—thirty minutes gone. The fact that a sling stone brought him down puzzled him, but squatters, if there were any, probably lived on what they hunted and gathered, and a sling was a cheap weapon, albeit one requiring practice and skill.

He stood, moved his head to free the tension in his neck and back before he walked straight into the bush where he thought his attacker lay concealed, but found only some broken branches and crushed Salal. Continuing his search, he recovered his missing pack near the edge of a gravelly brook, although his things had been dumped out and scattered over a meter or two of moss, and his cell phone was gone.

His mind went to his transport, Walter's boat, his only way home. He didn't want to spend the night on the island, and he couldn't call in. He grabbed his pack and hurried to the beach where he'd left the craft and was relieved to find the blue and green aluminum sitting where it was supposed to be. His phone, now smashed, lay on the seat. Archie cursed his luck. He wanted to go but decided that after the attack he could not now leave the remains of the murder victim unattended and unprotected. He hurried back to the cave, unholstered the SIG, entered, found the box and opened it. The skull still gleamed in its nest. He lowered the lid and carried the coffin outside.

Half an hour later, with the box secured in the bow, he ran his boat to deeper water and jumped in. As soon as he cleared the shallows, he dropped the engine leg and pulled the starter. The motor coughed and chortled and then hummed. As he glanced one last time over his shoulder, a stocky figure appeared at the forest edge and quickly disappeared. Archie briefly considered returning but decided against it, at least not until the box was safe at headquarters. He checked his direction, set a course for Harsley harbor and twisted the throttle to full on.

CHAPTER 2

Cal Fricke kept his back to Archie, his antique sports jacket presenting a broad wall of Donegal tweed topped with a thin-haired, gray-fringed geological dome that was the back of his head. Archie tried to amuse himself by comparing it to rock types and settled on snowflake porphyry. He wanted out of there. Having briefed his boss on what occurred on the island, he was now wasting time waiting for a decision. At last, the mountain moved. Fricke grunted, turned to face Archie and scowled.

"Couldn't you just go to the site and scope things out like I wanted, Archie?" he said. "Now I got a skeleton in a box from a sacred burial place or whatever, and I'm going to have political problems up the yin-yang. Dammit, I told you to take a partner."

"You heard what happened, Cal," Archie said. "I needed to remove it, and I'd do the same under the circumstances. We got a murder victim, and she's a recent addition to the cave. Plus, like I said, the box and the blanket are quite valuable and couldn't be left after the attack on me."

Fricke half-closed his eyes and scratched behind his right ear.

"So you said. I'll wait until Detective Kydd confirms the bones are recent, if you don't mind. And I don't know nothing about no treasures. Since when are you such an expert?"

"I don't need to be an expert," Archie said. "It's true Patsy Kydd knows much more about skeletal remains, but I have enough experience for the preliminaries. When is she going to examine them? I've got things to do and I'm sick of hanging around your office."

"Too bad for you. She's on her way here now. Try to get along."

"What do you mean?"

"I mean work out your personal stuff on your own time, Archie."

"I plan to. Plus, there's nothing to work out."

The door opened. Archie kept his eyes on Fricke. Patsy walked past him and took a chair opposite so he couldn't avoid her. She glanced at him, turned to Fricke, gave Archie her profile, which he liked. In fact, he liked all of her, her Halle Berry features, the coffee tone of her skin, the wave in her hair, the small of her back—all of her. He took it all in without thinking. She caught him glancing at her and frowned.

"The Detective Sergeant is right," she said. "The victim is Caucasian—about twenty-two, I'd say. I guess she's been dead for five years or more. Someone cleaned the skull and other bones. It's like an ossuary burial. The shot above the left eye likely killed her, as there's no other trauma. I'm not sure why Detective Sergeant Stevens didn't call for a team to come right away so the body remained *in situ,* but he didn't—so."

"I'm not about to explain my reasons for doing anything to this officer," Archie said. "I'd like a detailed report as soon as she can manage it."

Patsy rose, walked towards him until she stood directly in front of him, crowding him—something else she knew he didn't like. She looked up at him. She was about to speak, her mouth half-open, ready for the word. Instead, she made a sound like an aspirated *bah,* motioned as if to brush him aside with her right hand and left the room. Fricke moved over and closed the door behind her.

"This sort of crap better stop, Arch," he said. "No call for it. This is a cop shop, not a fucking domestic whatever. You can be civil and professional and so can she."

"I don't understand."

"Bullshit. Anyway, you're going to be working with her because I'm putting her back on your team."

Archie didn't reply.

"Hear me?"

"Hard not to."

"So tell me. Give me your thoughts on this thing."

"I'm starting with missing persons. I'll do some more work and get back to you. I need help to do some of the research for starters. Plus, I'm pretty sure I'm in trouble with the Tribe, and I'm not sure how I'm going to deal with them."

"You sure as hell are in trouble," Fricke said. "You made your bed, buddy. I wish you'd let me handle the political stuff upfront. I told you to take a partner. Sometimes you're a pain where a pill don't reach."

"So you keep saying."

"Why don't you talk to ex-chief Pete Wilson—he's a buddy of yours, isn't he? He's got a lot of pull with the Nation."

"Perhaps," Archie said. "But I'm not going to ask him to stick his neck out. I doubt if he'd see things my way anyhow."

"Get the fuck out of my office," Fricke said.

Archie was already half out the door.

"Archie."

Archie turned back.

"I promoted you over the heads of other detectives with more seniority, but you can be demoted too. Don't make me look bad."

"I didn't ask for it."

"No, you didn't."

Fricke shook his massive head and turned his body so he once again showed Archie the tweed mountain and took up his position at the window facing Auchterlone's Bakery—a straight shot across the parking lot.

Archie stalked down the hall thinking about the case, about Fricke's final comments, about how he had been fooled back on the island. He slammed a doorjamb with the side of his fist, making the dispatcher, Delia John, start. She rolled her eyes at him as he passed her desk.

The murderer—or someone else—had manipulated him, and Archie had half-ruined his own investigation as a result. Was it salvageable? Was his reputation? Likely not. He briefly considered resigning but wasn't about to quit. He was in a mess, but he would get out of it. He still needed to identify the victim and solve a murder, not to mention locking up the creep who knocked him out.

He returned to his office, tossed his jacket on a chair and sat down in front of his computer screen. For the next hour, he opened file images of missing women. In the reception area someone shouted his name, demanding and insistent. Archie thought he recognized the voice. He minimized the set of pictures he was studying and waited.

Bobby Carpenter was the founder of a youth camp on Velasquez Island and an old antagonist from boyhood days. He came with a delegation of people, none apparently local. He entered, crossed the room and leaned forward pugnaciously over Archie's desk.

"Who the hell do you think you are, going into a burial cave without permission?" he said. "Your granny or your Uncle Tony could wise you up to what's not allowed. Common sense should tell you anyway, man. And you take a coffin box out of there, with goddam bones in it. What were you smoking?"

"Come in, welcome," Archie said.

"Stick your welcome, you sarcastic bastard. This ain't no friendly visit."

"A criminal investigation takes precedent, Bob."

"Screw that."

"Yeah, well, we disagree. Anything else I can do for you? I'm working."

Carpenter had a lot to say. No shortage of insults either. Archie sat back, listened and got comfortable with the situation. The others members of the party could be Salish—eight people in all, including a formidable-looking man with short gray hair and an air of command about him, and a very pretty young woman with piercing black eyes. Other than Carpenter, no one said anything. The middle-aged man seemed bored; the woman amused. Archie wasn't quite sure who they were, and he couldn't tell if they were present because Carpenter insisted or for their own reasons. No matter. The people Archie needed to talk to, the chief, the council members and other tribal officials, were not there, and he asked Bobby Carpenter why.

"How the hell should I know? Sitting on their fat asses likely, which is beside the point. I want those bones, Stevens."

"Not going to happen, Bob. We're dealing with a murder victim who was not Native American, in spite of where she was found."

"Is that so? You an expert on dead bones all of a sudden?"

"Why do you think it's bones?"

"I been in burial caves. It's always bones, smart-ass."

"The department has an expert," Archie said. "A specialist who testifies in court on the subject of skeletal remains."

Archie reached across his desk, pushed the button on the intercom.

"I need you here, Patsy."

He added a *please* and waited for her confirmation, which she didn't rush to give.

"I don't care about this shit," Carpenter said. "You've got no right to be in there or to remove anything. On behalf of the Sxeesh Nation, I officially claim the bones and demand they be returned."

Archie laughed.

"You'll need an injunction, Bob, but I don't think you represent the Nation, not at the moment, anyway."

His small office was so full of people he didn't see Patsy until she tapped Bobby Carpenter on the shoulder. Carpenter stepped aside, almost knocking over an elderly woman in his haste to let her pass. Most men stepped aside for Patsy, but she seemed unaware of the effect she had on them.

"You wanted me, Detective Sergeant?" she said coldly.

"I wouldn't call you otherwise."

She glared at him.

"Okay. I'm here."

He checked himself before replying, knowing it would seem like a domestic dispute was being played out at work. The attractive younger woman with Carpenter figured it out anyway and smiled.

"Mr. Carpenter wants the subject of our investigation and her coffin," Archie said. "He thinks the remains are Native American, and I say they aren't. What is your professional opinion?"

"The skeleton is that of a young, Caucasian female," Patsy said. "And she was almost certainly the victim of foul play."

Carpenter seemed unsure about how to proceed. Archie got the impression he thought he would get what he wanted without a fight and had no plan other than the one he came in with.

"I don't do anything on the say-so of the police department," he said. "I want those bones and the box. No further investigation, no nothing. Not at this stage, anyway."

Archie remembered how much he disliked Bobby Carpenter.

"An official request from the chief and council would naturally be considered," he said. "Although you don't seem authorized to make demands. You're not carrying a court order, are you, Bob?"

Carpenter's face reddened.

"I'm leaving, but I'll be back, you prick. You're making trouble for yourself, Stevens."

"I'm used to trouble and might even like it."

Carpenter brushed past the rest off his party, his eyes flashing on Patsy as he left the room. The delegation, unsure of what exactly was to be done, lingered a moment and followed after him out. The gray-haired man, second to last to leave, grinned and said, "Good move," on his way out. The woman tilted her head and shot him a strange, unsettling birdlike look and departed.

"Who was that older man?" Patsy said. "And who was that girl? I thought she must know you."

"Other than Carpenter, I don't believe I've ever seen any of those people before."

She searched his face, studying him.

His thoughts were elsewhere, thinking about the past. Patsy tapped his desktop with her knuckles. He looked up.

"Is there anything else?" he said.

"You wanted me to give you my summary of what I've found. Remember?"

"Right. Give me what you've got."

"Okay. As I said, the victim was female, approximately twenty-two or twenty-three years of age. She stood five foot sixish. No significant childhood injuries or disease. Good teeth, evidence of orthodontic work. She has a supra-orbital bullet hole, left side, exactly three centimeters above the superior edge of the orbit; the slug appears to be about a thirty-two caliber, and it was still inside the vault."

"Something rattled when I moved the skull."

"Yes, that'd be it," she said.

Having delivered her assessment, she folded her arms across her chest and leaned back against a cabinet.

"This is too difficult, Archie. Can we clear the air and put our other stuff aside?"

"How would we do that?"

He turned away, retrieved a file folder from his desk. She shook her head.

"Okay," he said. "Let's go to the lab. I want to examine the victim in good light."

He signaled for her to lead and followed her down the stairs, through the half-glass door and into her lab. She had laid out the skeleton on a surface covered with the white paper doctors used on examining tables.

Thomas Lee entered the room. He had been an important part of Archie's first investigation and was an excellent and methodical detective, but lately he was more involved with the political and administrative end of policing.

"Aren't you more a budget guy these days, Thomas?" Archie said.

Lee nodded.

"It's a lot safer," he said. "I'm not likely to get shot like when I was working with you before. Anyway, Fricke thought I should drop by to see I could help out."

Archie nodded.

"Good," he said. "We're at the early stages, but your perspective is always appreciated."

"Archie Stevens admitting he could use help," Patsy said. "It's a miracle."

"Not really. Otherwise it would just be me and you, and I'm not sure how we'd do."

"I can be professional much easier than you, Archie," she said. "I'm delighted that you're here, Thomas, and part of the team."

"Thank you," Lee said.

"If you two are finished," Archie said. "Perhaps Patsy will bring you up to speed."

Patsy mocked him with a salute and told Lee about the note and Archie's experiences on the island; about how he found the remains in the cave, about how he was attacked, about how he brought the box away with him. She outlined her conclusions about the subject of the investigation.

Archie watched Lee's face, saw the raised eye-brows at the mention of removing the victim from the scene. He motioned them to an empty lab table, opened the file he carried and spread out the contents. He moved to the skeleton, ran his fingertips down the hard line of the tibia and then picked up the skull, examined it closely and returned it to its place. He pulled out a photograph of a smiling young woman, attractive, with long red hair.

"Earlier, I did a quick search of the missing persons file and came up with three possible matches," he said. "Now, especially after Patsy's examination, I think this person is the best candidate. Her name is Stella Picard. She comes from what the officer filing the report called 'a solid middle-class background'—no poverty, anyway, which would explain the health of the bones. She was twenty-two years of age when she went missing, and a graduate student in anthropology at the university. The last time anybody saw her was five years ago. There are two other missing women in the same age range, but they don't fit. One was a prostitute who worked the streets and the other was a mill-worker. The mill-worker was heavyset; the hooker was too old. If Patsy can eliminate them for sure, we'll focus on Picard. Patsy will coordinate DNA tests."

"That will take a week or so," Patsy said. "Longer, perhaps, and why are you looking at me like that? You know it takes that long."

"Still, the sooner the better."

"It's not up to me. It's up to the lab."

They locked eyes.

Lee coughed, his irritation obvious.

"You've got a list of things for me to do, no doubt?" he said.

Archie took the opportunity to end whatever contest he had been having with Patsy.

"I do," Archie said. "We need to figure out where the coffin came from first. It has to be from a museum, a university, or a private collection. I'll take on some of this, but I'd like Thomas to search computer databases and the like and Patsy to analyze the note, checking for prints or DNA evidence—not that I'm expecting any. Also, we want information on the composition of the ink and where it's available. And we could use more about the murder weapon and how the body got into the cave. Anything else?"

"The attack on you," Patsy said. "Shouldn't we try to figure who did it first?"

"I'm not sure yet if it wasn't something out of left field and totally unrelated. Let's put it to the side for now. The art is key. I'll talk to Ron Helerstone at the university. He's an expert on

Northwest Coast art, and I know him, or used to. I think our carved bent box is by a famous artist from the 1800s, which would make it priceless. The blanket could be an antique too. Helerstone might know the entire history of these things, their owners and everything about them."

He left them to their work and returned to his office. Although he was not sure if he was keen on touching base with Helerstone again, the professor might be able to provide some of the information Archie needed to solve what might turn out to be a very pedestrian crime. Most murders were banal, after all, even those involving treasure.

CHAPTER 3

Ron Helerstone's reaction when Archie showed up at the Faculty Club and greeted him was uncharacteristically awkward, like a shoplifter caught with his pockets full of contraband. He got out a greeting, but Archie could tell he had thrown the man off balance.

"You haven't changed, Archie," he said.

"That's good, I guess."

"The years take their toll, so staying the same is grand. How you been? How's police work?"

"I'm good. It's good."

"What brings you out here? Are you just dropping by to say hello, or can I buy you a coffee?"

"Sure, I can interview you over coffee," Archie said.

"Interview?"

"Yes, I'm afraid it's business this time."

"Involving me?"

"I don't think so. Why—did you do something?"

Helerstone laughed.

"Sure, lots of things. But what's *this* all about?"

"I'll tell you while we walk," Archie said.

Helerstone grabbed a blue hoodie from a coatrack and pulled it on over a long-sleeved T-shirt, checked his reflection in the wall mirror and ran fingers through his graying hair. Archie followed him through a side door to Compass Mall, the pedestrian thoroughfare that ran through the center of the campus.

Helerstone walked briskly, waving to students he recognized as he passed. The two men talked as they walked, about old times, about Archie's time in anthropology, about why he gave it up, about why a promising student would quit a program to go into police work. Archie said, really, he wasn't sure, but it seemed like a good idea at the time and dodged the question. He had his reasons but no desire to share them. Telling people he became a cop because a serial killer murdered his mother was something he wouldn't do. Not with most people.

Bert's Campus Coffee kept space in the back reserved for faculty. Archie followed Helerstone to a room where about a half a dozen professors occupied tables or lounged on couches.

"I'll get you coffee," Helerstone said. "How do you like yours?"

"Black."

"Something to eat?"

"No, I'm fine."

Helerstone sat down heavily, no longer the slim surfer-dude professor of earlier times when he lived the life of a frenetic, party-loving workaholic. Archie saw none of that now.

"What can I help you with?" Helerstone said. "What are you interviewing me about?"

"Mostly I want your opinion on some artworks."

"Okay."

Archie opened his computer tablet and pulled up images of the artifacts. He put the device on the oak tabletop and turned the screen towards Helerstone, who scanned the shots. Archie expected a reaction, but the other man barely blinked.

"A Haida bent box and a Chilkat blanket," he said. "What about them?"

"I hoped you might recognize these things or at least give me your thoughts on them. Zoom in if you like. I think there's a 3-D function there too, so you can rotate the objects if you want."

"I don't need to rotate them. These are likely recreated versions of historic pieces, but I could examine them in a few weeks if you insist, just to be sure—I'm pretty busy right now."

"Take a look at this one again."

Archie reversed the image to show the Edenshaw "Mickey Mouse" but didn't draw Helerstone's attention to the unique detail.

"This one's good, wouldn't you say?"

Archie watched Helerstone's face for a reaction, but the other man's expression did not change.

"The workmanship seems okay," Helerstone said. "These modern pieces are nothing out of the ordinary as far as I'm concerned. Why are the police interested in them?"

"Nothing I can discuss at the moment. We have an investigation going on. Artwork is sometimes stolen, and I thought you could value these for us."

Not exactly a lie, Archie thought. Not the answer to the question, though.

Helerstone shook his head.

"Workmanship's not bad. I'd say a few thousand dollars for both. The market for new work fluctuates."

Archie hadn't expected this, the professor lying through his teeth, and he picked up on something else too. Worry—or fear?

"Sorry to do this to you, Ron but I'd like you to come to the station tomorrow morning to view the items. I won't make an official request, of course. You'd be doing me a favor. This is important to my investigation, and I'd appreciate anything you can tell me. Perhaps something might occur to you when you examine them in person."

"I've got lots on my plate right now," Helerstone said. "Contemporary artists are outside my purview, but I can think about it. Shall I get back to you?"

"Sure, but the request stands."

Afterwards, Helerstone tried to pump him for information about the case and, when he was unsuccessful, made ready to depart. Archie let him think the interview was over before he asked his other question.

"By the way, we're also interested in locating a young woman named Stella Picard. Do you know her?"

Helerstone hesitated before he answered. He shook his head.

"No," he said. "I don't think so."

"She did anthropology here a bit ago and might have been a student of yours, so I thought I'd ask if you recalled teaching her?"

Helerstone scrunched up his face like he was trying hard to call something to memory. He's overdoing it, Archie thought.

"I don't think so, Archie. The name doesn't ring a bell. Anything's possible. I taught a lot of graduate students, and I don't remember them all."

Archie hadn't mentioned the graduate student part.

"You're sure?"

Helerstone tapped the air with his finger. More overacting.

"Wait a sec, I do remember her. She worked for me on a project six years ago or more. Haven't seen her since. A pretty redhead—yeah, quite attractive."

"She'd be your type, I guess. Any idea what happened after she left you?"

"My type? No, you're thinking of other days, Archie, when the rules were looser. I wouldn't take a chance now. In any case, I don't think I heard what she did after the project ended or where she went. Is this anything to do with the art you showed me?"

"She wasn't an artist or collector, so far as I know."

No lie there. He wasn't going to give Helerstone anything. The man might be telling the truth, but Archie was doubtful. He rose from his seat.

"I'll let you go, Ron. If you think of anything else, call me. Let me know when I can expect you tomorrow."

"Absolutely."

They shook hands. Helerstone departed. Archie waited until he was out of sight before he reversed himself. He headed for the university library where he went to Special Collections and asked for Wilson Duff's unpublished papers, particularly one he remembered reading on Charlie Edenshaw and his art, and when the documents arrived, he found the one he wanted and started to read.

CHAPTER 4

Ron Helerstone needed the seclusion of his private office to work things out. Archie Stevens's visit bothered him, especially after seeing images of an Edenshaw box and Tlingit blanket he thought hidden and secure. When he contacted Coyote for advice, Coyote's icy calmness and his false reassurances set Helerstone's nerves jingling instead. Now Helerstone wasn't sure what he ought to do. If he asked Archie Stevens for protection, he would certainly go to jail, so that option was off the table. A vision of Stella Picard popped into his mind as he remembered Archie's questions about her. Still, he thought he handled himself well, and he thought it unlikely the police knew anything about what happened to her.

He was now much more worried about his own skin. He didn't want to screw up and, certainly, he did not want to die like Porteous. Helerstone had had close calls himself and knew how to be careful. You couldn't do the kind of things they were doing without crossing boundaries most people couldn't see or sense. Coyote always said going deep into the underworld was like walking a tightrope over Niagara, which was why he, Coyote, was intolerant of error.

Helerstone was thankful for his secret office and lab—the forgotten basement suite beneath the museum, which few people realized existed. Years before, as department head, he took the space out of the rotation and changed records and diagrams to obscure its existence. Now, officially at least, it did not exist.

To avoid being seen, he used the back door, took the service stairs and went through an electrical room to the vast basement room that fronted his lab. This was the *Cemetery*, the artifact storage area where steel shelving held countless cardboard boxes, plastic containers and shallow trays filled with the relics of long-ago expeditions, now largely forgotten. As Helerstone hurried along its darkened corridors, motion sensors clicked lights first on and then off. When he reached his destination, he slid behind a wooden cabinet and, half-concealed behind it, keyed in his code on the number pad and entered. Inside, old-fashioned fluorescents flicked to brightness. He walked to his desk, threw his keys in a carved-stone Marpole

Phase bowl, took out his laptop and started the machine.

He checked his database, pulling up images and data on art treasures and valuable collector pieces locked away in storage areas all over the world, just like the one outside his door, in museum basements. After Helerstone picked out treasures, Coyote's thugs would steal them and substitute perfect copies made in Asia—the basis of a very profitable business model. Work helped Helerstone put his experience with Archie Stevens out of his mind; the fears of the day passed and he took a break to make tea.

He crossed to the small kitchen and put the kettle on before he went to the fridge and retrieved a plastic container on which the original owner had printed, "*This is not yours!*" in purple marker and in bold capitals. Helerstone opened it—macha macaroons apparently. He didn't remember the container or the macaroons, but he was often in a hurry and took many things from the communal department fridge. Besides, he was hungry.

The cookies tasted funky and herbaceous, slightly unpleasant like corked wine. Helerstone rinsed his mouth with tap water and dumped the empty container. When the kettle finished boiling, he made his tea, returned to his desk and continued his work. He pulled up and scanned more images of priceless artifacts, unknowingly sent to him by his graduate students who often got permission to work on otherwise ignored pieces, especially with the letters of introduction he provided.

As he calculated totals and made notes, his mind began to wander and soon he felt he was losing his focus and experiencing a disturbing confusion. His jottings made less and less sense to him too. Before long he forgot what each image represented and why he was staring at it, and he could no longer recall his own name. Archie Stevens seemed likely, but he wasn't sure, and in any case the name seemed to dodge and skitter away before he pinned it down.

At first he panicked, but the new sensations he experienced quickly offset his fear. His senses were more acute and his world became one of scintillating color and mesmerizing sounds. He heard every noise, even the footsteps of the bugs and spiders roaming the basement, and he could even listen to voices in the tree-lined pedestrian square many feet above the vault where he was working, which meant the sound traveled to him through forty feet of fill and concrete. He gulped more tea and the surface of his tongue grasped flavors like the tentacles of an octopus.

At first the experience was deeply pleasurable but suddenly, like an opened door letting a cold wind into a warm, cozy space, everything changed and the world darkened. Alarmed, he strained to focus his mind on reality and to organize his thoughts. His reason returned briefly, enough to let him know that someone had drugged the macaroons. He coughed and shivered. Purging the drugs from his system became his obsession and he rallied his will, braced his hands on the edges of his desktop for support, rose, stumbled to the sink, forced a finger down his throat and vomited out a pitiful trace of thin and bitter bile.

His legs grew weaker and he staggered back across the room, head down like a drunkard, and fell back into his chair. Terror stalked him. He endeavored to lock his computer to protect his secrets, but his hand on the keyboard refused to obey him.

Something drifted into his view, a solid object defying gravity. He could not turn his head, but his eyes tracked the thing. He recognized the ancient soul-catcher from the *Cemetery* that Coyote took from him years ago, desiring the carved, abalone-studded tube of human bone more than anything else in the collection. Impossibly now, it hovered and darted about like a bird, paused, turned on its axis and then stopped a few inches from his eyes, the mouths at each end contracting and expanding, breathing in and out and speaking; words flowed out and enveloped him, tickling his neck and humming around his ears. He wanted to brush them away like irritating flies, but his arms were leaden and the words settled on his hands and face like ash from a fire.

And then he experienced a new sensation. His body was changing. He shrank in size, growing smaller and smaller alarmingly fast and, unable to resist, he entered the soul-catcher, drawn in by one long, horrible, sucking breath. At first this terrified him, but when he bested his fear and accepted the change as a natural, organic process, he saw new wonders.

Inside the tube, a thousand niches stretched away, each containing a carved and living mask exhaling a powerful miasma of resin odors and smoke. And then Coyote appeared wearing his bedraggled cedar cloak. Laughing, the shaman looped a thin spruce root cord around Helerstone's wrist and led him like a child out of the hollow world and into a high-roofed wood-planked room. Each time Coyote moved, his tattered cloak sparkled and lightning shot out of the folds. In the haze, Helerstone glimpsed a figure — a red-haired woman with her back to him. When she turned to greet him, her eyes were hollow and frightful wounds on her head and legs oozed blood. He cried out and called to her, but when only nonsense words came out of his mouth, she screamed a curse, spun on her heel and ran away down the tunnel. He fell to his knees, sobbing.

Coyote reappeared, belly laughing silently, mime-like, as if Helerstone and his situation were the funniest things ever, a huge joke his victim missed. Coyote wagged his finger in mock disapproval and capered around his victim, laughed even louder. Often he poked Helerstone with his sharp stick compelling him to cover his eyes with his hands as he stumbled along. The thousand masks in their niches sang at him, their chant growing in volume until the din was unbearable, and he winced and clapped his hands to his ears. Coyote capered past him and his stick darted like a snake — twice. Helerstone, blinded, ran terrified into blackness.

CHAPTER 5

Wilson Duff's article was long and detailed, and Archie took his time reading it and making notes from it; he didn't leave the campus for several more hours. On his way back to the station, he grabbed a bite to eat at Avril's Donut House. He also stopped at Roderick Burlingame's Gallery and showed the owner the pictures he had shown Helerstone. Burlingame recognized the telltale Edenshaw sign immediately and whistled with surprise.

"Nice pieces," he said. "Never seen them before, so they must have been in a private collection somewhere and uncatalogued. I'd be interested in buying them if they're for sale. I'd have to mortgage the house to do it, but I would."

Archie told Burlingame the pieces were not for sale, thanked him and left the gallery. Later in the afternoon, he returned to his office and sat down to think.

Thomas Lee arrived, took the chair closest to the door and, after brushing an imaginary crumb off the sleeve of a pale blue sports jacket, shot his cuffs.

"How'd your trip to the university go?" Lee asked.

"I'm not sure," Archie said. "I can't figure out why my good old buddy Professor Helerstone would lie to me."

"How so?"

"He knows pretty well every piece of American Indian art produced on the coast for the past 150 years—and he knows the artists and their styles. I show him photos of a Chilkat blanket that Roderick Burlingame says is likely famous, and what he suspects is a lost Charlie Edenshaw bent box, both of which are worth a lot of money, but Helerstone doesn't blink. Never saw them before, he says. Modern pieces, he says, which means he's lying through his teeth, and I want to know why. Plus, he tried to give me the runaround with Stella Picard."

"Interesting."

"He's supposed to come here tomorrow," Archie said. "Then we'll see. You got anything for me?"

"I did some more research on the missing women like you wanted. I made some calls. Now

I'm a hundred percent certain the deceased is this woman, Picard."

Archie rubbed his eye socket with his index finger. His phone sang. He reached for his jacket, pulled it from a pocket and answered. It was Patsy, wanting him in the lab. He told an amused Thomas about the imperious summons. Halfway down the hall, Fricke, returning from some mission to Delia John's desk, hailed Archie.

"You're off the hook for right now, Stevens," he said. "Some folks from the Tribal Council are coming by later to discuss matters. In the meantime, I agreed that the remains would stay put here until things get sorted out, so no returns by our people to the cave unless accompanied by a Council member."

"Is that right?"

"Yes, that's right. And you're welcome. Don't say I never did nothing for you. At least your ass isn't in a sling."

"Yeah, I'm lucky."

Fricke grunted and walked off.

"You don't cut the guy much slack, do you?" Lee said.

"I thought I did."

They continued through the area of cubicles and carried on down the back stairs to the basement. Patsy didn't look up when Archie and Lee walked in. She adjusted the finger bones of the skeleton's right hand and made a note on her tablet.

"It's a bit more complicated than I thought," she said. "Thanks for coming back down, boss."

Archie nodded.

"Check this," she said.

She pointed to the right femur. Archie leaned in. She passed him her loupe, and he saw the marks she indicated with the tip of her index finger. He exhaled, rubbed his fingers across his forehead and handed the loupe on to Lee.

"Cut marks," Archie said. "Through the flesh and right down to the bone."

"Yes," said Patsy. "I can think of several explanations, I guess, but one springs to mind."

"I'm not ready to go there but I understand what you're suggesting."

"No point beating around the bush," Lee said. "Somebody cut a chunk out of her."

"That doesn't mean they ate the chunk." Archie said.

"No it doesn't, but we can't eliminate the possibility."

"No, we can't."

Patsy pointed out other features of the skeleton, the fillings in the teeth, the epiphyses on the bones, the distinct sutures on the skull. She explained that the Rochville ballistics lab was analyzing the thirty-two caliber bullet she recovered from inside the cranium. First reports were that it was a competition load and a specialty item. Lee asked about the traces of a pink material in the foramen magnum.

"I'll get that out," Patsy said. "Some of the silicone from the mold I made stuck. I sent a cast of the skull to Werner Froese. He'll do up a reconstruction of the face of the victim for us."

Archie nodded. He scanned the skeleton, trying to memorize what he saw, called up a mental image of the person who had once animated the slender bones. The cuts on the femur shocked him. He remembered the knife in Helerstone's drawer and made a note to have Forensics examine it for blood. Patsy stood very close to him, close enough that he accidentally brushed her hair when he moved a hand.

"As I said earlier," she said, "Age is about twenty-two, good teeth, evidence of orthodontics when she was younger, so likely middle class. She stood five six or so. Even without facial reconstruction, I'd say she was pretty—quite pretty and a little delicate."

"When will we get the reconstruction?" Archie said.

"Within a week, I hope."

"Sounds good. Anyway, it's late and I'm sure we're all tired. We'll meet again in my office at eight tomorrow morning."

"Can't be me, Arch," Lee said. "I'm off for a few days. Martin Demio will take my place."

"Now you tell me?"

"It just came up and I got to be going. Anyway—it'll be Demio. I should be back in a week or so."

Before Archie could follow, Patsy blocked him.

"Martin Demio has a reputation. Not a good one either."

"I heard."

They stood without speaking, awkward. Archie liked being near her and she seemed to sense that. She moved forward a millimeter or so, barely perceptible but forward nonetheless.

"Just for the record," she said. "I'm over it, Archie. No need to pussyfoot around. We're colleagues and we can work together. Okay?"

Archie focused on her left earlobe, thinking that it might be over for her but not for him. The hardest thing for him was to be around her and not have her, but he wasn't about to let her know it.

"We can even be friends of a sort," she said.

"Of a sort—sure."

He picked up the faint scent of the herbal shampoo she used on her hair and that alone would have drawn him towards her, but his instinct for self-preservation kicked in and prevented it. He was a fool if he thought things were different. Still, he lingered near enough to her for a few moments longer than necessary.

"I've got things to do, Patsy," he said. "I'll see you tomorrow."

Archie turned away and made for the door. He knew her eyes were on him, but he didn't have the foggiest idea what he should do about the situation between him and her. Be friends, like she said, he guessed. It could work. He kept walking. In his office, the door closed, he busied himself and tried to take his mind off two things, the cut marks on the bones, and the perfumed hair of Patsy Kydd.

CHAPTER 6

Powerful emergency lights lit the face of the cliff where a firefighter on a safety line hooked cables to the hitch rings on a late model SUV resting nose-down in a thick alder break, preventing its further descent into the sea fifty meters below. The tow truck driver waited for Archie to confirm the start of the lift. Archie peered down, got the thumbs-up from the firefighter who swung away and nodded the go-ahead to the driver. The winch whined and the cable went tight. Branches snapped and hissed as the SUV pulled free of the trees and started its journey back up the hill. At last, it crested the bank and came to rest at the edge of the street clear of the crumpled guardrail it had destroyed on its way down. Their task finished, the firefighters hauled their colleague up the incline and returned to their trucks.

Archie had been down to the car already and been shocked to find Ron Helerstone dead at the wheel, but the cliff was too steep and high, and the vehicle too close to tumbling all the way down to the sea to do much more than a preliminary examination. Only after he had seen as much as he could below had he allowed the removal of the SUV.

Now he waited as the fire department packed up and the tow truck went away on to other business. Archie was glad to see them leave—too many procedural discussions for his liking and the inevitable bullshit that happened when emergency services overlapped at a crime scene. The ambulance stood ready to take the body away as soon as he gave the okay; the attendants remained near their vehicle, checking their phones or playing video games.

He turned back to the SUV, pulled on his gloves and tilted his head to get a better view of the deceased, whose head rested on a closed window obscured by condensation and blood. He considered angles, gravity, and the position of the seat belt. He wanted to open the door but keep the victim, as much as possible, *in situ*. Roger Chu, the medical examiner, appeared at his side, called out to the scene from an all-night poker game, he said. He guessed what Archie was thinking.

"The deceased is going to slump out no matter what you do, Archie," he said. "No point in being delicate."

"Yeah. I'll be a minute."

"You're the boss for now. Just let me know when I can get on with my job."

Archie, his hand raised in agreement, was already committing his immediate impressions to memory. When he opened the door, Helerstone, as he expected, slumped out sideways and down, held in place by the seat belt over the shoulder, exposing the blood-bespattered airbag that obscured the steering wheel. As the head lolled to the side, the bullet hole immediately behind the right eye became visible, an almost inconsequential mark set in a field of powder burns. Although the wound suggested suicide, the cliffside plunge and the bullet to the head after the fact didn't seem to add up. There was something else too—the passenger-side seat belt dragged free and the buckle end was not fully retracted. Did Helerstone take a companion on his last journey? If so, why was the passenger-side airbag not deployed?

"Any idea who the guy was?"

This came from Detective Martin Demio, who had just materialized at Archie's shoulder.

"Yeah. His name is Helerstone, Professor Ron Helerstone. He taught at the university. I knew him from my time there, and I saw him yester-day—alive."

"Yesterday? That's a coinky-dink."

"Yep," Archie said.

"Word is you couldn't hack university."

"Lots of things I can't hack. People too."

Demio stood, hands in the pockets of a worn, gray duffel coat. He had once held the same rank as Archie, Detective Sergeant but in Empire City. Why he'd been busted down in EC, and how he'd ended up in Harsley was a mystery. Fricke probably knew, but he wasn't telling. For the moment, Demio seemed content enough to play second fiddle to Archie, but Archie wondered how long that situation could last. Demio rubbed him the wrong way.

"Got any theories on how he got here, other than by SUV?" he said.

"Hard not to think that he drove himself over the cliff," Chu said in passing.

"After which he shot himself?" Archie said.

"We see weird things in this business."

"We do, but some things are less likely than others," Archie said.

When he shone his flashlight into the rear of the vehicle and around the seat backs, the beam caught the shine of black plastic, the grips of a pistol lodged upright between a binder and a laptop computer case. He moved around, yanked the back door open and flicked on his mini-light to get a better view of the Ruger semiautomatic.

"Or maybe not," Archie said.

Archie nodded in the direction of the gun and Demio leaned in.

"His gun, you think?" Demio asked.

"I guess. He once belonged to a shooting club and was some proud of his marksmanship, but the Ruger is more of a self-defense weapon than the target pistol he favored; but it might be his. We're supposed to think he shot himself with this, I suppose."

Demio made a nasal sound that Archie interpreted as a laugh.

"Why not? It'd do the job."

"We'll see, but he didn't use this gun in any case."

He turned away and walked back to where he'd parked his car, phoned in to set up the warrants for Helerstone's home and office. Then he leaned against the fender while Demio unhooked the seat belt and released the body, watched closely by Chu who was already doing his job. Archie wished for a hot coffee. The sky was lightening in the east, the air was chill and the ozone tang of the sea strong. He liked such early mornings, especially when he was alone. Not going to happen for this early morning, of course, not surrounded by flashing emergency lights and half a dozen squad cars like he was. Demio wandered away.

Archie went to the body, now on a gurney. Death had set Helerstone's face into a mask, happy—almost beatific. The bullet hole in his temple absorbed light, a black hollow blemish on the temple. Bullets were small things and the holes they left going in were always small compared with the destruction they caused on the way out. Helerstone wore the same clothes, Hawaiian shirt and cargo pants, as on the previous day when they met. Archie, studying the face, noticed a red dot, like paint and about the size of a dime, on Helerstone's cheek.

"Anything you can tell me right off, Roger?" he asked.

The medical examiner shook his head.

"You know better than to ask, Arch. He's got a hole in his head and he was involved in a catastrophic MV accident. You can quote me. Write it down in that little Rhodia notebook you're always carrying."

Archie expected the answer. He'd asked the question as much to get Chu's dander up as for any other reason.

"Yeah, I'll do that," he said. "I'll put it right under my new heading: Miserable Love-starved Medical Examiners."

"I get action, smart-ass."

"I can just imagine," Archie said. "When will you do the autopsy?"

Chu rubbed his eyes with the tips of his fingers.

"Since it's you—next month sometime," he said.

"Seriously."

"Later this afternoon, say, four o'clock when I can make time."

"Thanks, I'll be there."

He took out his notebook and jotted down a couple of impressions and scouted around until he sent the body and SUV away. The rising sun brought more onlookers who began to gather on the other side of the police tape. Archie was surprised to see the man with the gray crewcut from Bobby Carpenter's delegation among them. When he saw Archie, he smiled and flicked his fingers— a kind of a wave, turned away and left.

Archie, his mind on other things, went down to the broken guardrail, sidestepped it and went down the bank. On the opposite side, it was easier than he would have thought. He found and followed a narrow path down, a relatively easy de-

scent to where the SUV had rested, and he discovered a clear fresh footprint beside the drag marks,
very close to the where the passenger-side door of
the vehicle had been. He marked the tracks, of a
woman's boot by its size, called up for a techni-
cian and told her to bring casting medium for the
print.

CHAPTER 7

Archie picked up Martin Demio on the street in front of Ron Helerstone's house, and they drove up the curved driveway, parked, got out and headed for the front door. Demio fell in step with Archie.

"Nice digs for a professor," he said.

"He had a good house in Pilotage, but nothing like this," Archie said. "This surprises me."

"Oh, yeah, Pilotage," Demio said. "Where all the hippies live. Probably he inherited the money to buy this joint."

"Possibly."

In his student days, Archie attended a few of the parties Helerstone threw for students and colleagues in the old house. Another student once described that place as "funky" and Helerstone as "rad," and Archie felt accepted there. The welcoming, comfortable Bohemian atmosphere of the Pilotage house was not part of this ultramodern mansion with its high protective wall and long, cantilevered terraces. A wide walkway through high rhododendrons ended at an oversized wooden door, a work of art in itself.

"Serious money here, man," Demio said.

Archie nodded.

"Perhaps, but he sure wasn't rich in the old days."

"When you talked to him yesterday, what'd he say?"

"He was evasive," Archie said. "I think he thought he was putting one over on me. He said Stella Picard worked for him for a few months six years ago and he scarcely knew her and he didn't know where she went."

"How much did you believe?"

"I believed the she worked for him part," Archie said.

He picked his way through the bundle of keys he'd taken from the ignition of the dead man's vehicle, found the right one and opened the side door. Demio asked him how he planned to proceed.

"For now, focus on any signs Helerstone was about to kill himself—the note, if such a thing exists. I'll start upstairs and you take the downstairs."

"Beyond a suicide note, what are you hoping to find during this waste of time search?" Demio said.

"Don't know. You're a detective. Keep your eyes open."

"Aye, aye, boss."

"You don't need to be here, Martin. In fact, I'd prefer to do this alone."

"I'm staying because Fricke insisted you needed somebody to keep you focused on the fact we got a suicide," Demio said.

"So you're Fricke's man?" Archie said.

Demio shrugged. "He signs the checks."

They walked into a large foyer. Demio scanned the area, sissed through his teeth.

"I expected something different in here," he said. "The joint is rich from the outside, but inside it's a dump."

The nearest wall of the space sported a rack of dust-covered Melanesian war clubs, which Archie recognized. They were a relic of the former house and a sad reminder of the old Helerstone. Otherwise the hall furniture consisted of an old coatrack, a worn, government-style oak bench and a cheap veneer side table.

They passed through and entered a large two-level living room. Demio was about to say something when a woman wearing a loose T-shirt and little else appeared at the top of the stairs. She was a redhead, like Stella Picard, and she held a nickel-plated Colt .45 Government, which she levelled at them.

"Who the hell are you and what do you want?" she said.

The heavy pistol didn't waver. Archie raised his hands and he saw Demio do likewise, but also shifting his body so that he presented less of a target, with his gunhand, invisible to the woman now on the butt of his pistol.

"I'm Detective Sergeant Stevens and this is Detective Martin Demio, Harsley Police. Who are you?"

As he asked the question, he figured he already knew part of the answer.

"Do you have identification?" she said. "Anybody can say they're a cop."

Archie nodded, carefully reached into his inside jacket pocket and took out his badge case, which he flipped open so she could see his shield, but she barely glanced at it.

"He's the picture of a cop," she said. "You aren't. You're too good looking."

Archie didn't acknowledge the compliment but stood waiting, watching her eyes and the pistol.

"I suggest you put the gun down," he said. "Right now you're threatening police officers with a deadly weapon."

She let the muzzle of the big Colt droop. Archie thought he caught an instant of uncertainty in her eyes. Or was it something else, the opposite of un-certainty, satisfaction perhaps?

She stooped, laid the gun down, brushed a strand of hair back from her temple and stood away.

Demio drew his Glock out and pointed the weapon at her. She started when she saw it and took a step backwards.

"I put my gun down, so why are you threaten-ing me?" she said, as she presented them with a new avatar, the confused, possibly frightened girl.

"It's a precaution," Demio said. "We're going to have to arrest you."

"Wait a minute," Archie said.

He made the arrest call, not Demio.

"You're not under arrest at the moment," he said. "Holster your gun, Martin."

Demio snorted, and he took his time putting his gun away.

"Sure. I don't think she's carrying a concealed weapon."

He laughed, and Archie scowled at Demio's crudeness.

"You can relax, ma'am. Just take it easy. Tell me who you are," he said.

She dropped the frightened girl act, crossed her arms across her chest defiantly.

"Ma'am—I like your manners," she said. "So old fashioned. Anyway, I'm a houseguest, just staying here for a while. Ronnie said I could. My name is Tessa, Tessa Simons."

That much was consistent. Tessa Simons was the type of woman Helerstone liked to attract. Inviting a beautiful, intelligent woman like her to stay in his house was what he would do.

"What's happened to Ron?" she asked.

"What makes you think anything's happened to him?" Demio asked.

"Pretty obvious." She was in control of herself now, her nervousness gone, and her tone reflected her confidence. "A couple of cops break into the guy's house, so there must be a reason."

"Possibly, we're searching for drugs," Demio said. "Or we got a call about a domestic incident."

"Bull," she said. "You're not looking for drugs or anything else, and you're not asking for Ron, so something must have happened to him."

"There wasn't supposed to be anybody in the house. Members of the force knocked on the door and phoned the numbers. There weren't any lights on so, I guess they figured the house was empty."

Archie watched her. She walked down the stairs and sat down on one of the lower risers, hands on bare knees. Sunlight glinted off the vermilion lacquer on her toenails.

"Can I get my phone?" she asked. "I want to call somebody."

"Your lawyer?" Archie said.

"No."

"Later, perhaps. I'm wondering why you didn't you answer the door? Remember that even if you're not under arrest, anything you say can be used in court. That's a caution, by the way."

"Okay, but why should I open the door to callers? It's not my house."

Now she was past the preliminaries, Archie realized she wasn't going to cooperate.

"What was your relationship with Doctor Helerstone other than houseguest?" Demio asked.

"I study ritual dance."

The answer had a lot of "mind your own business" in it, and her tone was combative.

"Not an answer to Detective Demio's question," Archie said. "I think the idea is to find out if you were ever in a romantic relationship with the professor?"

His question seemed to irritate her.

"Were you in any romantic relationships, policeman?"

He stifled a smile.

"This isn't a conversation, Tessa—whatever you might think."

"No kidding."

She seemed to think she was starting to get the upper hand.

"I'm going to ask you to get dressed," he said. "I'll take a statement from you at the station, okay? If you want to contact a lawyer, you should do so."

"I don't want to go anywhere at the moment. What if I refuse to go?"

"I'd like to think you'd do it out of respect for Ron. Professor Helerstone is dead, and we suspect foul play. You are in his house without a reason we can verify. You have been less than cooperative; you pointed a gun at police officers. Even so, I'm not going to formally arrest you right now. I'm asking you to come with us as a favor."

"Ha!"

She reacted in a way he did not anticipate. She jumped to her feet and ran back up the stairs, disappearing down the upper hallway. Demio glanced at Archie, grinned, and charged up the stairs after her. Archie, who now had a sense of the layout of the house, walked quickly through the kitchen and past a workout room, found the garage door and opened it.

A bright red Porsche sat in a Lino-floored space that could have held five vehicles. He paused as a door to his left opened. When Tessa Simons ran towards the Porsche, keys in hand, he moved to block her. She ran into him, tried unsuccessfully to muscle him out of the way, said *fuck*, and then dropped to a cross-legged sitting position on the polished concrete floor. She brushed her hair out of her eyes and nodded in the direction of the car.

"The Porsche is mine," she said. "In case you wondered."

"It's a very nice vehicle, but what the hell were you thinking? Now I'll have to put you under arrest."

"You sound irritated."

"People often think I'm irritated when I'm not."

"You could have fooled me."

"In any case, you are *now* under arrest."

"I want my lawyer now."

"Of course," he said.

After Martin Demio left with Tessa Simons in the squad car, Archie continued his search of the house. First, he gathered up Helerstone's unopened mail, sealed it in a bag and left it near the door to take away with him. Demio's comments about the furnishings were apt. Archie recognized some pieces from the old house, including copies of famous treasures from archeological sites, such as a famous bull-headed rhyton from Knossos. He crossed over to a dilapidated easy chair, sat down to think, trying to understand what he saw, to create an encompassing and satisfying narrative around the grand, new, poorly furnished house, the smart, manipulative girlfriend with the expensive car, the lying about artifacts, and Helerstone's murder soon after the interview. He got the impression Helerstone acquired his money relatively recently and wasn't sure what to do with it. Underneath that wealth lurked fear; Archie sensed it. He rose from the chair, crossed the room and climbed the stairs to the upper floor where Tessa had been.

The upstairs rooms were mostly empty, but the master bedroom contained an unmade king-sized bed without a headboard, and two expensive-looking suitcases. The floor of the room was a mess, littered with clothing — two or three pairs of women's jeans, a couple of shirts, a camisole, several pairs of women's lace panties, a bra, men's cargo shorts and two men's flowered shirts. A small dresser contained, when Archie checked, other items of men's clothing, an empty wallet, a Laguiole knife and a current passport.

Archie closed the drawers and then picked through the things on the floor before examining the bed and the floor under it. Forensics would likely find evidence of a sexual relationship between Tessa Simons and Ron Helerstone—a person didn't need to be a cop to figure that one out. A slight breeze from the half-open patio door brought with it the scent of flowers and the not-too distant sea.

After several hours of searching and making notes, Archie left the house, put the most senior of two newly arrived uniformed cops in charge and drove home to Harsley and the luxury condo he housesat for a female friend who seemed to have no intention of returning. He tried to will away his fatigue; he wanted to be alert, particularly when he interviewed Tessa Simons again. She was savvy, and she would take advantage of any weakness he showed. His early morning at the crash scene and the previous late night weren't helping his thinking much.

The best thing about the condo he occupied was the privacy it afforded. He never saw anyone on the floor, and he wasn't sure if any of the other unit owners lived there. Most of them likely bought their units as investments just like his friend had done. Even so, Archie lived in the condo like he was camping and used only a few of the many rooms.

Now, in spite of his fatigue, he wouldn't sleep, not yet. He was hungry for one thing. He went directly to the kitchen, found only a half a jar of peanut butter and a half empty bottle of cola in the fridge. Not for the first time, he made a mental note to go shopping.

He took the peanut butter and the cola to the counter, found a container of honey and several slices of stale bread in the pantry cupboard. After checking the bread for mold and finding none, he made himself four sandwiches, took them and his drink to the computer and began building his file on Professor Ron Helerstone.

Once, Helerstone had been a prolific scholar, a young Turk who challenged accepted theories and often made enemies within the anthropologist community. But what was the situation now? As Archie searched for scholarly papers, conference speaking engagements and other markers of a successful academic career, he noted the change in Helerstone's output—a dozen articles and books a year and then, suddenly, very little. Helerstone's last important work was a journal article, dated five years ago, on the Swaixwe ceremony. This was a Salish ritual about which

Archie knew almost nothing, though he once witnessed a performance as a guest of his Uncle Tony. That unsettling experience had stayed with him; in one part of the dance a clown-like being did hilarious things, but no one in the audience dared laugh, especially when the clown tried to blind the costumed dancer by stabbing its protruding peg mask eyes with a pointed stick. Tony said it was all about the dancer being able to see into the other world and the other being trying to prevent this.

Next, Archie searched city records for real estate transactions involving Helerstone. No problem there. The records were open to the public. He figured the Falcon View house was a recent purchase and wanted to know when the professor bought the place and, indeed, Helerstone purchased the house four years ago and paid more than six million in cash for it. His salary as a university professor would be, Archie guessed, a hundred fifty thousand—not sufficient to buy the Falcon View mansion. The seller was the notorious land developer, Rafe King, a man few people had met and of whom little was known.

Archie finished his sandwiches, washing down the last of the peanut butter-coated bread with flat cola from the two-quart bottle. He burped and rubbed his burning eyes. Eating failed to alleviate the familiar queasiness in his gut but at least he felt drowsy. He dragged himself to the couch, stretched out on it and almost immediately blacked out.

He woke to the buzz of his phone, fumbled it out of his pocket, learned he'd been asleep for less than an hour, and checked the message—Chu's assistant informing Archie of the autopsy taking place that afternoon as promised.

Archie dropped the phone on the coffee table and sat up, not sure if he felt better for the three quarters of an hour worth of dozing or not. He went into the bathroom, stripped off his shirt, turned on the shower and leaned his head into the flow, so tired he almost fell asleep standing there. He pulled his head clear of the water and turned off the tap, cursed the water splashes on the front of his pants and went to the sink to brush his teeth. After finger-combing his hair, he put on a clean T-shirt and leather jacket, pulled on his cowboy boots and went to the elevator.

CHAPTER 8

For Archie, the only positive thing about an early morning meeting was that when it finished, he might be able to go home and catch another hour of sleep. Aside from the forty-five minutes of dozing in the condo, he had been awake for thirty-eight hours, and he felt it. Now, sitting in the room, his mind wandered. He absently focused on the top of Cal Fricke's head and decided he could count the few hairs covering it if he wanted. Archie started the process and got to seventy-five before Fricke's voice snapped him back to reality.

"Wake up, Archie. What you got for us?"

Archie met Fricke's stare.

"I'm treating Helerstone's death as a homicide," he said, "and I believe there's a link between the professor and Stella Picard, the victim from the burial cave."

Silence. Fricke shook his massive head.

"It's a better chance Helerstone is a suicide, in Martin's opinion," he said. "So why are we wasting department time?"

Fricke often left out important details in his summations, deliberately it seemed. The technique either forced his investigators to make a point a second or third time, or to give up. Archie was never sure if the ploy was deliberate or not.

"Let's leave Stella Picard aside for the moment, Cal," he said. "Suicide just doesn't make sense. A guy points his car at the salt chuck and goes over a cliff, discovers he's not dead, finds a gun, lines it up and, never mind the logistics, pulls the trigger. It doesn't make any sense to me. Roger Chu also figures Helerstone would be marginally conscious at best after the crash. Also, there are tracks near the passenger side of the vehicle—a woman's tracks. Could be a shooter. Besides, we were supposed to think the Ruger was the weapon and it isn't, so where's the gun he used on himself?"

"More likely a firefighter or spectator made the tracks," Demio said. "And a passerby took the gun. We weren't the first people on the scene. Also, the passenger side window was open and it could have fallen into the sea."

Fricke grunted.

"Occam's fucking razor," he said.

Archie leaned to one side, put his chin on his fist, and regarded Fricke. Occam's Razor said, in a nutshell, the simplest solution to a problem was likely the right one. The concept was attractive, but solving a murder wasn't that kind of logic problem. He was surprised Cal Fricke, an old-style cop, had even heard of it. Besides, murder was the simplest theory, not suicide.

"It's not applicable here," Archie said. "Not your way, at least."

"Let's get another opinion," Fricke said. "What does Thomas think?"

"I'm with Archie, but I'd still like to see more evidence," Lee said.

Fricke inclined his head in Patsy's direction. She steepled her fingers and leaned back in her chair.

"Detective Sergeant Stevens makes sense," she said. "The victim would need to rack a cartridge and so on, which would be difficult if he were almost unconscious. We could send a diver down into the water below the scene to search for a second gun and eliminate that option."

"I called one of our divers about that possibility," Archie said. "He's of the opinion that with the tide changes yesterday, the depth of the water, the rocks and so on, we're unlikely to find anything down there."

"I still think we got a suicide, as does Martin," Fricke said. "Tell us again why not the Ruger?"

Archie rested an elbow on the table and leaned his burning eye socket into the knuckle of his finger. He rolled the eyeball in an attempt to moisten its surface before he spoke.

"It's nine mil," he said. "In the first place, the powder marks on the skin would be heavier if the victim put the barrel to his own temple and pulled the trigger. Plus, the exit wound damage is significant, but it's not like nine mil damage from a bullet fired so close."

"I don't buy it," Demio said. "He held the gun away from his head is all."

Fricke let out a sigh like the rumble of an oncoming train.

"So, not unanimous, Archie," he said. "You haven't cleared up all my doubts."

"We still need the ME's report," Patsy said. "We'll know better then."

Fricke rolled his chair back, rested the side of his beefy face on his hand.

"Okay," he said. "Possible homicide. What's on everyone's desk workwise?"

"I've got a few projects, but I can spare some time," Patsy said.

"I'm basically clear until the beginning of next week," Thomas Lee said, leaning forward. "The case seems complex and worth thinking about. Anytime someone dies violently and we find inconsistencies and links, I think we have a responsibility to take a hard look."

He brushed an invisible fleck from the sleeve of his Armani jacket and settled back into his chair.

Fricke shifted his attention to Demio, who shrugged and shook his head as if in disbelief.

"Whatever," he said. "I can do a little legwork, I guess, but lots of things seem more complicated than they are, which I'd bet any money is the situation here."

Archie wasn't sure he wanted Demio, but the man made it difficult to leave him out. The omnipresent mocking grin didn't help. The story on Demio was that he always had his own agenda and cooperated with other detectives only when it suited him.

"If the medical examiner concludes that this is indeed a suicide, I'm closing you down, Archie," Fricke said. "Also, I'm not convinced that the bones in the box and this death are as connected as you think. I still lean towards suicide for Helerstone, but I'll wait to see what you come up with. And as for this meeting, we're done."

Fricke fussed with the papers in front of him before he focused his small eyes on Archie.

"Stay here, Archie. I want to chat. The rest of you—what the crap are you all waiting for?"

The others got up and left; Archie remained. Fricke leaned back in his chair, shifted his bulk, and got comfortable.

"Close the door."

When Archie finished doing that, Fricke pointed him back to his seat.

"How are things going personally, Archie?"

"Good. Why wouldn't they be?"

"Because I don't think you're being straight with me, for one thing. You got problems with sleep or gambling or something I don't know about?"

"No, Cal. I don't. At least, none I want to talk about. Why are you asking this now?"

"You're roaming the town at night for no reason, is why. Tracy Gillot said he saw you at the Eagle Wing Casino at four in the morning Friday. Plus, you don't look too great these days, so I'm checking. It's part of my job."

Archie knew it might come to this—Fricke worrying about his mental state—but he didn't like it. His recent stress leave hadn't helped much. Being busy is what would get him past the nightmares, not hanging around with nothing to occupy his brain. It was true he needed more sleep, but most cops had their sleepless times.

"It's nobody's damn business what I do on my own time," he said. "Especially not Tracy damn Gillot's."

"Relax. He wasn't ratting on you. Your visits came up in lunchroom conversation when Tracy was talking to Ray Jameson about winning at gambling. You're right about your life not being anybody's business. It ain't, except when what you do in your spare moments affects your work. If you need more time off, just say so."

Archie didn't like people talking about him behind his back. He raised a dismissive hand.

"Any other issues, Mom?" he said.

"Not that I can tell, no. That doesn't mean it's not happening. You haven't been acting normal for weeks now."

Archie pondered this. He hadn't expected his visits to the casino would become a topic for conversation and that his colleagues would tell tales even inadvertently. It wasn't that he liked to gamble—he didn't. He just needed to fill the time between midnight and dawn. The Eagle Wing was noisy and busy in the strange, isolating way in which all casinos are busy, and he could see others all around him who were just as screwed up as he was. Misery loves company. The only problem was that games of chance didn't last long enough; he was going through money way too fast, and he wasn't sure what he was going to do about it. He shrugged and made to leave.

"I'm here to talk, Archie," Fricke said. "Anytime."

"Thanks, but I've got work to do, Cal. I'm okay, so don't concern yourself."

He left Fricke's office and headed for the morgue where Roger Chu was waiting to discuss the results of Ron Helerstone's postmortem and where he could put other matters aside and concentrate on his investigation.

CHAPTER 9

After a tour of the body that left Archie light-headed, Chu showed him the thirty-two-caliber slug Forensics retrieved from the roof liner of the SUV—the bullet that had exploded Helerstone's brain. The trauma from the crash was severe, but Helerstone might have survived it, Chu thought, and he wouldn't rule out suicide. Archie searched in vain for an abrasion ring or a mark around the right thumb that would confirm that Helerstone fired a pistol and pointed out the discrepancy to Chu.

"Negative evidence doesn't mean much, Archie. Your colleague could be right about how he held the gun. What about a helper?"

"True," Archie said. "An assisted suicide isn't out of the question, although it would still be murder as far as we're concerned."

Chu nodded.

"There's something else I want to show you," he said. "See here."

He pointed to faint dark lines on the wrists.

"Something caused these," he said. "A thin cord perhaps."

"Forensics found nothing like that in the car."

"No, nor did we find cords in the clothing when we stripped the body," Chu said.

Archie lifted the dead man's hands and examined the staining, which suggested that Helerstone had been bound. If he then drove the vehicle over the cliff, where was the rope or cord used? Archie pointed at the discoloration.

"I'm curious," he said. "It reminds me of the kind of residue left by the woven spruce roots I've seen elders use for baskets and the like. Can you get enough to analyze? I'm curious to know what we're dealing with."

"I'll try."

Archie thumbed the lids, noted faint red dots — one on each lid.

"What about these marks?"

"I noticed those," Chu said. "I found one on his neck and one on each cheek. See them?"

Archie nodded.

Chu leaned in, moistened the tip of a cotton swab, which he touched to one of the marks. He held it up for them to examine the scarlet tinge on the fibers.

"I expect we'll get paint when we test."

"From the color, I'll bet you've got red ochre rather than commercial, modern paint. What else have you got for me?"

"I saved the best for last."

Archie followed Chu to a stainless steel counter lit by daylight fluorescents. Chu removed the cover from a rectangular glass container and showed Archie a pale green quid of masticated vegetable matter, which, except for its color, reminded Archie of the chaws of tobacco his grandfather Moise used to spit out.

"Where's it from?" Archie asked.

"Inside his esophagus, like he'd choked *in extremis* and coughed it up."

"Something he ate, you think, some salad or Asian food?" Archie asked.

Chu raised an eyebrow.

"Nothing so simple. We're not dealing with broccoli in red pepper sauce here."

Chu turned the green glob with the tip of his forceps.

"It's plant material, like he'd been chewing grass or something from the forest so he could get a buzz from the stuff. It doesn't sniff like coca or cannabis, but I think we've got drugs here of some kind. Possibly he tried to get himself high before he did himself in."

Chu's words jogged Archie's memory. He'd seen similar quids years before when, as an undergraduate, he'd attended a seminar led by an ethnobotanist who specialized in magical practices and the hallucinogenic plants shamans used to induce visions. She brought examples to show to the class and they were not too different from the mass recovered from Helerstone's throat.

"Serious hallucinogens, do you think?" Archie said.

"I couldn't tell you for sure at the moment, but I suspect so. The lab will part out the ingredients and you'll get a new and interesting angle to do some detecting around. I'd be willing to bet one of them is psilocybin. I removed a few grams and sent it off to the toxicology lab at the university about an hour ago. I've asked a friend of mine to take a gander at the sample and give you something by the middle of next week."

"That's six days away, Roger. Can't you hurry your buddy up?"

Chu dug his hands into his pockets and shook his head. For a man who cared about the contamination of samples, he seemed to attract all manner of debris to his person. The lab coat was stained with God only knew what; Chu still carried chopsticks in his breast pocket that might have been used for his lunch—or for some other medical examiner purpose.

Chu tapped his chin with fingers stained by potassium, embalming fluid and other things Archie didn't want to know about, gave his head a shake and swore under his breath.

"I've got most of the quid here," he said. "I can run a few of my own tests. The results will be pretty rough and ready, nothing I'd stand behind and nothing that could go to court, but you might get something you can take to Fricke, possibly by tomorrow. It's the best I can do, so take it or leave it. I'll have to cancel my dinner date tonight."

"I owe you."

"You could arrange a date for me with Patsy Kydd and we'd be even. You're not seeing her anymore anyway."

Archie, surprised at his gut reaction to what was certainly a joke request, tried to make light it.

"You got to stop inhaling that embalming fluid, Roger. Your mind's totally going."

Chu grinned, turned away.

"I've never denied the fact. Call me at nine tomorrow and I'll let you know what I found."

CHAPTER 10

Tessa Simons arrived at the interview with her lawyer, an Empire City attorney named Rob Ghent. Archie knew of Ghent by reputation—a skilled, perhaps unscrupulous, player with a more or less perfect track record of getting acquittals. He was also rumored to be very expensive, so the Porsche obviously wasn't Tessa's only financial asset. Archie made a note to check her financial records if a case developed around her.

In keeping with the situation, she had dressed simply in a casual outfit consisting of a loose silk blouse and fashionable jeans, and she wore her shoulder-length red hair caught in a gold clasp. Otherwise, a gold Cartier watch was her only jewelry. She seemed too classy for a police interview room, which he guessed was partly the point. Martin Demio entered the room late, grinned at Tessa, raised his eyebrows, sat down, leaned back in his chair and belched. Archie started the interview.

He asked standard how-and-why questions first, and these Tessa answered perfunctorily without volunteering much in the way of elaboration. She refused to confirm her staying at Helerstone's house, though there seemed to be little point in denying the obvious. Occasionally, Ghent intervened when a question seemed to be leading, but mostly he stayed quiet.

After a half hour, Archie called a break, and he and Demio left the interview room to discuss strategy. They stood side by side observing through the two-way mirror while Tessa chatted with Ghent about baseball. More than once, she glanced at the mirror as if she could see them, and smiled.

"She's pretty cool," Demio said.

"When you brought her in, did you say anything about the circumstances of Helerstone's death or give her any hint that we were pursuing this as a murder investigation?" Archie asked.

"C'mon. Talk sense," Demio said.

"I'm just asking."

"I'm not stupid, pal." Demio was becoming irritated. "I told her over and over we wanted to understand why the professor might want to off himself and how we wanted to put the case to bed."

"What did she say?" Archie said.

"She said a friend told her Helerstone would put her up, beyond which, there was nothing more to tell me, and she meant me specifically. She's not going to give us nothing she don't want to give. Did you check out the Cartier watch? I don't think she was desperate for a place to stay."

"I never thought she was," Archie said. "Let's go back in and see if we get anything worthwhile from her."

They reentered the room, and when Archie took his seat opposite her, Tessa looked past him, emanating pure disinterest. He'd seen that expression before, part of the arsenal of a possibly cruel woman who never doubted her beauty. Ghent posed a question.

"Suicides don't usually get this kind of thoroughness from you people," he said. "To be clear, is this part of a murder investigation?"

"It could be," Archie said. "There's doubt. We don't think the professor was suicidal, but some think maybe he was. I think murder is a possibility, but I honestly don't know the direction the investigation will take. If you think your client is being misled, we can end the interview for now and reconvene later when you've consulted with her."

Tessa leaned over and whispered in Ghent's ear. He nodded. Tessa examined one of her fingernails before she returned her attention to Archie, a nice little dramatic pause, which he noted.

"Whatever you want, Detective Sergeant," Ghent said. "Let's get on with it."

"Okay, Tessa," Archie said. "I'm curious to know if you'd seen Ron take drugs, or been involved with them in any way.

She shook her head.

"I don't remember seeing anything out of the ordinary," she said. "A little grass, perhaps, but I don't know."

"Did he party much or associate with people outside of his social circle, any strangers or people who seemed out of place at a professor's house?"

She twirled a lock of her hair between her fingers.

"No," she said. "At least not while I was around him."

"What about academic research?" Archie asked. "I get the sense he was into ancient rituals and ceremonies. Did he ever say anything about such things?"

"No."

Archie leaned back in his chair. He steepled his forefingers against his chin and studied her.

"I'm wondering, Tessa," he said. "If you could hazard a guess as to why he felt he needed to keep a Colt forty-five near him. Was he afraid of someone?"

"My client doesn't know anything about that," Ghent said. "She has nothing to say about drugs, or creepy people, or weird ceremonies. As to the gun, who knows? It's not uncommon to keep a pistol in the house for protection these days."

"Your client had no trouble finding the gun," Archie said. "And yet, according to her, she was a visitor, nothing more."

"Whatever is that supposed to mean?" Ghent said. "The simple explanation is that she saw you as intruders. She's a young, attractive woman. She's alone. The gun came to hand when my client felt threatened, and she doesn't have any more to say on the subject."

"Fair enough," Archie said. "Let's talk about other things. Let's discuss the professor's professional life and why it went off the track. You told Detective Demio you helped him in his work, Tessa. In what capacity?"

"I helped him in the lab occasionally."

"Okay," Archie said. "I'm trying to get at his state of mind, and since you worked with him, it's possible you picked up on that. Did he ever act weird or out of character, or did you get the sense he was feeling frustrated or unfulfilled?"

She shook her head.

"He seemed fine to me."

"What help did he need in his lab?"

She hesitated, and Archie picked up on it.

"Okay," she said. "Not in his lab. I helped him with his marking and stuff like that."

Archie felt certain Helerstone had, in the past, researched the ancient Cannibal Society that once operated on the northern West Coast, and it might be true about shamans using hallucinogens. The quid Chu took from Helerstone's throat might be an indication the professor was more into his work than was safe. It was a long shot.

"I found notes Ron made on the old Cannibal Society. Did you help him with those?"

"I don't think so," she said.

She cast a sideways glance at Ghent.

"How much longer?" Ghent asked.

Archie leaned back, asked Demio if he had any questions. Demio shrugged.

"Nah," he said.

"I guess we're finished here," Archie said. He waited until they started to rise before he spoke.

"One more thing," he said. "Did Ron ever mention a woman named Stella Picard?"

The name meant something to her; he could see a flicker of emotion in her eyes. She folded her arms across her chest, tried to brazen it out, failed and turned to her lawyer. Ghent played his part.

"What is the purpose of the question?" he asked.

"It's simple and straightforward," Archie said. "I just want to know if Ron met this person. It may be germane, and it may not. I honestly don't know."

He held Tessa's eyes with his own.

"So, Tessa—do you recall Professor Helerstone mentioning Stella Picard?" he said.

Her eyes lingered on his as if weighing the consequences of remaining silent.

"He might have done," she said at last.

Archie felt like he'd struck pay dirt.

"When would that be—when he talked about her?" Archie said.

"Two years ago or so, at least, I think, but I can't remember for sure."

"Where did the conversation take place?"

"In this basement office he used, but I don't see the point of these questions. Stella was hardly even an acquaintance of his, as I recall."

This jogged Archie's memory. Helerstone once had a private lair in the basement of the Anthro building, but Tessa surprised him before he could frame a question about it.

"I knew her too, by the way," she said.

"*I hardly knew her* is a better way of putting it," Tessa said. "But yes, I met her years ago. I was at the university, took some classes, and then I left and did some other things. When I came back, Ron had Stella working for him. I think there was an understanding between them, but who can say."

"Is that the whole story, or is there something else you aren't telling us?"

Ghent leaned into the conversation. The harsh interview room light glinted off his shaven scalp.

"Be careful, Detective Sergeant. My client is cooperating."

"I don't like the tone of the question either," Tessa said. "I really don't like it."

Archie decided to back off.

"Okay. Sorry if you got that impression I thought you were hiding the truth. I'm clumsy with my questions sometimes. We are just curious about links between Stella Picard and Ron Helerstone is all."

"I don't see what this little tangent has to do with Ron's death," Tessa said defensively.

"It's early days, Tessa. We check under all sorts of rocks," Archie said.

"You can be insulting, Detective," she said, glaring at him. "Why do you want to dig up dirt on a dead man?"

Her tone was combative again. Archie still wasn't sure if her umbrage was real or feigned.

"We simply want to confirm certain facts and to get information about relationships or breakups that might help us understand what happened to professor Helerstone."

He was playing the empathy card, but he doubted she would pick it up.

"Ron had relationships with lots of women before I arrived on the scene," she said. "They don't mean anything to me and didn't at the time because I'm not the possessive type. I met Stella Picard occasionally at parties and once or twice in Ron's house or lab. She acted like she was Ron's girlfriend, and he seemed stuck on her. Naturally, the university has policies about professors and students, but I gathered that they became involved after she finished taking his course. I think they went on research trips together. Ron attracted bright, young women, but it wasn't what you, what most people, imagine. We all got something out of it. Whatever you think about it, it was worth it. Ron gave me something I never got from a guy my own age, and I'm upset he's gone."

She lowered her head. Did she have tears in her eyes? She seemed genuine, but a lot of liars could pull that off.

"I don't want to answer any more questions," she said.

Ghent stood up.

"I think it's time we left," he said. "Unless you thought of a charge you can hold her on. I wouldn't try the *threatening-a-police-officer* thing, or the firearms charge, because you'll just end up embarrassing yourself."

He shrugged off his suit jacket and hung it from a thick finger over one shoulder, a scorpion tattoo on the back of his hand clearly visible.

"So," he said. "Is she being charged, and if so with what?"

"She pointed a loaded weapon at an officer and took off, so we could hold her on two charges at least," Demio said.

"Bullshit. She didn't know who you were," Ghent said. "She was alone in the house. She got Helerstone's pistol from his bureau. What would you charge her with—trying to protect herself from intruders?"

Tessa glared at Demio.

"I didn't do anything wrong, and you both know it," she said. "I was waiting for Ron before you arrived. He never came home, and you won't let me see him now. It's hurtful. Can you arrange for me to view the body, Detective Sergeant? Would you set things up for me?"

Archie nodded.

"Sure," he said.

He put down his pen and closed his notebook. It was enough for the day. At least now he was certain Tessa Simons knew more about everything than she was divulging.

"I'm not prepared to charge you over the gun or anything else at the moment."

"Smart," Ghent said. "You'll avoid the police harassment thing, which would be the next step for me."

Archie took a business card out of his breast pocket and slid it across to Tessa.

"If you think of anything to help us, Tessa, or if you remember more about Stella Picard, I'd appreciate it if you'd give me a call."

"I'll think about it."

He officially ended the interview and switched off the recording. Demio opened the door for Tessa and Ghent and thanked them with such an obvious lack of sincerity that he made a mockery of politeness. After they left, he lifted hands and shoulders in the interrogative. Archie shrugged. Tessa Simons was no pushover, but she gave him much more than he expected to get. She had linked Picard with Helerstone and put herself in the mix too, and he was curious why she did so.

Patsy Kydd appeared at the door. She entered the room and sat down opposite Archie, told him that she'd watched some of the interview through the two-way mirror.

"I was in the neighborhood," she said. "So I thought I'd take a peek."

"And what did you think?" Archie asked.

"She's something. I don't buy those tears for a minute. She's got an edge to her that would cut leather."

"She seemed kind of sweet to me," Demio said.

Demio's irony made Patsy smile.

"Interesting that we know almost nothing about her," she said. "In fact, Stella Picard is less of a mystery than Tessa Simons."

"I was thinking the same thing," Archie said. "So that's the first order of business. Let's make investigating Tessa a priority."

"I can do it," Patsy said.

Archie nodded.

"Soon as you can, please," Archie said. "I'd like to know more, but let's call it a day for now."

Neither Patsy nor Demio lingered since it was already late. Demio seemed very anxious to get home, and Patsy said that she had things to do.

Both left within seconds. Archie packed up and turned off the lights in the interview room, glad to be on his own. He had lots of evening left, time he would use to visit the university and Ron Helerstone's office.

His dinner was a meatball sandwich from Avril's. He ate as he drove, his wipers on intermittent against the spotty effects of a light spring night rain. After picking up the key he arranged for earlier, he parked close to the Henry Wallace building, left a police identity card on his dash, went through the glass doors and entered the building. This was an old gothic revival relic of the ivory-tower age of universities and very busy during the regular school year. Now, however, with few students on campus, the halls were deserted and most doors closed.

Archie went up the marble stairs to the third floor, walked to the end of a long groin-vaulted hallway to number 313, Helerstone's office. He paused at the door and examined the bulletin board, hoping to find something of interest or even relevant. There wasn't much—a poster for a summer field school in archaeology at another university, the application due date long past, and three messages, two of them obviously from undergrads. The first message was friendly: "Came by. You weren't here. Call me, Love, R XO"; another was a complaint: "Professor Helerstone, I deserve a better grade. I tried to call you on several occasions. I waited for you here without result. I'm definitely contacting the department over this matter, Dougal Remy"; a third carried one laser-printed line, "The usual place at 3, King." Archie took note of this—King was the person who sold Helerstone the house in Falcon View. Archie un-pinned the notes and put them in his case before he opened the door.

Inside, dead plants and dust testified to the office's lack of use. Archie moved a coffee cup, its contents coated with a thick layer of bluish mold, picked up a file folder and thumbed through its contents—unmarked student papers from the semester just ended, among them Dougal Remy's effort. The desk's half-empty drawers contained only ordinary office supplies; the faint outline of a laptop in the desktop dust was the only sign of a computer.

The Henry Wallace office, Archie concluded, was little more than a letter drop for Helerstone, a place where he received papers and perhaps met with students. He did his real work elsewhere. He took more pictures with his phone camera before he closed and locked the door, sealed it and left the building.

CHAPTER 11

Splitting your aces was the right move, but Archie's new cards beat him on both hands and almost cleaned him out. Finally, after having watched most of his savings disappear, he gathered up his remaining chips, cashed them out and made his way through the faux-circus noise to the Eagle Wing Casino exit. A burly doorman nodded, said, "Arch," and waved him out. Archie congratulated himself on leaving with some of his money left, not a frequent occurrence of late, and concluded that there might be hope for him after all.

As he blinked his scratchy eyes to moisten them, he wondered what he should do with himself. He didn't want to go to bed; sleep would only invite his recurring nightmares of burning houses and burning people. He'd been forced to take a leave, which hadn't helped, nor had counseling, tranquilizers or sleeping pills. He muscled his thoughts back to his present case and the problem of the bones in the box. The cave was a perfect way to dispose of a skeleton when you thought about it. No one would search for the remains of a murder victim in a sacred burial place, one officially closed to visitors and rarely entered.

Of course, skeletonizing was critical. Scientists used *dermestid* beetles for that. Add traditional items like the Chilkat blanket for good measure, and you had a chief's prestige to contend with too. But who would throw away such treasures? And why send a letter to the police and more specifically to him, Archie? As for Helerstone, Archie suspected he'd known a great deal about Stella Picard's murder and, perhaps, the murderer feared Helerstone would tell what he knew and eliminated him for that reason. The plain facts of Helerstone's death, including the staged suicide, the quid of hallucinogens, the ochre dots on the dead man's eyelids, the plant fiber cord on his wrist, suggested murder as theater, or ceremony.

Helerstone could be secretive, and he'd been a player too. Archie recalled an incident when Helerstone hit on a woman named Hannah, Archie's girlfriend, for all the man knew, while she and Archie were talking in the cafeteria. When Helerstone reminded Hannah of a collection of Solomon Islands magical regalia he promised to show her, she had asked Archie to come along. Helerstone extended a reluctant invitation, to which Archie agreed. He was naïve in those days. But Helerstone was on the make—Hannah too, as it turned out.

Helerstone took them through the archaeology labs and the storage area to a private lab and office beneath the museum. Archie was so simple-minded he needed the better part of twenty minutes to figure out they didn't want him there, at which point he had taken his leave awkwardly. The next time he saw Hannah, she worked for Helerstone, marking papers and treating under-grads like him with disdain.

So where was he in his investigation? The im-promptu state of the Falcon View house and the barely used Henry Wallace office yielded little, so Helerstone's real working life must be elsewhere like, for example, in an out-of the way office hid-den under the museum. The office, if it still exist-ed, would be worth checking out, and Archie de-cided he would do so in the morning.

His queasy stomach now reasserted itself and, for want of a good idea, he returned to the casino and its buffet and loaded a plate with greasy food, paid for it, and took it to an isolated table. After a half hour, he felt marginally better. He dropped his second plate half-full on the busser's stand and like a sleepwalker followed a familiar trajectory to a blackjack table where he took a seat and began to play. Sometime well after midnight, he finished up, tipped the dealer, gathered his chips and left the table to go cash out.

Outside and half-stumbling with fatigue, he made his way to the 4Runner, which was now covered in dew. He unlocked the doors, pulled the backseats forward, laid them down and climbed in, swung the door shut behind him, curled up on the cold carpeting and fell asleep. For once, images of fire and burning did not return to torment him.

CHAPTER 12

Archie's cell phone buzzed him awake. When the screen lit up, he checked the time and the identity of the caller, saw Tessa Simons's name and answered on the penultimate ring.

"You said I should call you," she said. Her voice took on a husky quality that would probably be irresistible under the right circumstances.

"True. I did say so," he said.

The night cold, or something else, made him shiver. He needed to start his vehicle and get some heat going, but she kept him talking.

"You sound tired, or nervous," she said. "Should I ask what you're doing?"

"I'm not nervous. What did you want?" he said.

"I need to talk to you."

"Now? It's two o'clock in the morning, and I'm not yet home," he said.

"If you want me to tell you about Stella Picard, I'm ready now or not at all. Also, I drove past your vehicle in the Eagle Wing parking lot a half hour ago, so I know you're out and about. You're probably shivering in the cold right now, poor guy."

"Tomorrow in my office would suit me better," Archie said. "I do have a personal life."

"I heard different, but anyway, I'm feeling like talking now, and tomorrow I likely won't, so it's up to you."

There was nothing attractive about her ultimatum, intriguing perhaps, but not attractive. He told her again to come into his office during regular hours, but again she refused and hung up. After five minutes, he called her back.

"You win, Tessa," he said. "I'll come to you."

"Yes, we don't want to sit in your vehicle in the Casino parking lot like a couple of illicit lovers, do we? So where shall it be?"

Although he reminded himself that a detective meeting someone like her, a woman also connected to a murder investigation, in the middle of the night was stupid, he couldn't help being interested. When he suggested a safe coffee shop in Old Town, she laughed sardonically, said she needed a proper drink rather than a coffee and named a fashionable cocktail lounge. When he demurred, she told him to forget the whole thing and ended the conversation again. Deciding that he'd dodged a bullet after all, he rubbed his eyes to make them focus, started the 4Runner and pointed its battered nose towards home.

He was at the front door of his building, condo key in hand, when her Porsche, heralded by the low throb of its tuned exhaust, swung into the drive. Tessa parked her car at the curb and got out. She wore the full evening kit—a short skirt and the black patent leather high heels with the red soles Archie knew meant expensive. She had obviously dressed for a night out somewhere, and he figured she'd decided he would be her night-cap. She smiled when she saw him, arranged a pale green scarf over her shoulders to guard against the damp and came to meet him; stiletto heels clicked on the paving stones, light flashed on long earrings.

"I decided to take matters into my own hands," she said. "I'm not used to being at some-one's beck and call, and I'm ready to tell you things about Stella Picard."

"So you said, and I want to hear them."

He considered his options. He ought to send her away, to refuse to see her until he could inter-view her properly because the situation as it stood signaled professional suicide. Instead, he turned the key in the lock and swung the door open to let her pass.

"After you," he said.

She swept by him and walked across the lobby towards the elevator like she knew where she was going and he trailed her, too much like a lap dog, he thought. The elevator doors slid shut. She stood close and he could smell the subtle musk of her perfume.

"Rob said I shouldn't talk to you."

"Ghent?" he said.

"Yes, Rob Ghent."

"I'm curious. How did you settle on Ghent as your attorney?"

"I knew him slightly through Ron," she said.

"They were acquaintances, or friends. His card was at Ron's, and I called him."

"Happy with him?"

"More or less. He's a bit creepy," she said.

"You know he's got serious biker connections, I guess?" he said.

"I know he rides a Harley."

When they arrived at Archie's apartment, Tessa stood beside him while he unlocked the door and, taking a liberty, she preceded him inside before he could extend the invitation. He closed the door behind them and paused, thinking. She glanced back at him, shrugged off her light jacket and held it in her hand, waiting. He took it from her and hung it up.

"You're tired, Detective," she said. "I can see it in those brown eyes of yours. You're not getting enough sleep, obviously."

He smiled at the irony.

"Sometimes things come up," he said. "Night things. We could have talked in the morning, which would be better. This is not ideal."

She tilted her head and smiled.

"Why not?" she said. "I didn't come here to try to seduce you, Archie. You must be very full of yourself to think so."

He almost laughed at that remark.

"Never mind," she continued. "I felt the urge to get things off my chest. I was on my way home from a jazz concert, and I thought I could call you. I knew I wouldn't be able to sleep, so here I am."

"And now, for some reason, sleep is eluding me too," he said. "Okay. Let's talk. I'll set up a recording if you don't mind and make this official."

"Must you? Recording makes me clam up."

She put a hand on his arm as if to stay him. The touch made the situation more intimate than he wanted it to be, but he didn't resist either. She let her hand drop to his. As he decided he'd better end the discussion and send her home, she dropped his hand, kicked off her shoes, walked into the living room and crossed to the windows.

"You have a spectacular view, Archie," she said.

She stood on her tiptoes to peer through the high side window towards the lights of Old Town, showing him at the same time fine, strong calves, a marvelous dorsal curve and, when she turned, a glimpse of her breasts pushing against the translucent silk of her blouse. It was a nice move, sexy but subtle. He was quite certain now that a police-style interview was not what she had in mind. She turned and smiled at him. When she started to head for the couch, he called her to the kitchen and indicated a chair.

"Best we talk over here," he said. "So, what do you want to tell me about Stella Picard?"

She sat down, reclined in her chair and crossed her long legs. He found his notebook and took a seat opposite her, ready to record what she said. He hoped he seemed professional. She leaned forward, her chin in her hand, elbows on the table, studying him.

"I lied to you before," she said. "Stella Picard was a friend of mine, and I knew her well."

Archie pretended to be surprised by this revelation. Tessa peered at him as if she were searching his eyes for evidence she could trust him. Apparently, she saw what she wanted. Ron Helerstone was at the heart of it, she said, but there was much more. For one thing, she and Helerstone had been lovers, not just friends. Archie said he suspected as much and probed for details about their relationship.

"It started a number of years ago when I took some classes with Ron," she said. "That part is true—but our relationship started later. I left and came back and subsequently got work with him through an acquaintance. Ron was researching West Coast secret societies and he needed a gofer. Stella was around then, so sincere, so naïve, doing odd jobs for him."

She paused, like she was collecting her thoughts before continuing.

"Anyway, I liked her and we hung out quite a bit for a while. She got into what Ron was doing and became his full-time research assistant. She and he got a thing going and we stopped hanging out. She was jealous of me, I think. Stella and Ron seemed good, but one day I walked in on a big fight between them. Stella even threw an artifact at Ron once and accused him of dishonesty. I didn't get it all. She said something about him being a creep and ran out of the room. Ron made light of it at the time, but I never saw Stella again."

"And your relationship with Ron started soon after?" Archie asked.

She nodded.

"I was already in the picture, as you might guess. Ron couldn't stick with one woman for long, or be faithful. It wasn't in him. We had fun, and I was happy enough. I got who he was, plus I'm a bit like him. Ron told me Stella went back to her family in the East and I was relieved because she was a genuinely nice person and I didn't want to hurt her. Ron and I got closer and became friends with options, shall we say."

"But the relationship ended for a time?" Archie said.

"Yes. About six years ago, Ron met this guy he called Coyote, and things started to get weird. He would leave for weeks, and every time he came back from one of his trips, which often involved Coyote, he would be changed."

"Changed how? What do you mean?"

"Sometimes he would say and do things that scared me," she said." Once we hiked up to top of Raleigh Escarpment. He got weird and began to jump and caper around at the edge of the cliff. He even dragged me to the brink and said if we jumped we would fly like birds. There were other things too. He started to …"

Her phone beeped. She left off the conversation to retrieve it from the small purse she carried with her. She read the message and paled.

"I've said enough," she said.

Frantically, she went to each of the windows in turn as if searching for an intruder.

"Can anyone see in here?" she asked.

"We're ten floors up, so no."

She retreated to a place behind a partition out of sight of the windows. He sat for a moment before he followed her. She turned the screen of her phone towards him.

"It says to keep your mouth shut," Archie said.

"And it also describes us and where we are."

"Yes, it does," Archie said.

"How would they know?"

"A guess," he said.

"The message described your kitchen and my outfit."

"The kitchen is standard, nothing remarkable. The person saw you earlier this evening, followed you here perhaps."

She closed her eyes, took deep breaths to calm herself before she spoke.

"No, I changed just before I came to meet you. I didn't go to a jazz concert. I came from the house, and I didn't see anyone. Now I don't know what to think. Would you be able to protect me if I needed you to?"

"I might be able to do something if you start being completely straight with me," Archie said.

"Close the blinds—please. Can you check the sky for a drone?"

He shrugged.

"Okay."

He went out onto his balcony and searched the dark sky, but there was nothing. When he came back into the room, his front door stood open and Tessa was gone. He swore, grabbed his jacket, checked his pistol and went after her.

CHAPTER 13

Having bounded down fourteen flights of stairs, Archie arrived at street level just as the red Porsche squealed out of his building's drive. Two minutes later, he was speeding down the road in the 4Runner, heading towards Helerstone's Falcon View house, although catching the Porsche was a pipe dream. He cursed, flicked on his emergency lights and slammed his foot down on the gas pedal.

When he got to the darkened house, he spotted her car parked near the side door and pulled up, contemplating his next move. Was she afraid for real, or was this whole episode some trick? He suspected the latter.

A lamp winked on in a rear room where no doubt Tessa would be getting ready for bed, tired after an interesting and entertaining evening. The sensible thing, Archie knew, would be to call a squad car to watch the place and leave when it arrived. Instead, he got out, shut the 4Runner's door quietly and hiked up the path to the house.

When he was still fifty feet or so from the house, the front door opened. Tessa came out and stood silhouetted by the light, watching for someone. Archie slowed, keeping to the shadows and wondering what the hell he was thinking. If she hadn't seemed genuinely frightened, he would have gone home. Correct that—he *should* definitely go home. When he heard a man and a woman arguing, he eased closer and he was still listening, or loitering, when they grabbed him and began the beating.

They were professionals, stripping him of his gun right away before the first wicked punch almost doubled Archie over. He recovered enough to slam an elbow into the face of the one assailant before a second man pinned his arms and another swung an ax handle hard into Archie's ribs, winding him.

As he shrugged out of the grip of the man holding him, he took a jab from a burly individual, wearing biker denims like the others. Archie drove a knee into a nearby groin and heard a satisfying grunt of pain before another swing of the axe handle knocked him off his feet. Falling sideways, he rolled down the slope and deep into a tangle of shrubs and rhododendrons, a fortunate break, although Archie knew his attackers would find him if he didn't keep moving. He kept his head down and slid under the bushes like a snake, away from the sounds of pursuit.

When he had a chance, he probed his face and torso with his fingers—a bruised cheekbone and aching ribs—and considered his options. Identifying himself as a police officer might work in his favor, or it might not. He decided in the negative. After three or four minutes, he crept out of the shrubbery, but spotting the biker with the axe handle on the path ahead of him, Archie eased back. He was almost in the clear when he stepped on the dry branch. As the biker turned to face him, Archie charged, knocked the man down with an elbow smash, picked up the axe handle and continued on his way. Running now, he collided with Rob Ghent and bowled him over. Ghent yelled for help as he stumbled to his feet and the bikers converged on the spot. They circled Archie, waiting for an opening, but Ghent, brushing the dirt off his clothes, waved them back.

"Archie fucking Stevens," he said.

"You got that right, Ghent."

"Are you here stalking my client, Detective Sergeant?" Ghent said. "It seems so."

"You're in a lot of trouble, Rob," Archie said.

"I don't think so. I'm here to protect Ms. Simons from creeps like you."

"What are you talking about?"

"She called me," Ghent said. "It's true. Ask her."

"I'd like to talk to her for sure."

"Look—you get your wish," Ghent said.

At this point, Tessa appeared out of the darkness and seemed surprisingly nonchalant considering the evening's events.

"You shouldn't be here, policeman," she said. "I thought I made it clear to you that I have no more to say, and I'd like you to go."

"I will go when I'm ready," Archie said. "What's going on, Tessa?"

Ghent laughed.

"Please leave, Archie," Tessa said. "This is too weird."

"You heard her, Stevens," Ghent said. "As her attorney, I can tell you a charge of harassment is likely, or even something worse."

"I'm not worried, Ghent."

"We're done talking here, Detective Sergeant," Ghent said.

Archie's phone chimed.

"Plus, I put in a call to your boss," Ghent said.

"And you might want this."

He handed Archie back his pistol. Archie holstered it and answered his phone. Fricke came on, growled out a few syllables, the short version of a good old-fashioned reaming out. Archie cut him off, muted his cell and watched Ghent and the bikers head up to the house with Tessa. Nearly delirious with lack of sleep, he touched the still wet blood on his lower lip and, feeling like a whipped dog, made his way back through the gardens to his 4Runner.

CHAPTER 14

Still feeling the effects of the fight of the night before, Archie, accompanied by Martin Demio, arrived unannounced at the offices of Andrea Dhillon, the university's president. It was clear from her reaction that a police visit was unwelcome, so Archie tried to be extra polite and did his best to be charming—Patsy always said he could turn it on when he wanted something. However, whatever progress he'd made with the president evaporated when Archie asked to see Helerstone's other office, the one under the museum, at which point Dhillon shifted from welcoming mode to something less congenial. When she said she doubted the existence of any such office, Archie persisted, and at length Kari Fletcher, her secretary, produced a handwritten list. Dhillon tut-tutted.

"This should all be on the computer, Kari," she said. "How I am supposed to know what's what if I can't find things in my efiles?"

"President Porteous kept this apart," Kari said. "He liked to keep some things out of the database. He had his own way of doing things, as we've discussed."

"So stupid and inefficient."

"I just did what I was told, but I'll make whatever changes you want."

Archie listened to this seemingly staged interchange with interest. Kari retrieved a tattered folder from a filing cabinet drawer and gave it to Dhillon.

"You might want this too, Andrea," she said. "It might save us from additional intrusions."

Dhillon nodded, flipped through the folder, tutted, and handed Archie a plan containing a sketch of the department basement. This showed the area of artifact storage labeled "*The Cemetery*" in pencil. Archie noted the date. Twenty years ago.

"Normally, this space would be open to other scholars," Dhillon said. "Why am I surprised? People tend to claim things and hang on to them in this faculty, and if something is missed, so much the better."

Archie told her he needed access to the lab and she said she would arrange a key for it from Physical Plant.

"I have a conference call soon," she said. "The earliest I can meet you would be in three hours."

"I'll see you at the museum at one then," Archie said.

"What'd you think of her?" Demio said, as they walked away.

"She fits the role. She seemed surprised Helerstone kept the office, but I'm not so sure she was."

"I thought she was datable."

"You would."

"I'm not dead, man."

"I'm not sure she's your type, Martin."

Demio left soon after to take care of some business of his own, the nature of which he kept to himself. They would meet later in the day in order to interview other professors in the Department of Anthropology. Archie decided to take advantage of the interval to snatch a nap and remembered a quiet, shaded grassy area within a commemorative grove of oaks near the Associated Students Building. He walked there, found a likely spot, sat down with his back against the bole of a tree and fell asleep within seconds.

When he woke and checked the time on the clock tower, he realized he had slept for over an hour. Still groggy, he hauled himself to his feet, checked his messages, found nothing pressing and made his way across campus to the museum.

Andrea Dhillon was waiting for him at the main door with the necessary keys. To his surprise, she insisted on accompanying him, and he couldn't think of any easy way he could prevent her from so doing. Besides, he was convinced she wasn't quite as uninformed as she pretended, and he needed to learn what exactly she knew about secret places under the university.

He followed her as she walked briskly through the galleries, her shoe heels clattering on the laminated floors. They bypassed the curating area and carried on to a connecting passageway leading to stairs going down to the basement. When Dhillon opened the cellar door, they entered a vast storage area with the long aisles of metal shelving loaded with boxes, trays and artifacts. This was "*The Cemetery*." Archie knew it anyway. All archaeology students visited the place at one time or another. Dhillon, however, seemed lost. Twice they ended up in blind corners. She studied her map for a moment and then refolded it.

"This thing is no help," she said. "I'll need time to locate Professor Helerstone's illegal office.

I'll talk to Kari. I think it might be better if you came back another time."

Archie didn't like being stalled, which is what seemed to be happening.

"That won't be necessary," he said. "I am somewhat familiar with this area. I'm here now conducting a police investigation, and I want to see what I came to see. The Arkies call this the "*Cemetery*" because it's where research projects go to die. As I recall, there are almost a hundred years' worth of artifacts stored here from digs all over the world."

She jammed the map into her jacket pocket.

"Since you know so much," she said. "Lead the way."

Archie nodded. He still remembered the general layout, which seemed reasonably easy to figure out—basically a grid pattern on a north-south axis. He found a cross aisle and then followed a wider passage to a door half-hidden behind a tall cabinet. He pointed this out to her and waited while she opened it but stopped her before she could step inside. When she protested, he said, "You can stay if you like, but I don't want you touching anything in here."

"I have every intention of staying," she said. "I want to make sure the university's reputation is protected."

"Fair enough," he said.

She frowned, fondled the single string of heavy turquoise beads that hung around her neck and made a sweeping motion with her other hand.

"What's this all about anyway?" she asked. "I thought Professor Helerstone took his own life."

"No, it's a homicide, which means your reputation is not as high on my list as it is on yours. I have to ask you why you haven't been honest with me."

"What do you mean?" she said indignantly.

"You have been in here since I made the request. Which makes me wonder why you were pretending to be lost."

"Pretending!" she said. "How dare you suggest such a thing?"

"I'm not suggesting anything. I'm telling you, President Dhillon. You left a footprint."

He pointed to the mark in the dust inside the door left by a high-heeled shoe. He watched her for a reaction, but if she was surprised or shocked, it didn't register on her face.

"I have every right to go anywhere on university property I please," she said.

"Usually, yes, but you cannot contaminate a crime scene, which this might be, so I'll need to know what you did in here?"

She flushed, less, Archie thought, with embarrassment than with anger.

"I did nothing wrong," she insisted. "I simply wanted to check out what was what so I found the place and peeked inside."

"And you lied to me," he said. "I do not want you in this room again until I say so. Clear?"

"How dare you instruct me?"

Archie ignored her protest.

"I'll also need access to any records Doctor Helerstone might have left with the university."

"With the appropriate warrant, of course, I can't stop you."

"With a warrant, no you can't."

He opened his jacket and touched the edge of the folded document he had picked up from the office earlier in the day. Delia John was adept at such things and had expedited the paperwork. He thought Dhillon might want to peruse it, but she didn't seem interested once he caught her in the lie. Archie wasn't sure if she was more bothered by his accusation, by the intrusion into her territory, or by something else. He was still trying to get a good read on her.

"Would you like to examine the warrant?" he asked.

She shook her head in real or pretended exasperation.

"I hope this isn't going to require too much involvement from staff."

"I doubt if the university will be involved much. Naturally I can't promise anything at this stage. In the meantime, I would appreciate it if you could make parking available for my team and me? Some of us will be on campus again."

"I might arrange it. I guess you'll take what you need anyway."

He shrugged.

"I'm not trying to make your life difficult, President Dhillon. We won't be here too long in all likelihood. I'd prefer to use the rear parking lot, so my people can come in the lower door. That way you won't have us moving through high-traffic areas like the lobby or the galleries, plus any police vehicles will be out of sight for the most part. It will be less visibility as far as the university is concerned, and it's better for us too."

"I definitely don't want police officers wandering around campus any more than is necessary. Now, before I go …"

She brushed past him, peered inside Helerstone's office, making a point he supposed, turned on a stiletto heel and left without saying another word. Archie had the office to himself, which was what he preferred.

He went inside and closed the door behind him, savored the deep quiet of the space for a few moments before he took rubber gloves from his pocket and pulled them on.

He began his investigations in the kitchen area, examining cupboards, counters, and the fridge, which held some expired juice boxes and an empty and clean plastic container on which someone had printed, "*This is not yours*," in purple marker. The cupboards, the cutlery drawer, the microwave and the space under the sink were spotless. He took pictures and moved on to the office proper.

He wondered if Helerstone had been here the evening he died. It would have been quiet, with no music player or radio to break the tomb-like silence. Even now, Archie could hear no sounds coming from the museum or even from the main labs, which were not so very far away.

Archie wondered what kind of work required so much privacy, secrecy even. He read through the papers on the desktop, hoping to find a clue to Helerstone's recent activities, but these were mostly copies of old emails and notices about conferences and publications. When he opened the drawers, one by one, he found only commonplace things—paper clips, pushpins, pencils, ballpoint pens, and a power cord for a laptop computer, though the computer itself was missing.

A file safe alongside the desk contained a mound of reprinted scholarly papers. Archie leafed through these, mostly dated articles on shamanistic ritual and the meaning of objects used in magical ceremonies. Beneath the pile, however, he found something else, a small red box of pistol ammunition—Eley Tenex thirty-two caliber, a type he didn't recognize. He retrieved it and flipped the lid; five rounds were missing. He photographed the empty bullet nests, pulled an evidence bag from his pocket and slid the box inside and put the package in his pocket.

He took out his now-charged mini-light, dropped down to his hands and knees, bumped his head, cursed, and began to search under the desk. Near a far leg, he recovered what appeared to be green-tinged coconut, and he eased a sample of it into a plastic bag with the tip of his pen. He also picked up fragments of a post-it-note on which someone had hastily scrawled abbreviations, word fragments and numbers, including a large K, the number 10, most of the word *ceremonial* and the word *plants*. These went into another bag.

He stood, rubbed the tender spot on his head and then walked across the room to the door, which he opened before he returned to the chair and swiveled it so he could look out, wanting to know how much a person could see from inside the office. Beyond the line of deep shelving and artifact trays stretched along the back wall, this was not much.

He rose and walked to the shelves. Some trays seemed out of place, containing anthropological rather than archaeological artifacts; most were dusty. Some, he recognized—raven rattles, an *amhalait* from the north, possibly Tlingit. The main aisle was swept clear of dust so no footprints showed.

One of the trays sitting on its own shelf, separate from the others, caught his eye. This held *Ts'onaqua* dance masks and other Cannibal Society items that Archie felt odd even touching, but he could tell that somebody *had* been handling the items, and recently, too. Most of what he saw appeared to be shaman paraphernalia, but what this might mean to his investigation, Archie could not tell.

He pulled off his gloves and tucked them back into his pocket. Now at least he knew Helerstone's research into shamanism and secret societies continued, but otherwise, he had found nothing to help him to easily solve the professor's murder, or link his death to Stella Picard's, for that matter.

He considered the ammunition he'd found and remembered Helerstone once owned and cherished a target pistol, a finely balanced thirty-two caliber Walther GSP-C, a gun that shot the same kind of bullet as the one that killed Stella Picard. Archie would need to find the Walther if he hoped to have ballistics match the slug to the gun, if it still existed.

He finished his search of the office, took a police seal from his pocket and used it to secure the door before he crossed it with crime scene tape from jamb to jamb. He wondered how President Dhillon would react to the sealed door. He figured it likely she would return once he had gone.

CHAPTER 15

Archie divided up the task of interviewing Helerstone's colleagues between himself and Martin Demio. The Anthropology building stood on the north slope of a low bluff overlooking the strait, and most of the offices there had fantastic views. Archie hadn't been there since his student days years before, and he wasn't sure how he felt about returning.

He led the way. They entered a large garden of indigenous plants and crossed a Japanese demon bridge spanning a dry streambed of river cobbles, carried on past groups of exchange students talking or working on their electronic devices to the main door. Demio occasionally checked his smartphone and generally seemed uninterested. Archie tried to read him. He couldn't tell if what he saw in Demio was derision or envy or something in between.

They stopped at reception. Archie expected to have to confront the formidable old gargoyle that once manned the gate, but instead a friendly young woman greeted them and asked their business. Once Archie showed his badge, she gave him a list of professors, their office numbers and contact information while Demio scanned showcases with tribal objects, walls decorated with posters and bulletin boards pinned with job postings.

"What a fucking waste of space," Demio said at last. "I got no use for these eggheads. I could see learning business or something useful, but this is lame, and so are the people working here."

Demio had said little since they'd left the station, and Archie wondered how much of the comment was directed at him.

"We'll do better if you keep your thoughts on the subject to yourself while we're here," Archie said. "We're in the asking questions phase. No point alienating these folks."

"Like I give a damn. This is a pretty dumb activity anyway, investigating a murder where there isn't one. I still say the professor offed himself. Case closed."

Archie didn't reply. He checked the list of those still at the university and those out in the field. He knew one—Emily Frizell—but not the others, professors Larry Aberle and Robertson Foley. Aberle was not on campus, and the secretary did not know when he might be back.

Archie led the way down the familiar hallway to Emily Frizell's office. Her door was open and she was working at her desk with her back to them, apparently unaware of their presence.

Demio rolled his eyes and banged on her door. Archie noticed the buds in Emily's ears and the lead connected to a computer tablet, chuckled and called out her name. At length, she turned to face them, frowning until she noticed Archie, at which point a smile immediately replaced the frown.

She removed the earbuds, rose from her chair, crossed the space between them and hugged him. After releasing him, she stepped away and peered up into his face.

"Archie Stevens," she said. "I'm so glad to see you."

"I'm glad to see you too, Emily," Archie said. "It's been years."

He introduced Demio and told her that they were investigating the death of Ron Helerstone. Frizell shook her head, compressed her lips.

"Poor Ron," she said. "So sad."

Archie waited for more.

"He was a good man—for the most part, anyway. Can I get you tea?"

She lifted a kettle and a cup, but he refused the offer.

"What do you mean by *for the most part?*" Archie asked.

"Nothing in particular," she said. "Ron had his idiosyncrasies like everybody, but he meant well. He could be difficult if he wanted to be, more so as he got older. They say that one ought not speak ill of the dead, so I'll say no more."

"This is a police investigation," Demio said. "We've got work to do. We don't want tea, and we don't want our time wasted."

Frizell set down the kettle and the cup. The porcelain clattered.

"Really?" she said. "You don't want me to waste your time? You must be very important? In fact, I don't want *you* to waste my time. I'm extremely busy, and I'm through with this interview. You can make an appointment through the secretary if you like, and I'll decide at that time if I'm interested in speaking with you further. Sorry, Archie, but that's the way things are. Good manners would be nice, even from a cop."

Archie raised his hands, a gesture of surrender. He inclined his head in Demio's direction.

"Detective Demio has other business," he said. "It'll be just you and me, Emily."

Demio shrugged, said he would go see Professor Foley—strong emphasis on the word *professor*—and left the room. Archie picked up the cup and kettle and held it out to Emily. After a moment's hesitation, she took them from him.

"There was no call for the detective to speak to you the way he did," Archie said. "He comes from big city downtown and has his own style. Emily, I would appreciate it if you might spare the time to talk to me."

She shrugged.

"I meant what I said about manners," she said.

"I know."

"I heard you'd joined the police, but I never understood why, and I'm not sure I like it."

"As I've said, I had my reasons."

She lifted the tea jar, showed it to him.

"Want that cup of green tea? This stuff is pretty good—High Mountain, I think."

This time he accepted the offer. She directed him to a chair close to hers, poured the water into raku cups and handed one to Archie, took her seat and sighed. He was not aware he'd been studying her until she wagged a finger at him.

"Oh yes, your wonderful stare," she said. "I guess you're assessing me, probing me with those brown eyes. How am I doing?"

"I was thinking is all, and staring off into space. Nothing more."

In fact, he was assessing her, as she guessed. She had changed since the old days when she was the most glamorous and energetic young professor on campus. The once gloriously long, chestnut-colored hair cut short now and streaked with grey, and she carried a bit more weight. Fine lines etched the corners of her mouth and eyes. Not that she wasn't attractive still—she was, with finely drawn features and a beautiful nose, a perfect nose. He'd always liked that nose. He noticed other signs of age, a world-weariness —or exhaustion. And cynicism was there too; the enthusiasm of the youthful professor he had known gone forever, and in those eyes a hardness, or sadness perhaps. He pulled himself out of his reverie.

"How *are* things around here?" he said.

"You've some change at the top, I think."

"Have you met our President Dhillon?"

"Yes," he said. "My first stop on the tour."

"What'd you think?"

"Seems efficient. A bit of a bean counter, but I guess that's part of the job."

"She's more than a bean counter, let me tell you," Emily said. "She's got an agenda, and she will sink any poor schmuck who crosses her. She's the embodiment of the university as a big business, which is what a place like this is now, pure and simple, but at least she's got academic credentials."

"You don't like her?"

"The most diplomatic thing to say is that the jury's still out. If you compare her to old Gates when you were here, or even to Jeremy Porteous, there's no comparison. They were academics first and bureaucrats second. Not like her. She's the other way round."

"Porteous liked to follow the rules, as I remember," Archie said. "Always a form to fill out for everything, and a proper procedure too."

She puffed out her breath, a loud rebuttal.

"You could get around Jeremy easily," she said. "You can't get around Dr. Dhillon unless there's money involved. But you're here to talk about Ron Helerstone, not to discuss faculty politics. You took classes with Ron, didn't you?"

Archie got his notebook out and snapped the cap off his pen. He could imagine how Emily had got round Porteous.

"Yes, I did take classes with him—one or two. He was on my committee briefly as well."

"You liked him?"

"Sure, but right now I'm more interested whatever you can tell me about him, about his activities, his friends and enemies, his work, anything at all."

"So you can build your theory, which is—"

"Too early to say, Emily."

She laughed. He sipped his tea.

"Too early to say—perfect," she said. "You haven't changed, Archie. You always told me the same thing whenever I asked you what you were working on. You kept things to yourself then and now."

"This time it's true," he said. "I don't have a theory."

"Sure you don't."

She poured out more tea for herself and offered him a refill, which he declined. Leaning back, cup in hand, she examined him, too intently for his liking, almost like she was flirting. She glanced out the window towards the distant mountains as if gathering her thoughts, and when she looked back at him, her eyes were now hardened and the flirtation gone.

"Ron seemed a little burned out to me—and changed," she said

"What do you mean?"

"His work shifted focus about five years ago; he used to be into the development of power structures but changed to shamanism and ceremonials and got into secret societies too. He might have published on the subject, but I'm not sure. I didn't like the new direction and told him so."

"How did he take your criticism?"

"Not well, and soon we had, at best, a professional relationship and nothing more. We weren't friends anymore, is what I mean. By then, he was in thick with Robertson Foley, whom I don't like. Foley's got contacts with shamans up the coast, and Ron went away with him often. After a time, Ron wasn't in his regular office all that much, which is not in this building anyway."

"So I understand. Do you know of any women in his life? Was he in a relationship recently, or dating?"

She shook her head.

"That's what you ask?"

"Yes."

"I'm not sure. He always found someone to spend time with, as you know. Ron is, or was, glamorous and handsome. He attracted women, and in the old days, they usually chased him, not the other way round."

"Sure," Archie said. "What about anybody recent?"

"Not that I'm aware of," she said. "His women have always been on the young side, which make sense, I guess—date an attractive, charismatic bachelor professor, fun to be with. It's a little dangerous and a career path all in one. I wouldn't be surprised if there was someone, but I can't say for sure."

"In these times? How would he get away with dating a student?"

She laughed.

"Dear me," she said. "There are ways and ways. Things are not always what they seem."

"Are you sure Ron was the innocent in the mix? I'm not."

She set down her cup and sighed.

"It makes me cross, listening to something like that about a colleague, even from you, Archie, Archie the cop. People always assume the man is to blame, if that's an appropriate word even. You're an anthropologist—or were. You know how things work with exchange systems. Remember what Marcel Mauss said—there's no such thing as a gift. Young women hooked up with him, seduced him, I would say, and used him to get fellowships and TA jobs. He got something out of it, but they benefited most. They got careers. So what if he got a little sex in return? You can tell I have mixed feelings about him."

"I'm not judging him, Emily," Archie said. "I'm not the university disciplinary committee. I'm hoping to find something to help me to understand why he might, say, kill himself, if that's what happened, or why somebody might murder him."

"I can't think of any reason why Ron would kill himself—no," she said. "I think the murder idea is better than the suicide theory, but what do I know? I'm sorry, Archie, I don't have anything else to tell you, and I must get back to my notes. The conference is coming up, and I'm sure you understand."

There was nothing subtle about her change in mood. She wanted him gone, but he was convinced she was omitting something important and certain too that the rumors that a younger Emily Frizell had been Helerstone's student and lover were true.

"I'm sorry too, Emily," Archie said. "I just have one or two more things to ask and then I'll leave you alone."

"What?"

"We met a young woman named Tessa Simons who associated with him," he said. 'Do you have any thoughts on her?"

"Tessa, really? I wouldn't believe anything Tessa Simons says. She's a compulsive liar."

"You must know her well?" Archie said.

"No. I've never had very much to do with her."

"You hardly know her but you call her a compulsive liar?"

"I talked to her on the phone a few times but not recently. She promised to do something for me and didn't. She did a couple of other things and made trouble for me. I've seen her around, but I've never actually met her formally, so I'm not telling an untruth."

"What did she do? What upset you?" Archie said.

"It's private, Archie."

"What is it, work-related?" he asked.

"I said it's private," she said. "And I mean it."

"Yes," he said. "By the way, do you know a woman named Stella Picard?"

"No, I've never heard of her," Emily said.

"Perhaps in connection with Ron, not a student or friend or employee?"

"No, nothing. I've never heard of her."

"Okay," Archie said. "One more thing, and I'll be on my way."

"Shoot."

"Do you know what Ron was working on when he died? I'm getting different stories on this, and I want to pin down his most recent research focus."

"You could check his files, his computer," she said. "Or the office might know. You could ask up there."

"That's right, I could, but I wondered what you thought?"

She regarded him with something like disgust.

"You really are a cop, aren't you?"

"Yes, I am a cop, and I have a job to do. So, if you can help, I'd appreciate it."

She seemed to soften a little after that. Archie sensed that Helerstone had meant more to her than she let on but decided not to push it. He figured she was telling the truth when she said she didn't know about Helerstone's research, since there was no reason why she should.

They finished up in small talk, in false promises to visit again over a drink or dinner, the time left unspecified and the location vague. She agreed to call him if she thought of anything that might help his investigation, and then she walked him to the lounge area where he was to meet Demio, where she hugged him, kissed him on the cheek and said good-bye. Then she turned on her heel and went back down the hall in the direction of her office.

Archie bought a coffee from the machine in the lounge area and went to the seating area. Absently, he stared into space until Demio arrived moments later and interrupted his reverie. Demio grunted a "Hi" as he sat down on one of the low square upholstered blocks that passed for furniture, put his elbows on his knees, spread his feet in their polished shoes wide and began tearing an empty paper coffee cup to pieces, obviously delighted about something.

"What did you learn?" Archie asked.

"Foley speaks Vietnamese," he said. "We spent half the time talking about some ancient kingdom I never heard of."

"According to the faculty lists, Asia was once his research area. Did he talk about Helerstone?"

"Lots—once I got going on him. He didn't like the deceased much, said Helerstone didn't follow the rules, spent too much time 'fucking his students'—Foley's words. Also he doesn't like this other prof, Aberle, either. Can we get out of here?"

"Yes. I'm done," Archie said. "What'd he say about Aberle?"

"Mostly he didn't like him."

Demio seemed upbeat; a condition Archie decided meant the other detective figured he got the better of somebody. They walked towards the exit.

"Did Foley know what Helerstone was working on?"

"No, I asked but he said he didn't have a clue. He suspected Helerstone had woman troubles and killed himself because of it, which rings true for me too."

He grinned, chuckling to himself. There seemed little point arguing with him about his conclusion, but he picked up his pace, forcing Demio to walk faster. Soon, the other man was struggling to keep up. Finally, he stopped.

"Slow down, Stevens, for Chrissake," he said. "I thought you liked being here."

"Where you get that idea?"

"I just thought."

"You thought wrong."

CHAPTER 16

They continued in silence. Archie, with his mind on the university and big business, on professors and secret knowledge, and on Emily Frizzell, was too preoccupied to say much. He'd glanced at her computer screen while they talked. She had lied about working on a paper for a conference. The material on her display was not anthropological at all, nor recent, which meant she'd opened a file when she'd heard them arrive and minimized what she was actually doing, and he wondered why.

After a few minutes, Demio suggested lunch, to which Archie agreed. They met at the New Gold Restaurant. With its dusty windows and ancient "waving cat" figurines, the New Gold seemed to scream health-code violations, but Demio insisted the restaurant's appearance didn't matter much.

Inside, the restaurant was busy and very noisy and almost everyone was speaking Cantonese. Its organized chaos being typical of better Dim Sum places, Archie guessed Demio made the right choice. They sat down at a table and a portly waiter in a stained white shirt dropped off the menus as he passed. When Archie reached for his, Demio waved a negating hand over the faded red volume.

"Don't need those," he said. "We'll see what they bring."

Fifteen minutes later, a waiter brought heaping dishes of food, side plates, chopsticks and jasmine tea. Demio didn't wait; he loaded up and began to eat. Archie took a portion of an unfamiliar chow mein, some Kung Pow chicken, garlic pork and chop suey and samples of other dishes he didn't recognize. Half an hour later, he pushed himself back from the table, his gut full to bursting. Demio leaned back too.

"Best Cantonese food in town," he said. "A fuck of a lot better than the crap you get downtown. They used to be in Empire City. All these guys care about is food and gambling. I laid off them a couple of times when I was in uniform, and they don't forget."

Archie frowned. He didn't like dirty cops.

"What'd you need to lay off them for?"

Demio grinned.

"Bullshit stuff," he said. "One thing more important than the others. The guy working the wok is named Wong. His old ma don't speak a word of English. She's about eighty and into loan sharking at the casino. Her daughter is still at it. With the old lady there wasn't much money involved and no strong-arm stuff. Somebody complained, I guess, so I went easy on her."

"What about the daughter?" Archie asked.

"Nothing much. She's okay."

Archie was thinking about what it meant. Not that he cared. He never thought Demio could give anybody any slack, unless the person could do him some good. Demio seemed to sense Archie's ambivalence. Archie wasn't feeling judgmental, but Demio made a gesture of reconciliation.

"So you still think this case is about more than a suicide?" he asked.

"Seems obvious to me," Archie said. "I'm also convinced Stella Picard and her murder somehow involve Helerstone. Why doesn't anyone seem to remember Stella, I wonder? Anyway, let's talk about Professor Foley and what he said to you."

"Professor Foley," Demio said. "He starts off by telling me Helerstone did great financially. After Helerstone bought that new place of his, Foley says he seemed depressed about the way his life was going. Foley says Ronny-boy had a hard time dealing with getting older too. Seems some young babes like those who used to want to party with him disrespected him and, naturally, the guy ended up in the dumps. Said Aberle was a bad influence on Helerstone."

"And your assessment of Foley?"

"He's a smart dude, for sure. He tried to pull some superior shit, but he caved pretty quick when he saw I wasn't buying in."

"And he figured Helerstone killed himself."

"He said so about three times. I got everything I could from him so I begged off."

Archie wondered at Foley's insistence on suicide, like no other explanation need apply. It seemed strange.

They paid the bill and left. Clouds blown in from the sea obliterated the distant mountains and the wind blew biting cold. Demio said he needed to make some calls and they parted, with Archie going to the 4Runner and Demio his Chevy. As they crisscrossed, a heavyset woman wearing a ball cap got out of a parked pickup and raised a shotgun to her shoulder. At the same time, Archie caught movement to his left, a man unlimbering an automatic rifle. He yelled at Demio to get down, spun to his left and dove between two cars as bullets stitched a line of holes up the hood of one vehicle and smashed out the windows of the other. For a moment or two, nothing more happened.

Archie dispatched an "officers in need of assistance" code and drew his pistol. As Demio sprinted past, a shotgun blast caught him and he fell to the ground, sprawling. Archie jumped out of cover and started firing, even hitting the guy with the machine gun. The woman screamed something and emptied her shotgun at him, covering her partner who limped to their vehicle. He unleashed a final burst of automatic rifle fire before he jumped in. The truck squealed away in a cloud of blue tire smoke and was gone. In the distance, sirens wailed.

Archie caught his breath and turned to attend to Demio, who seemed surprised by the way things had happened. As Archie came up, he tried to stand but then crumpled, sat down hard on the curb, put a hand to his side and gingerly touched the spreading patch of wet blood on his shirt.

"Goddam it," he said. "This stings."

Three squad cars roared into the street, halting in a protective ring around the two men while Archie bent to examine the holes the double ought buckshot had made in Demio's midriff. Demio grimaced, his face pale from shock.

"What's the verdict, Stevens?" he said.

"Nothing to worry about. You'll be fine."

"I guess I'll be taking some time off all the same. What a screw-up."

Then he swore, slumped down, leaned forward and would have fallen head first to the pavement had not Archie caught him and eased him down. A few seconds later, when medics arrived to take charge, the other detective lost consciousness.

CHAPTER 17

After checking on Martin Demio recovering from his wounds in the hospital, Archie attended Helerstone's funeral, partly because he once liked and admired the man, and partly because, as a policeman, he needed to see who else showed up.

The service was held in an interfaith chapel on campus, and the university was well represented there. Heidi Hungerford, the office manager and doorkeeper of old, sat near the front of the room, and Archie suspected she might have organized the show. He took a seat with a good view of the room over which a large picture of the deceased, smiling and wearing a Hawaiian shirt, presided.

As more guests arrived, Archie scrutinized them, trying to guess their motives and to discover connections between the players. Academic colleagues from other departments and universities occupied the center pews, talking amongst themselves as if waiting for a visiting scholar to appear and present some new and noteworthy finding. Several attractive women in early middle-age who seemed more town than gown and who all radiated grief could have been former lovers. A few people who vaguely resembled Helerstone were likely distant relatives; Archie knew Helerstone had no close kin. Students arrived in small groups mostly and found seats together. Archie could only speculate about them. Probably most came out of love, or out of loyalty; others came to make an appearance so those who mattered might note their presence.

When the room was almost full, Andrea Dhillon showed up. She wore a somber business suit, picked a prominent seat, the proper place for Helerstone's former boss to sit, and checked her phone for messages. Tessa Simons, tastefully dressed as usual, entered through a side door and headed for the back of the room. She glanced at Archie as she passed. Was there a brief, wintry smile there? He couldn't tell.

Archie rechecked his mental list. Emily Frizzell, high on that list, arrived seconds before proceedings began. She came in through the main door, paused to sign the book of remembrance, took her time scanning the audience and sat down in a pew near the podium. Almost everyone who should be at the service was present, with the exception of Larry Aberle and Robertson Foley. It might not mean anything, but their absence set Archie wondering.

The celebration seemed destined to be a long one. Too many people made speeches and gave testimonials to the point of tedium, reminding Archie how much he hated sentimental remembrances of the newly dead. A simple, traditional funeral was best, he thought, or better still those ancient ways of his people which were designed to keep the dead happy and coincidentally to prevent them from returning to vex the living. As far as Archie was concerned, sentiment found no lodging in the land of the dead. The dead were not sentimental in the slightest. He left as soon as he could do so without disrespect.

Back at his 4Runner, he checked his messages. He had asked Thomas Lee to interview the security guards on duty around the time when Archie suspected Helerstone last used his hidden office, which was on the night he died. He also wanted to review the footage from security cameras installed near the Department of Anthropology buildings. Lee's message said that the recordings were set up and ready to view.

Archie texted Lee back, set a time for them to meet at the campus parking and security services office and left the chapel lot, happy to be gone. Besides, he planned to stop at the Harsley Pistol Club, a place he knew well since most cops practiced at the club range and where he needed to check something out.

At the turnoff, he eased off the highway onto the metalled side road, passed the range signs and continued on until he reached the low buildings that fronted the shooting area. After parking the 4Runner away from a Jeep already in the lot and turning off the engine, he got out and walked across the wet gravel to the office. The hammer booms of a heavy rifle cut the still air. The range manager, a Harsley old-timer named Bud Marsden, came out of his glass-fronted office to greet him.

"I'm here as requested, Archie," he said.

"I appreciate it."

"You want to shoot some, too?" Marsden said. Marsden was a talker. Usually, Archie tried to get the sign-in over with as quickly as possible as Bud could generally waste fifteen or twenty minutes in small talk. But, this time, Archie needed the talker to talk.

"Not today, Bud. I'm working on a case." Marsden leaned in.

"Something to do with the range?" he asked.

"Yeah—one of your shooters died," Archie said. "You heard about Ron Helerstone?"

"I heard."

"I'm tidying up some loose ends."

Marsden scratched his belly, shook his head.

"Too bad about Ron. He will be missed. I remember when he first started shooting—"

Archie interrupted him.

"Bud, maybe you can help me connect the dots on something."

The heavy rifle boomed again. The muzzle of the rifle poked out fifty feet away. As he watched, the tip jumped a millisecond before the gun cracked and expelled a tiny puff of blue smoke. Marsden passed a hand over his smooth crown.

"That's a guy I never seen here before. American Indian," he said. "Older guy. You might even know him. Uses a 30.06 Huskie. Good shot too. Take a gander. He's at three hundred yards."

"I don't know everybody, Bud."

The rifle boomed again, followed by the clash of a bolt action, but the shooter remained invisible behind the shooting booth partition. Archie checked the target through Marsden's scope—the black center torn out by a tight group of shots. Scary good.

Marsden grinned, rolled his eyes.

"Nice shooting," he said.

"Seems like it," Archie said. "Perhaps I should meet him."

Marsden nodded, locked his office, put a "Back in five minutes" sign on the window and led Archie to the pistol lockup at the other end of the shooting line. He pulled out a key, opened a steel door and switched on the light. Archie asked for the membership book, which Marsden retrieved from under the photo-veneered bar. Archie flipped open the plastic-coated binder and scanned the list of sixty-two members. Ron Helerstone was number twenty-four and Emily Frizell, to Archie's surprise, was number thirty-seven.

"When was Ron last here?" Archie asked.

"Not for weeks—or months. He renewed his membership in January, but he didn't stay to shoot."

"What about Emily Frizell?"

"Emily?" Marsden said. "She's a regular. She shoots at least once a week. She was here a couple of days ago. I think Ron introduced her to the sport."

Another surprise.

"What does she shoot?"

Marsden should know.

"A foreign pistol. Not a target pistol—a self-defense kind of gun. I'm pretty sure it's an Astra—the little one, smaller caliber."

Marsden squeezed the corners of his mouth between his fingers, blew out his breath.

"I think she shoots an Astra M40 Firestar," he said.

"Never a thirty-two caliber anything?"

"Not that I've seen, no."

"I'd like to check Ron's gun locker. I'll need the key?"

"You got a warrant, I guess?" Marsden said.

"I do."

"Okay. I got to ask. The owner has a key and I got a duplicate. I'll have to go back to the office. You okay, here?"

He left Archie to find the key he needed. Archie positioned himself so he had a good view through the window of the access passage to the shooting booths, which were now quiet. A man carrying a rifle case appeared near the shadowed side at the entrance, his face obscured by a hoodie, paused like he forgot something, took an item from his pocket, examined it and then disappeared. Archie was curious. Hurrying to intercept the man, he almost collided with Bud Marsden. Marsden twirled something small and bright between his fingers.

"Guy said he knew you. Said I should give you this."

He handed Archie a thirty-two caliber cartridge. It was match ammunition, a wad-cutter, an Eley Tenex casing. Archie closed his fist and ran to the door, but the Jeep was already accelerating out of the lot.

He went back to the desk, hauled out Marsden's register and scanned the sign-ins. The scrawl the shooter left read "*Archie Stevens*."

"Don't you read the names when people sign in, Bud?"

Marsden shrugged.

"Usually, but the guy was yakking at me about baseball," he said. "He seemed like a good guy. I missed it this time."

Archie showed Marsden the name. Marsden peered at it.

"God."

"I'm going to need to take your book."

Marsden nodded.

"Okay. You still want going to check Helerstone's locker?"

"You bet."

They returned to the clubroom. Marsden led the way to the bank of steel-fronted lockers to Helerstone's at the end of the second row, which Marsden opened. It contained two polished wood pistol cases. With his gloves on, Archie opened the first and examined the 9mm Browning High Power; the second held a .357 Magnum Cobra.

"You're supposed to carry the key with you, right?" he said.

"Club rules." Marsden said.

No locker keys were found on Helerstone's body nor anywhere else.

"Where's Ron's Walther target pistol?" Archie asked.

"It ought to be here. No one signed it out."

"It's obviously not here," Archie said. "Dammit, Bud—do you know when you saw it last?"

"A week or two ago, maybe."

"A lot can happen in a week or two."

Archie replaced the pistols and shut the boxes.

"I'll give you a receipt," he said. "These are coming with me, so list them and their serial numbers, please, and I'll sign it."

Marsden nodded and closed the locker door, the mechanism engaging with a loud click. Archie took a police seal from his pocket and affixed it. As they turned to go, Marsden glanced at Archie's gun secure in its holster.

"You get a new SIG, Archie?"

"No, why?"

"Your gun had a chip out of the checkering on the grip. Your new one don't."

"You're thinking of some other gun. This is the same one I've had for quite a while."

"If you say so," Marsden said. "I don't usually get gun details wrong, but you'd know."

"Yes I would."

He put the gun boxes under his arm and left the room. Marsden followed him out. Back in the 4Runner, he drew the SIG. It seemed like his gun, felt like it too. He ran a finger across the checkering. Had the grip been damaged before? He couldn't remember. He didn't obsess about guns much. The SIG was a tool of his trade, nothing more. He slid it back into its holster and started his vehicle.

CHAPTER 18

The wheels of the 4Runner cycloned fallen rhododendron petals as Archie drove into the lot behind the campus security building. He nosed his vehicle into an open spot in a bank of marked spaces with reserved signs and killed the engine. Thomas Lee arrived moments later, scattered another pink cloud and parked his BMW close to Archie's 4Runner but so it straddled two spaces. Archie guessed he didn't want to take a chance on Archie swinging open a door and damaging the Beemer's pristine, blue coachwork. Out of his car, Lee regarded the 4Runner with its scratched grey paint and bullet holes and shook his head ruefully.

"Is this any way for a Detective Sergeant to present himself to the community?" he said.

"What do you mean?"

"Your so-called vehicle is what I mean."

Archie shrugged his shoulders.

"At least I don't worry about scratches."

"If that was mine, I'd welcome scratches. Plus the bullet holes from your last case are still there. Did you ever think of going to a body shop? Better still, you should sell the junker."

"I like it the way it is."

"More's the pity. Sorry to hear about Martin Demio, by the way. Close call?"

"Seems like. I checked up on him and he's going to be okay. He'll be off work for a while, but otherwise he'll be fine."

"Lucky."

"Yes. Considering the attackers were pros."

"Incidentally, Archie. I keep turning up the name Rafe King in my research. He sold the house to Helerstone, plus he gave money to one of Helerstone's projects, and Helerstone got an invite for a week on King's yacht. Know much about him?"

"Other than the fact that he's publicity shy and unscrupulous, not much. I wonder what those two had in common."

Lee opened the glass-panelled door to admit them and followed Archie inside. A blue-uniformed guard stood at a counter arguing with two kids over a parking ticket. One of them with dreads piled up under a Rasta toque possessed enough legal knowledge and erudition to talk rings around the guard, which didn't help with the fine, though. The guard nodded to a greeting.

"You must be the cops we were notified about?"

"We are," Lee said.

The guard grunted, turned away from the counter, hit the button on an office intercom, said something inaudible and got a metallic okay in reply.

"She's on her way," the guard said.

He returned to his argument, which revived with added intensity. A stocky blue-shirted woman wearing a Sam Brown belt loaded with gear appeared and beckoned them to follow her through the door at the end of the room. Inside, she turned and faced them, cross-armed.

"I'm Sandy Fitter," she said. "I assume you've got ID?"

Archie flipped open his badge wallet; Lee pulled his from the inside pocket of his cashmere coat, opened it, showed ID. Sandy glanced at the shields and then led the way past corkboards with grey-toned surveillance stills of vandals at work, wanted posters and bulletins. She stopped at a metal door, opened it and let them into a small audio-visual room where she sat down in front of a bank of computers. She motioned Archie and

Lee to take the seats she had already positioned behind her.

"I've set it up for you. These are from relevant cameras. It's what they saw on the night of May fifteen, the night you wanted and the hours you wanted. I've cut out some footage that shows no activity."

She flicked a finger over a pad and called up an image of the side door to the lower wing of the Anthropology building. The camera had been positioned poorly. A person leaving would be easy to identify but someone entering would need to turn to face the lens. Otherwise you got the back of a head at best.

"You only have the one camera there?" Archie said.

"Just the one. It's not considered important, security-wise," Fitter said. "But I get what you mean."

"Start it running, please."

Sandy tapped the electronic pad. For several minutes, only the numbers on the digital clock at the lower right of the image frame changed. The scene, partly obscured by an overhanging branch, was static. Archie thought about the tedium of watching such videos, waiting for something—anything—to happen, when a figure appeared from the left side; a wind gust moved the obscuring boughs. The man stopped at the door, put a key in the lock, opened the door and went in. He might have been Ron Helerstone, but the peak of a ball cap obscured the face and it was impossible to make a positive ID.

"Any other people go through there that night?" Archie asked.

"Nobody else went in," Sandy said. "The camera's on all the time. He came out though—see."

Fitter launched an item on a pull-down list. The video fast-forwarded two hours to the same scene. This time, the tree branches moved less and at one point a large raccoon wandered through a frame. At last, the door opened and Helerstone stepped out, though now he wasn't wearing a ball cap and his coat was unbuttoned. He carried a computer bag over his shoulder and shook his head twice as if to clear it before his eyes settled into a fixed gaze. Several times, he fiddled with his wrist.

"Freeze that and zoom in," Archie said.

Close up, the thin cord attached to Helerstone's wrist was visible. Helerstone tugged at it once more and then fumbled in his pockets as if searching for something, and after some long seconds produced his keys. The door had already shut behind him, but Helerstone tried to reopen it, tugging on the handle and trying different keys.

He dropped them once, glanced at something or somebody off screen and mouthed words. Finally, he shook his head as if in anger and walked away; his movements seemed awkward and confused. Archie got Sandy to reverse and slow the video.

"Anybody here read lips?" he said.

"He says *leave me alone, get home* and then *SUV* and then *problem*," Thomas said. "And then, *you want the computer not me.*"

Archie raised an interrogative eyebrow.

"My mother was deaf," Lee said.

"The guy's loaded," Sandy said. "Usually, it's students. Profs are more careful, but this guy, I don't know."

"He does seem drunk. Is he planning to drive, I wonder?"

"Do you know what parking lot Helerstone used, Sandy?" Archie asked.

Sandy flipped a page in a notebook.

"He's got a spot out in Lot B1, which is not too far from the Anthropology building. Detective Lee has already requested the video, so I have it for you. You can't see much out there—not with where the cameras are located. Professor Helerstone's vehicle wasn't there though. His parking space was empty."

"What else have you got?"

She scrolled down to access another file. It opened in a new window beside the now paused image of Helerstone leaving. This showed a scattering of vehicles in numbered stalls, but Helerstone's SUV was not among them.

"Where else might he have parked?"

"Because of your request," Fitter said, "Staff and I examined a number of lots, even got some street angles that should show what you need, but we haven't turned up the professor's vehicle yet."

"How the hell did he get from the university to the cliff he drove over?" Archie was thinking out loud.

"I've checked taxis for fares from there, but so far, nothing," Lee said. "He must have left the SUV away from those lots covered by video surveillance."

"Or he got picked up. Somebody got him after he left the Anthro building. Do you have footage of the Main Boulevard near Ambassador Avenue, Sandy?"

Fitter nodded.

"It's a good place to pick people up. You must know your way around here."

Archie grunted. Sandy swiveled her chair so she could access another keyboard and then ran through file folders identified with acronyms and numbers. After ten minutes she clicked on one.

The camera took individual shots, rather than continuous footage, and the resolution was low.

"What is the interval?" Archie asked.

"Ten seconds."

"Show us the footage."

They watched the scratchy, green-tinged image lit by overhead lights and surrounded by shadow. Seconds rolled through the counter before Helerstone came into sight. He stood, turned his head to the left, stared off into the distance and wrung his hands. The nose of his SUV appeared. The wind blew tree braches around blocking their view for several frames. When they could see again, Helerstone had vanished. Archie took a deep breath, stood back.

"That's inconvenient," Lee said. "At least, any doubts anybody had about murder are out the window now."

"Damn," Sandy said. "There's no controlling the wind."

Archie rubbed his eyes. They would get nothing else here. He straightened up, stiff from leaning in and watching videos.

"It's not perfect," he said. "But I'd still like copies of the footage sent to our shop. I think we've seen all we can for now. I appreciate what you've done, Sandy."

"My pleasure," she said. "Sorry about the last part."

They took their leave and left the building. In the parking lot, Lee opened the door of his car and stood with his hand on the roof.

"Too bad about the interruption," he said. "We came very close there."

"Horseshoes and hand grenades, as they say," Archie said. "We saw Helerstone being picked up, so we know he wasn't alone on the final night of his life. Now, we need to ID the driver. If we can do that, we might have a case."

CHAPTER 19

When Archie assembled his team in the meeting room, Ray Jameson joined them, surprising Archie. Jameson dropped into a chair in a corner, picking his teeth with a toothpick, apparently disinterested. Archie didn't like the other Detective Sergeant much and, so far as he could tell, the feeling was mutual. He walked over to Jameson and put the question to him.

"What are you doing here, Ray?" he asked.

"It's Fricke's idea, not mine," Jameson said, returning to his teeth.

Archie shook his head and returned to his place at the front of the meeting room. He referred them all to large panels where he gathered diagrams and photos important to the investigation—photos of the deceased in the SUV, stills from the CCTV footage, the interior of the SUV, the trajectory of the dead man's vehicle, the placement of the gun, the slug and other details.

On another board, Archie had posted pictures of Stella Picard, the bent box, the skeleton *in situ*, the bullet wound, the partly flattened thirty-two caliber slug taken from the skull. At the upper-right corner of the first and near to the second panel, he had pinned a headshot and a full-length photo of Tessa Simons. Red lines connected various images and maps, but there was only a large question mark beneath Tessa's picture.

Lee was about to make a point about forensic evidence from the scene of the crime when Fricke entered. Fricke paused, glanced around the room, walked to the board, peered at the image of the vehicle approaching Helerstone as he stood waiting by the curb.

"What's he got his hand sticking out for?" Fricke asked. "He must think he's carrying an imaginary parrot or something."

"We were wondering about it ourselves," Lee said.

"He appears drunk or stoned," Patsy said. "It's like he doesn't even know where he is."

"Or like he's hailing a cab, which he wasn't," Lee added.

Fricke harrumphed.

"Tell us where you're going with this, Archie," he said. "You seem to be automatically connecting these two murders. I don't know. You might be right, but you got to be careful. It's easy to lose track of one case while you're focused on another. Get my drift?"

"Sure," Archie said. "I'm aware of the risks."

"Have you figured out anything like a motive yet?" Fricke said. "Or are you going on hunches?"

"Not yet, but I'm close," Archie said. "In the meantime, I'm focussing on the Helerstone case, and we've got some interesting things to check out. We're searching for a missing gun, for one thing, and a key to the gun locker."

"Okay," Fricke said. "What else?"

Archie gestured to Lee who rose from his seat, crossed to the bulletin boards. He turned to face the others, opened the file folder he carried and removed several images. The first was a detail of the footprints Archie noted at the Helerstone crash scene. He passed around copies to the others.

"I've analyzed these and run the pattern through the database," Lee said. "These are the tracks of a small man, shoe size eight."

"They look like the prints of a woman," Jameson said from the back of the room.

"They're from a man's hiking boot," Lee said. "With a special lugged sole. I can give you the make, the year they were made and the model number, if you want. It doesn't mean a woman couldn't wear them, but they are men's boots."

"I'm not convinced it's a man," Archie said. "The print should be deeper if a man made it. It could be a man, but women occasionally wear men's footwear. In any case, somebody was down at Helerstone's vehicle that morning *before* we arrived on scene. We need to know who and what happened."

"I sometimes buy boy boots," Patsy said. "They're more rugged."

Fricke's bass rumble alerted Archie to the fact the chief was about to speak. He coughed a warning and the room went quiet. Fricke launched right in.

"Okay. I see your pictures and lines, Archie," Fricke said. "What I don't get is the sense you're close to arresting anybody, or even knowing in what direction your investigation is headed."

Archie crossed his arms across his chest.

"Nope, no arrests, Cal," he said. "We're working on it."

"Is that what you call it?" Jameson said from the back.

"Yep."

"Seriously, Archie," Fricke said. "Plus, have you made any progress nailing Martin Demio's assailants? That should be a priority."

Fricke knew Demio was expected to recover. Archie had alerted police forces up and down the coast to be on the lookout for Brenda Volio and Jeff Riggs, but so far nothing had turned up, and Fricke was well aware of the fact.

"We identified the two shooters," Archie said. "You already know that, Cal. They're contract killers from the mainland who often work here. You know I have an all-points out on them, so why are you on my ass about it? I'm not about to put murder cases on the backburner because somebody shoots an officer."

"I just don't like to see an assault on a cop going unpunished is all," Fricke said. "Okay, I'm done for now. You can continue with the briefing, but don't let the Demio attack slip below the radar."

"I won't."

Fricke nodded, grunted, detached himself from the rear wall, grabbed the back of a chair, spun it around so the back faced Archie, and sat down. The metal and plastic chair squealed under his weight.

"I got budget to think about and manpower too," he grumbled.

Archie tried to feel sympathy but failed. Fricke was always complaining about the same things. The investigation was less than two weeks old, and he didn't care much about Fricke's problems, not with two murders to solve. By now he was also sure the shotgun blast wasn't meant for Demio, but he kept his suspicions to himself.

He laid out his plans for the next week, including division of labour, emphasizing the need to establish motives for both homicides. For the time being, Archie said, they should operate under the assumption Helerstone had killed Picard but not be wedded to the idea. Perhaps, he said, there was a motive for Helerstone's killing there. Archie asked Lee to talk about the missing target pistol and the locker key.

"We've checked everywhere we can think of," Lee said. "Patsy and I think he likely sold it and lost the key."

"Maybe, but I don't think so," Archie said. "I know for a fact he used the pistol a few months back, and there's no record of a sale. I asked Bud Marsden, the shooting range manager, about it."

"I thought the Tribe wanted that skeleton back?" Lee said. "What's happening there?"

"I'm not sure." Archie turned to Fricke. "Has the press got wind of the burial cave thing yet?" Fricke shook his big head.

"Bobby Carpenter never went to them," he said. "I don't know why. He seemed pretty hot under the collar. We don't have the press to worry about yet, which can change, of course. In the meantime, we can't access the cave. The Tribe put a twenty-four-hour watch on the place and no-body's been allowed to enter since you were there. We could go the heavy-handed route, but I figure it's not worth it right now. I'm not sure what other evidence you would find there, but the scene of the crime is safe for now. The other thing is that I want Ray to be part of this. You can use the man-power, and Ray will give you a chance to ease back a bit, bring in some clarity."

Ray Jameson stood; his chair slid noisily back. Jameson was a hollow-faced, lanky individual who looked like an emissary from one of the levels of hell, the one where they specialize in bar fights. Fricke's plans were obviously not to Jameson's liking.

"I thought we'd settled this, Cal?" he said. "You know I got my own stuff to work on. I came along today and I'll help out with Demio, but there's a limit. I'm not used to playing second fiddle to another guy the same rank as me."

Fricke leaned forward in his chair, arms crossed over the backrest, watching Jameson through the tangle of his eyebrows. He wasn't the kind of supervisor who liked to be organized by his underlings.

"I decide what you work on, Ray," he said. "You going to give me any shit on this?"

Jameson shook his head.

"I'm just saying."

Archie didn't want help from Jameson. Jameson was capable of sabotaging an investigation if his nose got out of joint, plus he was notoriously prickly, but Fricke had his agenda, and Archie didn't feel like pushing the point. He reminded the detectives of their tasks and ended the meeting. When the others were gone, Fricke stood, yawned and stretched.

"Did we accomplish anything here today, Archie?" he asked.

"Tons."

"Didn't seem like you did."

"What were you hoping for?"

"More," Fricke said.

"It's too soon. Tune in next week."

"I will."

Archie nodded a good-bye and left before Fricke could add anything else. Patsy Kydd, who had been waiting in the hall, caught up with Archie as he made his way to his office. She seemed to want to talk, so he slowed his normally brisk pace and they walked side by side, the top of her head at the level of his shoulder.

"You need to think about how you handle Cal," she said. "You're probably out on a limb on the skeleton, Archie. You need him."

"How so?"

"You didn't follow procedure when you pulled that box out of that cave. I hate to tell you this, but you don't even know one hundred percent you got the right person—the right box with the right remains."

Archie had considered that possibility and then had done his best to dismiss his doubts. Trust Patsy to remind him he'd been too rattled to make sure he got the right box, even though he hadn't noticed any others in the chamber. Fricke had been right, he knew. If he'd taken a partner, he could have done things properly and wouldn't now be a victim of his own pride and his stupid, guarded independence. On top of which, problems around protocol now prevented him from reexamining the crime scene, and this fact left him with the unsettling certainty he had been engineered into doing exactly what he was supposed to do. He picked up his pace, hoping Patsy would get exasperated and leave him alone. She didn't. She quickened her pace to match his and stuck to him like a barnacle.

"Having said that, though," she said. "You must go back to the cave, Archie—as soon as possible. Take a warrant or go without one."

He shook his head.

"You heard Fricke. You want me to piss off more people?"

"You didn't finish the job is why."

"I know what I need to do, and I don't need you to tell me."

"Nevertheless."

The trajectory of the conversation vexed him. His phone rang and he checked the call display, saw Fricke's number, answered and listened. Patsy watched him, head cocked to one side.

"Now Fricke wants me in his office," Archie said.

"Good news—I hope."

"I doubt it. Not if tone of voice means anything."

He started to walk away. She frowned, gave him a quick palm up wave, turned on her heel and strode down the hall, shoulders swinging.

Fricke seemed occupied with organizing the bowling trophies on top of his filing cabinet when Archie entered his office. After a moment, Fricke turned, sighed, pointed to a chair and sat down behind his desk. He seemed to be thinking, to be choosing his words. He glanced down, checking out a brownish stain on his shirt where it stretched tight across the curve of his belly, like he was expecting the stain to move. Archie waited.

"What's the deal, Cal?" he said finally.

Fricke raised his head, leaned forward, linked his fingers over his desk blotter and studied Archie's face.

"How's the sleeping these days, kid?"

"I sleep like a baby. Why?"

"Because you still look like hell, is why. Plus, you almost ran your vehicle into a row of cruisers this morning. You're dangerous. So the deal is this—either you take care of the problem, or I'll put you on health leave again."

"We have health leave? Cool."

"Don't get sarcastic with me, Stevens," Fricke said. "You'll be on leave if you don't straighten this out. You can take that to the bank."

"Am I done here?" Archie asked.

Fricke shifted his bulk, glanced at his bowling trophies, swung his chair back so he faced Archie.

"For now, yes. But you've been warned. I'm not fucking around. Get some sleep. Give some work to Jameson. Ease back a bit. Understand?"

"Yes, boss. I'll be good."

"Aw shit, get out of my office."

Archie stood, turned to go.

"Archie," Fricke said.

"What? You mean we're not done here?"

"You're a good detective, but right now you're hurting yourself."

"Okay."

Archie left the building through the rear door to the parking lot, got in the 4Runner and then drove down Brotchie Street in the direction of Moffat's Bar. His sleep, he figured, was none of the department's business.

CHAPTER 20

Archie hadn't been in Moffat's for over a year, but not much had changed in the interval. A new bartender, pretending to wipe the draft beer taps in the center of the bar, grunted a greeting as he entered. Archie headed for the pool table in the corner where John Robbie was practicing eight ball, slamming shots into pockets, one after the other. He didn't look up as Archie approached, stayed low across the rail for his shot, lined up the cue tip with the cue ball, snapped the shot and rattled a combination into the end pocket before he moved around the table ready to set up his next move. He acknowledged Archie with a slight wave of the cue tip.

"How you do, buddy?" he said. "What's up?"

"Reasonable — how about you, John?"

"Couldn't be better. You here for social reasons?"

"Got time to talk?" Archie asked.

Robbie nodded.

"Get a cue," he said.

Archie walked to the rack, selected a stick, eyeballed it for straightness and took his position at the table.

"Your shot, Arch. I'll give you the six ball."

The six was hanging on the rail almost touching and half behind the thirteen, with no clear hole to receive it making for an extremely difficult shot.

"You're not making it easy for me."

"Which is how the game is played," Robbie said.

"Or we could rack them up." Archie said. "And start over."

"Come on. Play the ball. I'm curious."

Archie scratched the blue chalk block across the tip of the cue, examined the problem and then hit the thirteen, which trickled into the corner pocket. Robbie grinned.

"My ball," he said. "Thanks."

He holed two more balls. Archie made one and missed one, after which Robbie sank the rest one after another.

"Pool's not your game, Archie."

"I guess not. Rack them up."

"Bet ten bucks on the outcome?" Robbie said.

"All right."

They played two more games, and Robbie took thirty dollars from Archie—ten for the first game, twenty for the second. He tucked the twenty into his shirt pocket and passed a hand through gray-flecked hair.

"Do you want me for something other than pool?" he asked.

"I need your help, John. I have to do something that could get me and whoever helps me in trouble."

"I owe you, Archie, but not enough to screw myself around."

"No problem. Are you going to give me a chance to win my money back?" Archie said.

Robbie laughed.

"You're going to go broke at this rate."

"Thanks, Mom, now what do you want to play for?"

"How about your thirty and twenty more—fifty?"

"Okay, fifty. I'll let you break."

Robbie racked the balls. Archie broke and sunk two before Robbie got three in a row. This time, however, Archie played slightly better and even hooked Robbie. On his next turn, Archie sunk the eight ball and ended the game.

"You got lucky," Robbie said. He tugged out his wallet, pulled fifty dollars from the bulky mass and fanned the bills out. "How about we go double or nothing?"

Archie won the next three games easily. He left the final wager—five hundred dollars—on the rail.

"You hustled me, you son of a bitch," Robbie said.

Archie grinned.

"It's how the game is played, John."

Robbie swore, unscrewed the sections of his cue, found the box that held them and laid the parts in their nests, closed the lid and snapped the clasps shut, took the case to the bar, handing it to the bartender before he returned with his pint. Throughout, Archie watched the ritual with interest.

"Jeez, what a rigmarole," he said. "Are you done?"

"Yep. What's on your mind?"

"I still need your help, and now I've got the money to pay for it," Archie said.

"Seriously?"

"I told you I was almost broke, and now I'm not."

Archie walked over to a table in the corner, sat down, kick-slid a chair out for Robbie who called out for more beer and took a seat.

"I'm going to tell the bartender my beer's on you, Arch."

Archie nodded acquiescence. Robbie's shirt needed washing; the legs of his jeans were shiny with dirt and oil, and he carried the faint smell of woodsmoke with him. The beer came—Archie's Blue Buck and Robbie's Miller. Archie sipped; Robbie chugged.

"Just out of curiosity, are you still camping out on Velasquez Island?"

Robbie squinted, his small, blue eyes almost disappearing beneath heavy eyebrows.

"This cop business, or friend business?"

"Bit of both, but you'd be doing me a favor."

Robbie stared at the worn red flannel on his sleeve, turned the edge over in his fingers, and considered the fabric for several seconds before he brought his head up.

"I've got one of the old hippie cabins above Siwash Beach. It's not bad, all cedar and hand-made. I've got a little generator, even got Wi-Fi, and lots of driftwood for fuel. It don't get no better. Bonnie Tran left me her place in her will, which I never expected. I sold the old Zuider Zee and put the dough in investments. I could live anywhere I want, but I like being where I am."

"I heard about the will," Archie said. "It makes sense. Tell me about your neighbours."

"Tell you — like how? I'm not going to rat on anybody, if that's what you're hoping."

"You know me better. What I need is for you to go and check something out and not be seen while you're about it."

"Where would that be?" Robbie asked.

"Do you know Bobby Carpenter's place?"

"I do."

"I want to make sure about something there," Archie said. "And it'd be better if someone other than me went there and checked things out."

"You want me to sneak around?"

"In a manner of speaking. There's five hundred in the deal for you."

Robbie, obviously considering the proposition, slouched back, raised his beer glass, took a gulp. He set the glass down.

"Seems okay," he said. "Tell me what you want."

Archie told him about the cave and the remains, Bobby Carpenter's possible injunction and about the possibility someone else, maybe Ray Jameson, would take over his investigation. Robbie listened, leaning on one elbow, eyes focussed on some spot to the right of Archie's cowboy boots. When Archie finished, he nodded.

"So, that's it," he said. "I take pictures inside the cave and watch for Carpenter in case he visits the place. I can do that for you, Arch. I never liked the guy. Don't like Ray much neither. It shouldn't be hard getting there unseen. When?"

Archie checked his watch.

"As soon as you can."

Robbie nodded, finished his pint, said he needed to pick up groceries before he headed back to Velasquez Island, and left the table. On his way out, as he stopped to talk to the bartender, he turned his head, pointed to Archie and pantomimed lifting a pint of beer. When the bartender nodded, Robbie grinned widely, waved and swaggered through the door.

After he had gone, Archie flipped through his notes and continued to search for patterns linking the two homicides, the attack on Demio and Tessa Simon—all the parts of the jigsaw. If he could find Helerstone's missing pistol, he could confirm it had been used in at least one murder and perhaps two—or eliminate it. Of course, if the killer had fired the Walther, the easiest way to dispose of it now would be to toss the thing into the chuck, in which case salt water would soon reduce it to a lump of scaling iron on the bottom, but Archie thought this unlikely. Somebody, he convinced himself, still had the weapon, and that person was probably the murderer.

CHAPTER 21

The shotgun pellets the doctors removed from Martin Demio's side and upper thigh occupied a small glass bottle next to Demio's hospital bed. Magnified by the water, they seemed to be the size of .45 slugs, deadly at close range. None had hit a blood vessel or organ, but the lead left what was likely a painful wound. When Archie entered his room, Demio interrupted the game of cribbage he was playing with his young son and made introductions. He dismissed the teenager to the cafeteria for snack food.

"Next time ask me," Archie said. "I came to find out if you wanted anything."

"Thanks, but he needed the break. Any word on our attackers?"

"Nope. Ray found the pickup in the Alfonse Park lot, but that was stolen. No prints in the car, no nothing."

"The shooters were pros, I guess."

"Yeah. I recognized Brenda Volio even with the ball cap pulled down low, which means the guy would be Jeff Riggs. Those two work together."

"Hired guns, hey?"

He scratched his forehead and then pursed his lips.

"I was trying to think if I ran into them before, but no."

"Were they after you or me, Martin?"

"I'm not sure, but I'm going with *you*."

"Except they shot *you*. Yep, they sure did. You moved at the wrong time, but you saved me. I appreciate it."

"It could have happened either way," Demio said. "My bad luck is all."

"I guess."

He made ready to go. Something didn't sit quite right. Professionals like Volio and Riggs wouldn't usually attempt a hit in broad daylight, especially on a cop. He also wondered how they figured out where he and Demio would be. It didn't make sense, nor did the fact that Demio hadn't recognized the shooters. He would have run into bikers and gangsters in Empire City and on the mainland too where the two were notorious.

"Fricke says he's giving you a holiday, Martin. Lots of time to heal up."

"I guess I'll take it."

They talked a little about the case, but they soon ran out of conversation. When Demio grunted with pain, or boredom, Archie got his chance to leave.

"I've got to go. You want the nurse?"

"Not right now. I can tolerate the discomfort, and it's too easy to get to like those opioids too much."

Archie nodded.

"I've got an appointment with Roger Chu. You sure I can't get you anything?"

"Be careful, Archie. They won't give up just because they missed this time."

"I'm not worried, just take care of yourself."

The son returned with coffee and donuts, and Demio waved them off to a side table as Archie took his leave, glad as always to be leaving rather than entering the hospital. He considered going back and asking Demio straight out what was going on, but thought better of it. He had enough on his mind with two murder cases to solve and political problems he couldn't wish away without building in more complications. He said, "Fuck it," to himself and walked out the door into a warm, May drizzle.

Roger Chu was passing through the medical examiner's office reception area when Archie arrived. Chu motioned with his head for Archie to follow him and led the way down the hall, though a glass-fronted door and into a spacious lab lined with multi-level worktables and floor-to-ceiling storage cabinets. To Archie's surprise, Patsy Kydd was there, bending over a binocular microscope. She straightened when she became aware of the two men, caught Archie's questioning gaze and shrugged.

"I'm getting age and condition data from Roger," she said. "I didn't know you'd be here."

"Change of plan."

Chu brought Archie to the microscope; Patsy stepped aside for him.

"You should see this."

"She's right," Chu said. "This is from the blanket the victim's bones were in."

Archie positioned himself at the eyepieces and looked through them at the strands on the slide.

"It's hair of some kind," he said. "Or fibers."

"It's hair—cat hair," Patsy said triumphantly.

"Cat hair? Interesting."

"Indeed it is," Chu said. "From a tabby, I think. Given time, I might even be able to tell you the breed."

Archie pondered the new information. He congratulated Chu and asked Patsy if she knew if anyone they'd interviewed possessed a cat.

"Not that I'm aware of, no, but we'll keep looking."

"It's important. What else have you got for me, Roger?"

"You wanted info on the vegetable matter from Helerstone's throat?" Chu said.

Archie nodded.

Chu retrieved a notepad from the capacious pocket of his lab coat, flipped back the first page and put on his reading glasses.

"It's a strange mix," he said. "Some stuff from nature, some exotic and some local, and some synthetic pharmaceuticals. There's *datura*, *psilocybin*, peyote and *Astragalus*, also called locoweed. Most of the rest was a cocktail of opiates and amphetamines. There were traces of coconut too, and macha—like a macha macaroon. A cookie like that would whack anybody's brain."

Archie mentally catalogued the plants, dividing them by geography. The components came from the north, the coast and the southwest desert. The *datura*, or locoweed, suggested a *brujo*, a sorcerer who cooked up potions with such plants. *Datura* was scary as hell by all accounts.

"How much of it reached his gut, do you think?"

"Enough. I'll send you the complete analysis this afternoon. By the way, that knife you found at Helerstone's was clean, very clean."

"So, that's a dead end," Patsy said.

When he got another call, Chu excused himself and left them. Archie felt strangely awkward being alone with Patsy. She seemed to pick up on it.

"I think we have some serious leads here. Why don't we grab lunch and talk about it?"

He explained that he'd left his vehicle on the other side of the boat basin.

"Even better," she said. "I feel like a walk."

"Okay."

"By the way, I checked on the ink and paper like you asked me, and it seems like it comes from a source in Asia. It's expensive."

Archie took in the information.

"Good work."

"Yeah," she said. "It is. Also, you asked me to dig around re: Tessa Simons, which I did."

"And you found?"

"Brace yourself, Archie. Officially there is no such person."

"What do you mean?" he said.

"I mean she has no past, no records, nothing."

Archie focussed on the path ahead. He knew something wasn't right about Tessa, but this was a shock.

"All right, keep digging. Thanks for this, Patsy. This is good police work."

"You're welcome."

They crossed to the head of the wooden stairs leading down to the promenade. She went first. He lagged, watching as the sun highlighted the loose auburn curls on the crown of her head. She almost hopped down the steps, talking to him all the while, about the weather and other matters that were neither personal nor work-related. He found the experience delightful, like old times.

When she reached the bottom of the staircase, she slowed to let him come up beside her, now so close he brushed against her. She turned her head and shot him a warm smile, and he smiled back, said something nonsensical about the day. They turned towards the esplanade and continued on walking side by side, almost like a couple. While Archie was searching for something to say, she broke the impasse.

"I'm quite curious now about your burial cave," she said. "I'm sorry I suggested that you didn't get the right body. In fact, the cat hairs confirm it. I don't know why I put my oar when I did."

"It was a fair question. No need to second-guess yourself."

"I'm not sure where it's all going. Do you understand how it all interconnects? We have two murders complicated by lots of noise. Are we getting anywhere? What's your guiding theory, Archie?"

"The theory question again—no. Anyway, I'm not tempted to come up with a theory and go searching for the facts to support it. I like to work the other way round."

"Just like Sherlock Holmes."

"Exactly."

They loitered, unsure. The wind rattled the shrouds of sailboats moored in the harbor; loose halyards wind-chimed against masts. Patsy cocked her head to listen.

"I like that sound," she said. "I grew up listening to it. We lived in a house at Burt's Harbor, up on the hill above the moorage."

She had told him little of her family or background before. He was curious but reluctant to pry. Now he was hoping that too much interest on his part would not lead back into something that would poison their working relationship.

"Cool."

She seemed to sense his unease and laughed.

"Don't worry, Archie. I'm not interested in you, not in that way, not now. You're not a good candidate for a boyfriend. You really fell for another woman, and I don't think you're over *her* yet, but it's better if we're comfortable with each other, don't you?"

He nodded but kept his eyes focussed on the sea.

"Yes, it is," he said. "Much better."

"Where do you want to eat?"

"The Weatherglass is close."

They carried on past the end of the wharf, skirted a small treed park, and strolled Thermopylae Road to the Weatherglass, a harbour-side restaurant that had a respectable wine list and good food. Not too stuffy either, which Archie liked. They were climbing the steps to the broad porch when his phone sounded. It was Fricke outlining a deal he'd worked out with the Tribal Council. He would also back off on a possible medical leave if Archie promised to get more rest. When Fricke finished explaining, Archie, having little choice in the matter, agreed to the terms. He thumbed the "end call" icon, jammed the phone into his pocket and let his eyes wander over the ranks of moored boats.

"Well?" Patsy said.

"I have permission to go to the cave, but I'll be taking observers when I go."

He glared at a passing gull and cursed, a loud expletive. The gull, in the manner of gulls, ignored him.

"What do you mean—observers?"

"It's what Fricke wants—or what Bobby Carpenter wants. Fricke says that it's optics. We'll have a so-called shaman and Larry Aberle with us."

"Larry Aberle—you're kidding?"

"He's an anthropologist from the university."

"I know Larry. What's wrong with him coming?" Patsy said.

"I'm not sure if there's anything wrong. I'm just not into having to watch my p's and q's. Anyway, I wanted to talk to Aberle, so things might work out okay."

Patsy was obviously trying to read his face, her head cocked to one side looking at him.

"You got the other name, I guess? Fricke's voice carries."

"Morris Denton?" she said.

"That's the name."

"You know him?"

"I've heard of *a* Morris Denton who was a chief from up island. I didn't know about the shaman part."

"Do you think he will be a problem?"

"I can't say for sure, but I'm not thrilled."

He nodded in the direction of the front door of the restaurant.

"I'm quite hungry. How about you?"

"Famished."

She put her arm through his elbow, and like they were a couple of buddies, they walked up the ramp and into the Weatherglass.

CHAPTER 22

Thomas Lee, supervising the loading and stowing of poly-equipment cases onto the boat, was ordering the rearrangement of the cargo too often to suit the young cop helping him. The constable caught Archie's eye and shot him a pleading glance. Archie shrugged, turned away, pulled the couriered letter from his top pocket, reread the contents, the upshot of which was that the Tribe gave reluctant permission for police to revisit the burial site but insisted nothing be removed from the cave without further consultation. The word *nothing* appeared twice, both times double underlined. As Archie folded the letter and put it away in his back pocket, a vintage Cadillac rolled into the parking area and Fricke got out, tugged up his pants by the belt and ambled over to talk to Archie.

"You get the correspondence okay?" Fricke said.

"I got the letter. I'm not sure why they think I need to be told twice not to move anything."

"Beats me, but let's see how it goes before you get your knickers in a knot. You don't know what you need to do yet, and you may not even think about removing anything anyway. The process could go great."

"Yeah, maybe."

"By the way, Morris Denton is the guy you should butter up, if such a thing is possible for you. He told me he's okay with you having a look-see."

"I'm just tickled that *Morris Denton* is onside."

"Relax, Archie. You can work on him. He's who they want, and he's probably under a lot of pressure to protect the cave's contents—or what's left of them. You're taking that Professor Aberle from the university too because he somehow wangled his way into the mix."

"Why Aberle? It makes no sense."

"It's not my doing," Fricke said. "He's done work with for the Tribal Council on ancient burial practices is all I know, and they want him."

"It's bullshit. Since when do police investigations need escorts?"

"I have to think about the optics. This calls for sensitivity, which is not your strong suit, Archie, so do your best to keep your mouth shut when necessary. You don't want to screw up your own investigation, do you?"

Archie shook his head.

"The thing is, Cal, we're talking about murder, and you're worried about politics."

"God, you're naïve sometimes, Stevens. Politics is pretty well the whole ball of wax, and you'd better learn the drill if you want to rise higher in the police force. So, do you want this, or do I give the case to somebody else? Thomas Lee could handle this part. Try to remember I'm your superior officer."

"How can I forget when you're on my ass all the time?" Archie said. "And, yes, I damn well want it."

"Okay, then I'm on your side."

He patted Archie on the shoulder and walked away to his car. Archie took a deep breath and looked to Pete Wilson's trawler, the *Cherish*, leased with the skipper for the day and ready to depart, but with Lee still fussing with gear and Patsy yet to arrive, they waited. Finally, Lee dismissed the constable who'd loaded the boat. The young cop said a loud, "Thank God," set his shoulders, climbed up the bank and headed for the black and white cruiser in which he'd arrived. Lee walked to where Archie stood, shaking his head.

"Young guy who thinks it might be better if he were in charge," Lee said. "Nice looking, but when you've said that you've said it all. The gear's loaded properly in spite of him. When is Patsy supposed to get here?"

"Now. We should be on our way. It's already midmorning."

"Tracy Gillot said he'd been talking to her. She had breakfast with him, apparently."

Tracy Gillot was a go-getter constable with designs on Patsy. Archie guessed he must have seemed perturbed, because Lee glanced at him and tutted.

"She has to eat, Archie."

"I have to question her choice of breakfast partner."

"Do you indeed?"

Archie recalibrated. He hadn't been planning on renewing anything with Patsy, so he ought not feel the disappointment Lee's announcement engendered in him. She could certainly spend time with, or breakfast with, anyone she chose, and she would definitely not hesitate to tell Archie so.

Lee also brought word about where they would be picking up their passengers—Larry Aberle, at his summer cabin at Wellspring Island a few miles up the coast, and Morris Denton at the community wharf at Sea Warrior Inlet, a little farther along. Afterwards, Pete would lay in a course to Velasquez. Lee picked at a mote of lint on his coat and flicked it away, mumbling something about time on his hands, strode off to the parking lot and his BMW. Walter George, Pete and Archie's friend, arrived in his three-quarter ton and announced loudly he would be coming along for the ride. Archie put his finger to his temple like he was going to blow his own brains out, upon which Walter contorted his face into an exaggerated expression of joy and pumped his fist. Archie laughed, and Walter went aboard.

After a moment or two, thoughts of Patsy with Tracy Gillot returned to tease him. Archie, arms crossed and head down, focussed his mind on the work ahead. He kicked a rock out of his way, crossed over the gravel skirt of the parking lot towards the dock and pondered how to adapt his investigation to the new paradigm.

When Patsy finally showed up alone, Archie felt better, but as he watched her car crest the berm and pull into the lot, a black and white cruiser swung onto Humboldt not far behind—Tracy Gillot following her like a lap dog.

Patsy, out of her vehicle now, lifted a hand in greeting and crossed the tarmac towards Archie. When Gillot started to follow, she reversed him, gave him her keys and sent him back to retrieve some of her additional gear. He returned a few moments later with the tackle boxes she used to hold her measuring and sampling gear. She motioned him on to the boat with them, and when he jogged back to her, she dismissed him to his cruiser. If she noticed Archie's amusement, she didn't show it. She asked to be briefed.

"Took you long enough to get here," Archie said.

"I had car trouble, and I'm lucky Tracy was in the neighborhood."

"Lucky for somebody," Lee said under his breath.

"So what's happening?"

"You tell her."

Lee nodded and explained about picking up Denton and Aberle.

"Them's the breaks, I guess, "she said. "I'm ready to head out if you are."

She glanced in the direction of the boat, where Pete could be seen through the gillnetter's pilothouse window flipping through the pages of a magazine, with Walter reading over his shoulder.

"Does Pete have coffee in there?"

"I think he does," Archie said. "And sandwiches — if you're brave enough to eat them."

She nodded, skirted him, crossed to the boat and legged over the rail, followed by Lee. Archie scanned the parking lot to make sure they left nothing important behind and went aboard. Pete leaned his head out of the cabin, raised his eyebrows in mock disbelief.

"Don't tell me we're finally getting this show on the road?"

"Start the damn boat, smart-ass."

Pete grinned and ducked back into the pilothouse while Walter, at the stern line, snickered at the exchange.

A minute later, the diesel rattled to life and black smoke shot from the stacks. Pete eased the seiner away from the float and into the channel. After a half hour of travel, he drifted the *Cherish* up to a well-constructed private wharf of what was obviously the estate of a wealthy person. The house was invisible except for a plume of blue smoke that marked its location behind a screen of dark cedars, so dense that the trees appeared interlocked. Professor Larry Aberle was waiting on the dock, daypack at his feet, drinking coffee from a thermos cup. He tossed the remains of his drink into the water, screwed the cup back onto the container, and stuck it into a side pocket on the pack before catching the line Pete threw him. Pete idled the diesel.

Aberle, heavyset and going to fat, slid his rear onto the rail and swung his legs over, his rubber-booted feet slapping the wood deck as he came aboard. Otherwise, he acted like he was getting into a taxi he'd just hailed, his New York vowels sharp in the flat air. Aberle grinned, stuck out a hand.

"Goddam warm for the time of year," he said. "You got to be Archie Stevens."

Archie took the proffered hand.

"Yes, I'm Archie."

"This can't make a cop happy, having people like me along, but don't worry, I won't get in the way."

Archie was thinking otherwise but kept his thoughts to himself. He shrugged, said, "It'll be fine."

"Too bad about Ron Helerstone. You and him went back a bit too, right?"

This was not the time to interview Aberle about Helerstone, but something like an interview started.

"Somewhat."

"And now you're investigating his death — must be weird."

Archie had no intention of being the interviewee.

"Some stuff goes with the territory. By the way, were you friends with Professor Helerstone?"

"We were colleagues, as you know."

"Friends also?"

"Not really."

He picked up his pack and slung it over his shoulder.

"I'll stow this in the cabin, I guess," he said.

Just then Patsy came out on deck. When he saw her, Aberle whooped a greeting, moved forward, threw his arms around her and hugged her.

"I was on the other side of the boat when you came aboard, Larry," she said. "How *are* you?"

He assured her that he was well.

"I didn't know you'd be here, Patsy. It's been a long time."

"Five years or more, and it seems like forever."

The fact that Aberle and Patsy were well acquainted surprised Archie and, as her boss, vexed him a little too since Aberle might even become a suspect, for all she knew.

"Are you a consultant on this thing, Patsy? They didn't tell me."

"Not exactly, Larry. I'm a detective on this case. I'm a cop."

Aberle seemed momentarily taken aback by this announcement. He probably couldn't imagine why a talent like Patsy would decide on policing. Archie often wondered too, even after they'd talked about it. Their conversations when they dated hadn't helped much. Something attracted her to the life, but she didn't seem to want to share the reason with him, beyond saying she wanted to do something to help women. When she asked him the same kind of questions, he clammed up, and she pointed out his double standard and did it in a way that made it seem like he had lots of those. He turned his attention to the interaction between her and her old chum.

"Not sure what to say about your career decision, Patsy," Aberle said. "It's an unusual choice, and I have to get my head around the new reality."

"You're not the first."

Aberle shrugged, said, "Talk to you later, girl," and went to find a place to sit.

When she took a seat next to Archie, he asked her about the internship and how she'd met Aberle. She said Aberle was a physical anthropologist, which was how she'd met him. Burial practices were a specialty of his, and she needed to learn about them as part of her training. Their conversation turned to the carved bent box the remains came in, with Pasty wondering if there might be more in the cave. Archie replied in the negative. He had seen no other complete pieces there.

She asked how people used such things in traditional society, and he told her that the best examples of the art, skillfully kerfed and steam-bent at the corners with their bottoms fitted and sealed to make them watertight, were prestige items. Chiefs, or *si'ems* — important men — owned the finest examples, like the one from the cave. Others became the poly-cases of their day, holding almost anything, from eulachon oil to blankets. His grandmother kept two in her closet, one for the grey wool she used to knit sweaters and one filled with old snapshots. The first still smelt faintly of ochre and fish oil. Ordinary storage boxes were simple and unadorned, but master carvers like Charlie Edenshaw created boxes of great beauty.

"And yet this one became a coffin. So sad."

Archie had already given this some thought.

"I don't think so. In a way, it's a great honor, especially with the accompanying grave goods, and that fact is worth thinking about."

CHAPTER 23

When they picked up Morris Denton at midafternoon, Archie immediately recognized him as the older man who came with Bobby Carpenter to Archie's office and was also at the scene of Helerstone's murder that morning when the SUV went over the bluff. Archie, curious, blocked Denton's path momentarily.

"You're Morris Denton?' he said.

"And you're Archie Stevens."

"We've met before."

"Not really. You seen me a couple of times, but what of it?"

For a moment, the two locked eyes. Denton, in passing, gave Archie the briefest snap of the head. It was like at weigh-in, two fighters sizing each other up. Archie nodded back and then made his way forward as the boat got underway. He took a position beside Pete at the wheel. Pete glanced at him over his shoulder.

"What's eating you?"

"What do you know about Morris Denton, Pete?"

"Only what I've heard. He's a hereditary chief—or could have been. Apparently he became a shaman the old-fashioned way."

"How's that?"

"They used to sit in graveyards with the finger of a dead man in their mouth, so the story goes."

"Denton did that. You're kidding."

"I heard it, but it don't mean it's true. He's a spooky dude, though. So, if anyone could sit in a graveyard chewing on a dead finger, it'd be him. I don't like having him on my boat when it comes right down to it. They also say he's got lots of dough."

"He's rich?" Archie asked.

"Word is he made big money in oil or property development or both, and now he's loaded."

"That's interesting."

"He don't seem it, though; rich, I mean."

"No, he doesn't."

Archie, thinking, concentrated on the surface of the green sea. The westerly increased in strength and soon they were fighting a heavy chop while a dark grey mass of clouds on the horizon indicated another squall might soon arrive.

"We got bad weather coming," Pete said, as if in confirmation. "She'll get crappy out here, but we should be at anchor in the lee of Velasquez Island by the time the worst gets to us, I hope."

As he finished speaking, the wind shifted suddenly southeast and a swelling sea broke hard over the foredeck sending a curtain of spray slamming into the windshield and drawing a curse from Pete. Rain began to fall.

"Damn," Pete said." Where the hell did that come from? There was no warning of that wave at all."

He spun the wheel and corrected his course. Archie fought for balance; his hand closed on a bracket and he set his legs against another sudden turn. The bow slammed through a yet bigger swell, most of which washed across the front windows, temporarily cutting off their view.

"Is there a waterfall here?" Archie asked. "I don't remember any on the map, but I can hear falling water."

"No, there fucking isn't no fucking waterfall. That's Jeremiah Strait. The whole flow of the Pacific goes through on every tide change, and there's whirlpools there ready to suck this boat to the bottom."

Pete cursed again as he changed his course, fighting the wheel, feathering the throttles.

"We're too damn close. The sea's pushed us into the strait too soon and in the fucking rip too! This wind is too weird. I got to get us out of here or we're going to be standing still. The old diesel can't do more than keep us in position in this sea. This is going to get rough, buddy."

Pete yelled out to his passengers to hold on, reset the helm and increased power to the screw. As the stern swung back into the flow of the current, another huge swell smashed into the hull as the *Cherish* turned towards the wind. His expletives competed with noise made by bodies colliding with walls and the hollow thump of polycases bouncing around behind the pilothouse and below. The nose of the trawler buried itself in white water twice more.

Archie braced himself again. The police gear containers they'd brought with them and stacked on deck were shifting and the pile sagging. The next wave or lurch of the vessel could loosen the last of the bungee cords after which the stack of boxes would collapse, and some might go over the side and be lost.

"I have to secure our gear," he said. "I brought too much expensive police equipment to lose overboard."

"Don't be an idiot," Pete shouted. "Wait until I can bring her around."

The *Cherish* lurched, spray darkened the windows and torrents of fast flowing water flooded everything between the gunwales.

"It's not safe on deck, Arch. Stuff ain't worth your life."

"Got to be done. Try to hold her steady."

"You're nuts, man. Be careful!"

The wind and current seemed to shift ninety degrees, and as it did so, the *Cherish* yawed wildly. Pete concentrated on keeping her from sliding into one of the many cream-edged whirlpools marking the streaming dark water ahead. Archie released his handhold and almost fell across the angled cabin floor to the starboard door. He threw it open, went out into the storm and secured the door behind him.

The narrow side deck was awash, but at least the rain had diminished. Archie grabbed a line and held on as a surge of water almost knocked him off his feet, and then edged his way back to where the cases were piled. A plastic box slid by his left foot heading for the stern and he grabbed it, and holding on to a cleat, swung it on top of a stack coming apart under its bungee cords. Then he released his grip, jostled the containers into a more compact bundle and tied the whole thing down with some of the ropes Pete kept coiled there.

When Archie felt satisfied that all was secure, he reached for the handrail, ready to get back inside the cabin, when the *Cherish* pitched so violently it threw him off his feet. Another surge caught him sliding and buried him in cold water. He turned his body sideways against the torrent to lessen resistance and grasped for a handhold. His fingers brushed a brass fitting and he extended them in vain hope, only to feel the metal slip away from his fingertips. The *Cherish* lurched again. For a moment, he found his footing, but then a massive wave hit him hard and swept him over the side.

For an eternity he resisted the immense forces trying to drive him to the bottom of the bone-chilling sea, but then he remembered his scuba training, remembered to use the current and to let it carry him along. At length, he surfaced, barely avoiding a shattered tree riding the same maelstrom; it careened past him and disappeared beneath the foam as he fought to keep his head above water. His vision cleared enough and he could see the stern of the *Cherish* not more than fifty feet away and also could see Larry Aberle framed in the streaming rear window of the cabin, watching. As the undertow dragged Archie under the frigid water and into the dark mouth of the whirlpool, Aberle held up a hand as if in farewell.

CHAPTER 24

Once they were through the strait and the rip slackened, Pete Wilson throttled back and let the *Cherish* drift out into open water while Walter scanned the water's edge for Archie. When he became aware that Patsy was watching him, Walter glanced at her and shook his head before glancing back at the skipper in the wheelhouse.

"No sign of him, Pete," he shouted. "There are too many whirlpools and too many deadheads, too much rough water to see far. Anyway, we got to go back to search for him."

"Damn right we're turning back."

Patsy joined Walter at the stern and grasped the rail as the *Cherish* came about.

"He couldn't have survived," Walter said, almost to himself. "It's too goddam cold for one thing."

Patsy let out her breath, a loud sigh.

"I don't believe it," she said. "He's got the strength and the luck. I know he's alive."

Walter studied her a moment and nodded.

"Me too," he said. "Pete will run this here channel until she's too dark to damn well see. Archie's our buddy."

Patsy nodded. She left Walter and crossed back into the pilothouse where Thomas Lee and Aberle were meeting with Pete Wilson.

"You did your best, skipper," Aberle said, his hand on Pete's shoulder. "You let the coast guard know we lost a man here. Not much else we can do here. Perhaps the detectives still need to go to the cave?"

"That's not going to happen," Lee said. "We'll go back if we're sure we've exhausted all chances of finding Archie."

"Tide's gone slack," Pete said. "We'll run up through the strait again just in case."

Morris Denton eased himself out of the bench seat he'd been occupying.

"You think it's worthwhile, do you?" he said.

"Obviously, I think so. We got a man overboard, for Chrissake."

"Be reasonable, skipper," Aberle said. "You're wasting everybody's time here. The frigid temperature would kill him even if he didn't drown. You know it's true."

"We're not giving up on Archie."

Pete kept his eyes on the stream. Denton mumbled something; the actual words impossible to distinguish but somehow disturbing. Patsy squeezed past him and went out on deck and took up her position near the net drum with a clear view of the canyon. Morris Denton suddenly appeared beside her and put a hand on her shoulder. She brushed the hand away.

"Keep away from me, Mr. Denton."

"Aberle and me are only being realistic. Archie Stevens is gone."

"I don't want to talk right now so please leave me alone."

She left him standing by the hold cover and moved to the bow. For a moment, she thought Denton might follow her, but he didn't, but Aberle, now on the deck too, spoke to her as she passed.

"Tough spot to be in," he said. "We all realize there's no hope, and yet we have to try to find our missing comrade."

"I don't believe he's dead."

"No, of course you wouldn't. The question is what we do now. When do you or Detective Lee take over the murder investigation? When can you make the decision?"

Meanwhile, Walter was on the move, clearing out a line ready to throw to Archie if he should appear.

"The boat is under the control of Pete Wilson," he said, over his shoulder. "He decides when we stop."

"I'm sympathetic," Aberle said. "But I can't be out here indefinitely on a rescue mission, and neither can Morris."

Walter shook his head. Patsy understood they couldn't extend the search forever. Lee was the senior detective and could call it off if he lost hope, but she thought it best to get Denton and Aberle off the *Cherish*. Walter had been thinking the same thing. He returned almost immediately with Thomas Lee.

"The coast guard is coming," Walter said. "Pete called another boat that should be here within a half hour. Anybody that wants to get off can climb aboard it and go home."

"Mr. Denton and Professor Aberle at least should go," Lee said. "Patsy can stay here, and I'll go back to the station to coordinate from there."

A few minutes later, when the relief boat, a trawler, came alongside, Denton and Aberle transferred themselves and their gear to it.

"I'm not sure what you can do here, Patsy," Lee said. "At least you'll have help with the search. The coast guard and sea rescue are experts in this."

"Yes."

"Good luck then."

He climbed aboard the trawler and it pulled away. Patsy turned and went back into the pilothouse to join Pete and Walter.

CHAPTER 25

Archie no longer fought the irresistible force of the torrent except, when guided by nothing more than a hunch as to which way was up, he pushed himself to the surface to gulp in a lungful of air. At length the stream backed him into an eddy behind a half-submerged boulder and released him. As he entertained the thought that his ordeal might be over, something massive slammed into his back and drove him under the water again, shattering his hopes. When at last, he surfaced, he found his attacker beside him; it was the cedar tree trunk he had glimpsed earlier. With his last strength he reached for its roots and wrapped his arms around a giant coil, but like a bronco fighting a rider, the log whipped out of the eddy and rolled over. Archie, holding on like grim death, with his lungs empty and searing, could feel himself losing consciousness, a sign the end was near, but then like the bolt from a ballista, the log shot out of the torrent, fell back and turned Archie side up.

The root mass now held Archie safe above the flow, cradling him in the giant basket formed by the swollen tendrils that once anchored the tree to the earth. He shivered convulsively, breathed freely and lay back, now too tired to move. How much time passed as he traveled on his strange craft, he could not tell, but at length, it slammed through another wall of white foam and drifted into a calmer patch of water. With land visible less than fifty feet away, and with some of his strength returned, he made a decision. He rolled off and began swimming. The log bounced and was swept onward; Archie glimpsed it once more before it vanished under a standing wave.

A side current helped him, propelling him gradually shoreward and he swam, as he must, although his stroke was ungainly and weak and almost ineffectual, like the half-dog paddle of a child. He paused often to gather his resources and somehow kept slowly angling towards shore. When an accommodating cross flow carried him into a lens of shallow, flat water and a tiny bay, he struggled to its narrow beach, little more than a rim of dirt and debris beneath a high cliff, and pulled his bruised and exhausted body onto the pebbly sand.

Weary and chilled through, he collapsed, ready to sleep but almost immediately, however, the feeling of cold water creeping up his legs signaled the turn of the tide and snapped him out of it. He could not stay where he was. Although he toyed with the idea of giving up and accepting his fate, he finally dragged his leaden feet up under him, rose and forced his numbed legs to move. As being upright alone wouldn't save him, what with the water coming up so fast, he searched in vain for a path up the high cliffs and then, at the lower end of the bay, he spotted his savior log where it had become wedged into the rocks, the trunk angled upwards like a ladder. He trudged through the rising, icy water and once there raised a foot to the slick, peeled surface and levered himself up.

His ascent was glacially slow. At the base of the precipice, the tide quickly obliterated the beach and sent standing waves dancing across the width of the now calmer waters of the strait. With no alternative but to go higher, Archie climbed. His fingers sometimes slipped from their slight handholds, and he fell back often, but at last he found a narrow place where he could rest and catch his breath.

As he leaned back into the rockface with his legs almost dangling over the edge, the *Cherish* came into view a hundred yards below him, hugging the far shore, searching. He saw Walter George on deck, moving quickly from one side to the other, scanning the banks. And then Patsy appeared, watching the waters off the vessel's bow.

Archie tried to call out, but his weak voice would not carry above the moaning hiss of water, and the stone he threw to try to catch their attention went unnoticed as *Cherish* continued on her way. Archie experienced a deep feeling of warmth and gratitude when he thought of his friends and their loyalty, but sooner or later, they must assume he had drowned and was gone, and after a time they would go home.

The day was passing away and he considered his options. He was too tired to go higher and going down was out of the question. The idea that he would die there, halfway up a cliff, crossed his mind, and he was not sanguine about the possibilities. Besides, he was losing visibility as heavy clouds moved in from the southwest and the darkness began to deepen. Still, he had too much work to do to give up. Massaging his salt-water stung eyes with the heels of his hands, he stood up gingerly and examined his perch. He could not avoid a cold and lonely night with little hope for the morrow, but he might at least be able to make himself even slightly more comfortable.

At first he saw little to encourage him, but then on the underside of a shallow overhang, he spotted painted marks that glowed scarlet in the crepuscular half-light. It was an ancient pictograph created by someone who must have climbed down the cliff long ago and that, he realized, meant there might be a way up. He braced his feet on the slanting surface of his ledge and edged sideways towards the red ochre stains. As he got closer, these resolved into the well-made portrait of a bear, which was Archie's totem, according to Tony.

The painted bear sniffed the air in the direction of a gravity-defying patch of scrubby alder. To Archie, this suggested a route marker into oblivion, but when a breeze moved the alder, a painted vermilion bear paw appeared. Archie moved to the image, the sides of his boots almost over the edge of the precipice. He reached out, grasped the knotty trunk of the alder, drew himself to it, extended a foot, swung his body out into nothing and let his momentum carry him to safety.

The platform was six feet or so wide, protected from the wind and bad weather by an overhang and two vertical arms of stone. Pictographs covered the rear wall. For a rock shelf many feet above a canyoned arm of the sea, Archie's refuge felt almost homey. It was even carpeted with grass and moss. From the little he knew about the customs of the old ones, this seemed like a place where warriors or shamans went to greet their spirit helpers. His Uncle Tony once told him that the bear was Archie's friend, and now the fact that the animal's tracks, albeit manufactured, had led him to safety made him almost believe it.

He saw the lights of *Cherish* once more before darkness fell and Patsy out on deck, leaning on the net drum, scanning the banks of the stream. He knew his voice would not reach her even if he could muster up a yell, and although he longed to let her know he was safe, he did not call out.

Later, a big Coast Guard zodiac made runs up and down the channel, the crew searching with powerful lights, but after a time, all activity ceased, and Archie knew the channel was empty. Now marooned and given up for lost, he felt alone, miserable and hungry, but his clothes at least were almost dry, and he drew comfort from that.

Without a light, he didn't want to move far, but he did explore the base of the rock shelter by feel, hoping to find enough dead vegetation to make himself a bed of sorts. He was successful in this, but he also found something else. A small patch of plants grew at the western end of the ledge, tucked into the rocky arm. He brushed the flowers with his fingers, pinched one off and held it close to his eyes. It was Chocolate Lily, an edible plant—his grandmother once showed him how to prepare the bulb. Indian Rice, she called it. He found a piece of a dead branch and scraped away the soil. The bulbs were composite and the bulblets felt like seed grain. He harvested a half a dozen, returned to the central part of the alcove, put his back to the wall and munched down a small and bitter supper that helped restore his strength and spirit.

For a time, he was immobile, doing nothing beyond thinking about his predicament, but when that process accomplished little, he got busy. He dragged in dead bracken and leaves and piled them around him and settled down, falling into sleep almost instantly. Once, during the night, he thought he woke up. A white bear, a Kermode maybe, sat at the opposite corner of his refuge, close to a panel of pictographs and studying him. The animal both alarmed and reassured him, a strange confusion of emotions, but he wished he could speak with it. At that moment, he felt a sharp pain in his shoulder, but the stinging sensation quickly passed. The bear dipped its head and then lifted its muzzle to test the wind. Archie closed his eyes to moisten them but when he opened them, the bear had gone and the dream ended.

Woken by the rising sun, Archie trembled with the early morning cold, and he got to his feet quickly, flapping his arms to warm himself. Below him, mist obscured the narrow body of water and certainly no vessel would risk the channel until the day burned it away. But something else on the breeze gave him hope—the sweet, harsh tang of woodsmoke. Archie lifted his head to try to sniff out the direction. People were not far off, and on his side of the canyon too.

He scrabbled out a couple more of the rice root bulbs and ate the bitter starch, which brought on a thirst intensified by the knowledge of the water below. His priority now was to find the route taken by those who made the pictographs and get from the ledge to the rim. He read and reread the markings, and it occurred to him to go to the spot where he dreamed of the bear, and indeed, at the narrow end of the platform, he found where, at some time in the past, people had enlarged natural declivities in the rock wall and created a kind of ladder up the cliff. He studied the rockface. It wasn't going to be an easy ascent, but he had no alternative but to try. He set his foot on the lowest step and reached for the handhold above him and went up. Several times, he slipped and caught himself before he fell into the mist-shrouded abyss below him, but finally he hauled himself up out of the canyon.

Relieved to be on flat ground again, he felt good, almost triumphant. The air was warm up top too, and he was already sweating. Since it seemed like a good time to check for injuries, he peeled off his shirt and examined his body for scratches and bruises. For the most part, he had been lucky, with only a large bruise above his hip and five curving red lines, rather like the claw marks of a bear, on the skin over his left pectoral muscle. He let the breeze dry away his sweat, put his shirt back on and set out in search of breakfast.

He soon picked up a deer trail that seemed to be going in the right direction and followed it. When he glimpsed blue smoke intermixed with a slight mist drift through the cedars near him, he reset his course towards the source and began to entertain fabulous visions of bacon and eggs, pan-cakes, pitchers of syrup and pots of coffee. He was famished.

CHAPTER 26

The cabin was a disorganized jumble of found wood and recovered objects built round a cobblestone chimney from which issued the blue smoke that brought Archie to the place. As he walked towards the structure, the door opened and John Robbie stepped out to greet him.

"I saw you through the window," he said. "Are you out for an early morning stroll or what?"

"I'm hoping for breakfast. Any chance?"

Robbie laughed.

"Why didn't I think of that," he said. "Why else would Archie Stevens show up *here* at seven thirty in the morning?"

He led Archie inside his cabin and indicated one of two lawn chairs at the end of a salvaged and battered wooden table. He rinsed a mug in a bucket of water, filled it with coffee from an old-fashioned perk, and handed Archie the cup.

"You want eggs or oatmeal?"

When Archie hesitated, Robbie shrugged.

"No problem. I'll make both."

Robbie studied Archie while he ate and held his questions until he finished his meal.

"They were searching for somebody down in the channel up until dark," he said. "Would it have anything to do with you?"

"Yes, I'm sure they were looking for me."

"You went overboard in that freaky weather yesterday, did you?"

"Yes."

"And you survived Jeremiah Strait. You got horseshoes up your ass, man."

"I can't argue with you," Archie said.

"Now what are you planning to do?"

"I don't know for sure. Have you got any way of communicating with the real world up here?"

Robbie struggled out of his lawn chair and went into another room, returning moments later with a laptop computer. He booted up the machine. He noted Archie's surprise.

"What would you think, Archie? It's the twenty-first century up here, same as everywhere else. I got solar panels, and I charge extra backup storage batteries every time I'm at Moffat's."

He spun the computer around so that the screen faced Archie, an email program already open and ready for Archie to use. Archie nodded his thanks, tapped out messages to Patsy, Pete, Delia John, Fricke and Thomas Lee. After that, he opened the local news page and read the copy below the "Police Officer Missing" headline. The replies came quickly—Patsy first. She didn't try to hide her joy.

"And folks are still searching for the body," he said. "I'm flattered."

"Yes, you're special," she said.

He told her what he would like her to do on the case and spent the next few minutes responding to other messages while he ate his breakfast.

"I've got to get to some place where they can pick me up, John," he said.

"That shouldn't be a problem. We'll go down to the cove."

They set off as soon as they finished the dishes, following a well-used trail leading from Robbie's shack into the forest. Archie's thoughts returned to the murders, particularly Stella Picard's.

"You know the burial cave on the south side, John?"

"There's two caves on Velasquez. Which one you mean?"

"Two?"

"Yes. The southern one is bigger with smallpox victims inside, and the little one is almost right in the center of the island."

"Can you take me to the second?"

"You got time?"

"I'll make time."

They came to a fork in the trail, and Robbie veered to the right and picked up a path along the island's sandstone spine. This descended into a shallow valley formed by an ancient slip fault after a few hundred yards. They skirted a mass of broom and negotiated the boulder-strewn approach, arriving finally at a horizontal fissure about two feet high to the left of a large red pictograph. Robbie pointed to the painted rock.

"Cool, huh? Can you read what the picture means?"

"No."

"Don't seem friendly, more like a warning sign."

Archie nodded.

"I'm going to check inside."

He hunkered down and crawled through the opening. The light from outside lit the cramped interior where bones and coffins had mostly disintegrated, but the living also used the cave as evidenced by a sleeping bag on a broad ledge, an electric lantern and some other supplies for camping out. A mortar and pestle and a shallow bowl containing an assortment of plant matter occupied a rocky shelf.

Archie needed a clean container so he could take a sample necessary because the material seemed similar to that Helerstone chewed on the night he died. Luckily, the camper had left a small box of sandwich bags with the gear. Archie pulled out a bag, scraped some of the rind that rimmed the mortar into it, and he sealed it. He did the same for the contents of the bowl, put both bags in his pocket and crawled back out.

"Somebody has been living here," he said. "That confirms what I saw."

"Which was?"

"I checked out Bobby Carpenter's place like you asked—easy to slip by the kids watching the place. I didn't see Bob, but another guy showed up who seemed to spook the young guys a bit, said he wanted to speak with the dead, or some such bullshit. He carried a sleeping bag with him."

"What did he look like?"

"Couldn't say. Short, but he wore a hoodie and hid his face almost like he knew I was there."

"You're sure it wasn't Bobby?"

"No. I'd recognize Carpenter, hoodie or no."

The compound consisted of a longhouse, a bunkhouse, an administrative building, a log dwelling, a small basketball court and a playing field. Because searching without a warrant was generally a bad idea, especially if one got caught, Archie walked straight up to the front door of the largest building and knocked.

When no one answered, he peered through windows, checked out the bunkhouse and headed across the field towards an open longhouse door. He was about to go inside when he heard a familiar, whistling whirr. His second sense saved him. At the last moment, he threw himself sideways. The hurled stone sang past his ear and echoed off a wooden wall; the sling whistled again as it gathered energy. Archie founded his footing, turned and charged towards the sound, his momentum carrying him head down into his attacker. He swung a fist, knocked the man to the ground and then looked down at Bobby Carpenter. Carpenter picked himself up, held his head back to stop the blood dripping from his nose and swore.

"You're in deep shit now, Stevens."

The hand holding the nose muffled the sound.

"So are you, Bob, and this isn't the first time you've used a sling on me, is it?"

Carpenter hesitated.

"I don't know what the hell you're talking about. I only know you're on my property."

"Your property or tribal territory?" Archie asked.

"It's not tribal land, and you're trespassing like I say, so hit the road."

"I'll go when I'm ready, and what's with using the sling?"

"I used one since I was a kid," Carpenter said. "I'm good with it, and you're lucky you moved so fast. I teach all my young guys how to use the sling in their survival courses. It works well and it's easy to make."

"You attacked me before near the burial cave, didn't you?"

"Go to hell. I never done nothing to you before."

Archie was not completely convinced, but Carpenter, stemming the flow of blood with tissues from his pocket, seemed sincere.

"I hope you didn't break my fucking nose."

Archie peered at the nose and shook his head.

"I don't think so. I didn't get enough on the punch, I guess. Why the hell would you want to whip rocks at me, anyway?"

Carpenter pulled out another tissue, tore off a piece, rolled it up and blocked the nostril with the wad, said "Ow!" and stuffed the rest of the tissues back in the pocket.

"In the first place, you're trespassing," Carpenter said. "In the second place, who knew it was you? I been threatened lately. I think somebody is trying to scare me—or kill me—so I had to protect myself."

"So you've never used that sling on me before?"

"No—why the hell would I?"

"We've had our run-ins. You were pretty steamed when you came to my office," Archie said.

"I got a right to be steamed. I don't want the damned authorities—so-called—messing about with ancestral stuff. It's the thin edge of the wedge, and it's a big wedge."

Carpenter seemed sincere, and for a fleeting moment Archie wondered if he had misjudged him.

"I don't completely disagree, Bob."

"Well, that's something."

"You got any coffee?"

"Coffee? You trespass, punch me in the head and you want me to give you coffee?"

"Past history and a new start," Archie said. "What do you say? I want to ask you some questions about some of the folks who came with you to my office last week."

Carpenter shook his head, tugged out the wad in his nostril, examined it and stuck it back in.

"Aw shit. Okay—follow me. Those were some interesting folks, especially two of them. They were strangers to me, but they seemed to want to help."

"Tell me more."

"Later."

He led the way to the administration building and into the small galley. He gestured to an old armchair before he flipped the switch on a coffeemaker.

"Sit there, Stevens. I'm going to go clean myself up. Pour us a couple of cups when she warms up. We'll talk some more when I get back."

He left the room, and Archie watched him through the window as he crossed over to the log house, mounted the porch and went in through the front door.

When the coffeemaker beeped, Archie rose, found mugs in a cupboard, flipped them up on the melamine counter and filled them with coffee. Then, carrying his, he went to the pictures on the bulletin boards, mostly shots of groups, including photos of young men with canoe paddles and other outdoor gear, and one or two of an older man he took to be Bobby Carpenter senior — the resemblance was plain. Archie also wandered through the other two rooms of the building but noted nothing out of the ordinary.

Bobby Carpenter had not reappeared, so Archie set down the empty mug and went to look

for him. He was crossing the short grass and gravel to the house when the muffled crack of a shot
echoed through the clearing. Archie ran towards
the sound. Bobby Carpenter was behind the
house, in a sitting position, his back to a post and
shot through the head. His sling bound him to the
post like a Spanish garrote. A pistol, which Archie
recognized as his own, the SIG Sauer with the nick
out of the butt grips, lay close to his hand.

CHAPTER 27

Archie tried to sneak into his office and thereby avoid discussion of his Jeremiah Strait experience, but Patsy and Thomas Lee were waiting for him. Lee said something about reading Archie's mind and Patsy even touched him on the cheek. Archie immediately shifted the conversation to work, asking them if they'd made any progress on the murder cases. Patsy laughed and shook her head.

"Typical of you," she said.

"We were searching for you, Archie," Lee said. "You were the priority. It would have been too late in the day to go back and do anything worthwhile, even if we'd wanted to, which we didn't."

"I'm sure you heard about Bobby Carpenter," Archie said. "I radioed in right after I found the body. It's either going to help our investigation or screw it up."

"I suspect the latter," Patsy said. "Ray Jameson's gone out there with his folks."

"Somebody has to go, I guess," Archie said. "But it brings him into our work more than I'd like."

They lingered a few moments, trying to draw some of what happened back in the strait out of him before they decided to go back to their own duties. Lee departed. Patsy paused and held his eyes with her own.

"I'm glad you're safe," she said. Then she turned and followed Lee down the hall.

After they left, Archie checked his messages. The first was from Ray Jameson saying he was back from Bobby Carpenter's compound and needed to discuss something with Archie urgently. Archie decided he wasn't in the mood to see Jameson, especially since the man hadn't seen fit to tell him what it would be about. There was also a brief message from Tessa Simons saying she'd like to connect again when Archie could make time. He was about to call her when Fricke messaged him to come to a meeting, and he didn't want Archie "fucking dawdling," as Fricke put it, on his way there.

Archie got some candy from the machine, paused at dispatch to wish Delia John a good morning and walked through Fricke's door fifteen minutes after he'd been summoned. Fricke didn't waste time. He said he was pleased Archie had not drowned and even shook Archie's hand before he lurched into what he wanted to talk to Archie about, the upshot of which was that Archie was going to get a holiday, whether he wanted one or not.

"You got to be kidding," Archie said. "I'm up to my eyeballs in work."

"I know this will seem like a new concept to you, Archie, but there are procedures when an officer uses his weapon and a death results."

"You mean Carpenter?"

"Of course I mean Carpenter. Your gun killed him. What do you think the media might do with this?"

Archie knew Fricke had no choice but to do something but figured there must be another alternative, because a leave would stop his investigation cold.

"Bud Marsden will confirm I was not carrying the murder weapon. How 'bout I work from my office for a few days and let Patsy and Thomas do the legwork?"

Fricke shook his head.

"It don't matter at the moment, Archie," Fricke said. "Obviously you didn't shoot Carpenter, but like I said, there are procedures. A cop is implicated in any way in a death and steps have to be taken. I'll see what I can do about desk duty, but right now, cool your jets, will you?"

"I guess I have to."

He got another text from Jameson, a summons more or less, which Archie wasn't in the mood to answer. He left the building, intending to work around his so-called leave, Fricke's injunction notwithstanding. He had a job to do, and now he also wanted to get his hands on the sneaky bastard who'd set him up, the murderer who outgamed him at every turn.

He passed down into the holding cell area and exited through the door they used to bring prisoners into the station and avoid cameras and reporters. In the absence of a real plan, he headed for his grandmother's house, now vacant since Archie moved her to a retirement home. Never sure if she recognized him or not, he still visited her every week and took her the chocolates she liked so much. Even now and with her absent, her house was home to him, more than his condo or anywhere else.

He crossed the river and passed quickly through his home village of Kokishilah, which stretched out along its banks. He parked the 4Runner behind the old bungalow and used his key to open the back door of the house, aware that the person who had occupied it would never return, and saddened by the thought. The silent rooms, even the one that was once his, smelled like old age, old salmon, old woodsmoke. He went to the stove, lit a burner, put the kettle on to boil and hoped his granny had left more in her cupboards than the stale biscuits she usually fed him when he visited, because he was starving.

Outside, dusk settled into the surrounding forest. In the somber half-light, Archie made his tea and then searched for food. In a lower cupboard, he discovered a large can of spaghetti and silently rejoiced. He took the can to a counter, found a saucepan, opened the can and heated its contents. He didn't bother with a bowl, just carried the pan to the big easy chair she always assigned him, pushed some of the crocheted covers aside, sat down, put his sock feet up on the old ottoman and ate. The house was close to the main road and the hollow gravel hiss of vehicles passing by lulled him. Soon, he dozed off, the saucepan handle still in his hand.

When he awoke it was full dark, but he made no move to turn on house lights or the television. Only occasionally now did vehicles pass by. Archie amused himself by identifying each one by type, a pastime from the old days before his granny got TV and there wasn't much to do. Suddenly, headlights flashed into the darkened living room and he heard a big pickup pull into the driveway, its tires crunching on damp gravel. He roused himself, set the empty pan to one side, retrieved his cowboy boots and pulled them on, worried about vandals more than anything else.

He moved away from the windows and took a position near the doorway leading to the kitchen. Automatically, he reached for the SIG he no longer carried. Against the wall, he found his grandmother's standing ashtray with a silver airplane on top—a heavy antique and possibly a formidable weapon. He took it up, let it hang loosely in his hand and waited. He'd give the intruders a scare at least, which would likely be enough to send them on their way.

The truck's door slammed and heavy footfalls sounded on the aggregate. A shadow passed a window. Someone knocked on the glass and rattled the doorknob. Seconds later, the door opened with a squeal of unlubricated hinges and a large shape stood silhouetted against the starlight. The shape spoke.

"You in here, Arch?" it said.

Archie set the ashtray down and let out his breath.

"I'm here, Walter."

Walter George entered quickly and closed the door behind him. Archie drew all the curtains and flicked on the light. Walter studied him and made a "sheesh" sound through his teeth. It was the first time Archie had seen him since the boat ride. Walter took him by the arms and then embraced him.

"Glad to see you, man," he said. "I was fucking worried."

"No need. I just took a dip in Jeremiah Strait is all."

"Very funny. Do you know how much diesel we had to use up searching for you when all the time you were at Robbie's eating bacon and eggs? Not to mention having to spend hours with Pete."

Archie laughed.

"I'll make it up to you both one day," he said.

"You're damn right you will, but right now you got to get out of here."

"What do you mean?"

"I mean that your Uncle Tony got hold of me, said to tell you to keep moving."

"Why's that?"

"Tony said your granny's house is not the best place for you. He was insistent."

Archie shook his head. The idea that Tony would send him a message through Walter seemed strange to him. Tony normally made his own calls—if he absolutely needed to talk to somebody, which was seldom.

"I don't buy it," Archie said. "This is as good a place as any for a cop to ride out a suspension."

Walter tilted his face towards the ceiling, an expression of exasperation and impatience.

"Right. All I know is Tony told me to tell you to go home and not to stay here. More dangerous than Jeremiah Strait, is what he said. He said Morris Denton would meet you at your condo and help you in some important way."

"Morris Denton? Why the heck would he want me to talk to Morris Denton?"

"I'm just telling you what Tony told me."

"You saw Tony?" Archie asked.

"No. He called me."

"He called you?"

Again, the strangeness of Tony making such a request bothered Archie. He always figured Walter was too honest for his own good sometimes, accepting as truth whatever people told him and therefore easy to fool. Unable to lie himself, it seemed he could not conceive of anybody else doing so.

"You think I don't recognize your uncle's voice?" Walter said, his frustration showing again. "I've known him all my life, man. He scared me enough for your safety that if you don't go, I'm going to have to stay in this musty old place with you, and there probably isn't even any food here."

"No, there isn't. Fine—I'll do what he wants, Walter. Okay."

"Yes, okay, you stubborn son of a bitch. I'll head home, but if you need me, call. I mean it."

"I know you do, Walter," Archie said.

After Walter left, Archie rinsed the empty can and threw it into the recycle box, washed out the saucepan and spoon and put them away. He straightened the throws on the furniture before he quitted the cottage, locking the door behind him. If ever his granny could come back, she'd find the place tidy.

On his way to town, he pondered the situation, deciding he might advance his investigation by learning more about Morris Denton, if it was Denton who had called Walter, which Archie suspected. As he parked the 4Runner on the street outside his condo building, the man himself came out of the shadows to meet him. Shorter than Archie by a head, he seemed harmless—even avuncular—but Archie knew better. As if he read Archie's mind, Denton grinned and lifted a hand in a friendly wave.

"Glad you were able to drag yourself out of the chuck, Archie. We're all relieved."

"Me too."

Denton whistled.

"You got nice digs for a kid from the Kokishilah. Being a cop must pay pretty well."

"Just average. Now if I can figure out what you're doing here, I'll be happy. We didn't exactly hit it off when we met last time."

Denton scanned him like a doctor making a spot diagnosis.

"Funny, I thought we did," he said. "Anyway, I came because your Uncle Tony asked me to check on you, and I was worried about you too after the incident on the boat. You sure got lucky there."

"So everybody keeps saying, but I don't need taking care of. How come Tony didn't send any word to me about you?"

"Must have slipped his mind, telling you, I mean. Anyway, you don't think you're vulnerable because you got your scientific mind working, but you're in more danger than you've ever been in, and you don't even know it."

"Aw shit. Not this again."

"Hear me out," Denton said. "We almost lost you in spite of me keeping an eye on you, but accidents happen. Your uncle wanted my help with you. You should respect his wishes."

Archie moaned.

"Can we go up to your apartment? You're too open out here. And when you're on display, I'm running risks too."

On the way up, Denton talked and Archie studied him. When they reached his floor, Denton surprised him again by taking a right turn off the elevator and leading them both in the correct direction, eventually stopping at Archie's door. When Archie expressed surprise, Denton shrugged.

"Don't ask me. I just went. It's not always clear how things happen. I've always been able to find things, to pick the right path, but I can't say I understand how it happens."

Archie took out his keys and opened the door.

The sun was dropping below the mountains but the condo, with its western exposure, was still warm. Archie slipped his keys into his pocket rather than leaving them in their usual spot in a bowl on the hall table. Denton pushed past him, said something incomprehensible in a language that sounded vaguely like the old Salish his granny spoke to her friends. Then, to Archie's surprise, Denton tossed a handful of powder into the air.

"Your enemy has been here," he said. "You have to be careful now."

Archie grabbed Denton's shoulder and spun him around to face him.

"I've got a good idea who's been here. You walked to my door and yet you've never been here before?"

Denton clicked his teeth together and grinned.

"The way it is, you're screwed, Slick. Your enemy isn't a person, and you don't understand what you did back on the island at the cave, and you were unlucky. Coyote is what your enemy is called. He was hanging around because of things not being right there, and when you showed up without any protection, you opened a door for him."

Archie's father used to call him "Slick," but no one had spoken the nickname for years. Archie felt a chill.

"I've got enemies, Morris, but they're not ghosts or spirits. They're people, and I can deal with them."

Denton aside, someone had been definitely been in Archie's condo. He sensed it. He pushed past Denton, went through to the kitchen and carried on into the living room. Everything seemed normal except in his den where the computer was running, which surprised him because he usually put it to sleep. He crossed to the desk and rolled the mouse until the screen flashed. A weirdly different desktop populated by unfamiliar icons and backed by wallpaper featuring images of coyotes and skulls greeted him. A line of text ran along the bottom, words in Salish he didn't recognize that appeared one after the other, the result of a hack of some kind. He started to sound them out.

"Idiot, don't say any of those words!" Denton yelled. "Are you crazy? You'll be speaking a spell he's left for you. It's a trap. This is what Tony was afraid of."

"I don't believe in that stuff, but I do believe the security on my computer is compromised, and I think you're involved somehow."

Denton rubbed a thick hand through his iron-gray brush cut and laughed.

"I don't even have one of them computers, and I wouldn't know nothing about doing something to one. You're in way over your head now, and you're goddam lucky I'm here or you'd be halfway down the Coyote's path by now."

"You keep talking about Coyote like you're trying to scare me. Don't waste your breath."

Denton looked at him as if he was a child who didn't understand that trains don't fly through the sky.

"Suit yourself. You're caught up with something that don't like you one bit. You're in deep doo-doo, and you can't never figure out why because your thoughts don't even go that way, which is why Tony is worried for you."

Archie shook his head.

"If you didn't screw up my machine, I've got a virus. That's the simple explanation and the most likely."

He walked back to the computer and started to read the words scrolling across the bottom of the screen. When he turned around, Denton was gone.

CHAPTER 28

Archie pried open stinging eyes, stumbled out of bed, searched for and recovered his phone and answered the call from Fricke who ordered him to report to work pronto. Even sleep deprived, Archie welcomed the opportunity to get out of the condo, the Morris Denton visit having unsettled him. He found a half can of cola in the refrigerator cup rack and gulped it down, and en route he picked up a to-go breakfast from Avril's. When he arrived at the station, Fricke leaned out of his office door, bellowed his name and motioned him inside.

"I'll say it again," Fricke said as Archie settled into a chair. "I'm damn glad we didn't lose you in Jeremiah Strait."

"I appreciate you saying so, Cal, but if I could get back to work, I'd be thrilled."

Fricke rubbed his boulder of a head like he was polishing stone.

"You're in luck. The police board met and, as of this morning, you're off suspension. Since we're paying you to solve cases, I want you to get your ass in gear."

"The police board was fast."

"It was a foregone conclusion," Fricke said. "We checked with Marsden who confirmed what you said, but more important is that you didn't have a weapon on you when you went overboard. The gun you carried remained on the deck of Pete Wilson's boat. You must have lost it in the excitement."

"I guess so. I climbed out of the water without the SIG."

"Yeah. Patsy found your pistol. She went back to check for it and discovered the thing wedged behind a net locker, plus there's the fact you don't have no motive to kill this guy anyway, except that to you, Carpenter was a pain in the ass, which is hardly reason for a cop to shoot anybody. If it was, there'd be a bloodbath."

Archie closed his eyes, thought of Patsy, grateful to her, appreciative that she believed in him.

"And now you want me to add Bobby Carpenter's murder to my investigation?" he said.

"Nope. Ray will be officially in charge of the Carpenter case. The weapon you normally carry is involved, after all, so it can't be you. You've got other stuff on your plate."

"Makes sense, I guess."

"Yeah."

Returning to his office, Archie thought about contacting Patsy to thank her, but he didn't know how to do it or even how he would begin. Before he could think it through, Thomas Lee showed up.

"I found something that might interest you," Lee said. "It concerns the president you met out at the university."

Archie waved him to a chair.

"Go on."

Lee opened the file folder he brought.

"I searched the files and researched old newspaper files as you asked, and one of the folks you were interested in was Andrea Dhillon, right?"

Archie nodded. Lee passed him a photocopied page. Archie studied it and handed it back.

"I'll be darned. She was let go by a British university—with cause. It's from seven years ago."

"With cause means it's serious. Likely something to do with money, I suspect."

"There's no way we can find out what the cause was, I guess?"

"I don't think so," Lee said. "Institutions keep such information confidential, and I'm absolutely sure a big British university isn't going to want to share it with a little police force on the west coast. I could try, but I'm not optimistic."

"Okay. This helps. It gives us something to think about."

Lee leaned back in his chair, straightened a very expensive silk tie, folded his hands across his belly and raised his chin. Patsy came into the room and sat down, lifted a hand in a kind of a wave.

"Not much of a holiday for you," she said. "Your suspension, I mean."

She'd given him a good lead-in, making it easy for him to thank her for finding his pistol on Pete's boat, which was an expression of loyalty that still astonished him.

"No problem, he said. The work has to continue, right?"

"Right. How's it going?"

"I did a bit more digging on Helerstone's colleagues. Hoping something like a motive might turn up. I didn't find anything. The guy Martin talked to, Robertson Foley, is absent right now, and I couldn't find much on him, not even a recent picture."

"Are you suspicious of Foley?" Lee asked.

"I'm not sure," Patsy said. "We just don't know anything about him is all."

Archie leaned back in his chair, glanced at the display boards. Then he reached for a fresh five by eight and a marker, printed Robertson Foley's name and drew a large question mark beneath it. He got up, walked to the Helerstone case board, found an empty space on the side, pinned the card there and returned to his seat.

"Okay," he said. "We've got to narrow things down, because Helerstone is only one piece of this mess. We've got the other deaths to deal with, the ones related to the burial cave and even Bobby Carpenter. Have we linked up one damn part to another yet?"

"Other than the links through the university for Picard, we've got nothing," Lee said.

Archie listened, but Lee's words seemed stretched out, slowing to the point where Archie began to lose track of them. He was also becoming hypersensitive to outside noise and the harsh fluorescent lights of his office and he felt irritable and impatient. Aware everyone was watching him, he tried to gain control of the dialogue and keep his focus.

"I'm glad we're getting somewhere," he said. "Good."

The word "good" boomed inside his head. Patsy leaned forward, stared at him, searching his face.

"Are you feeling okay, Archie?" she said. "You don't seem well."

He nodded, but his lips felt numb and sweat drenched him in spite of the coolness of the briefing room.

"Archie!"

Patsy's yell startled him. Aware he was slumping in his chair, he fought to stay upright. When he lifted his head, a stocky figure occupied the space between Patsy and Lee. They faded from the picture but the new arrival rapidly morphed through a series of avatars, first a clown, then creatures of various kinds and finally an enormous, leering coyote.

Archie slapped his forehead with the heel of his hand to try to clear away the vision. He heard people calling his name, but the sound of their voices seemed far away. Desperately, he focused his eyes on his hands, hoping to attach his consciousness to reality, but when he raised his head, the coyote had gone, replaced by an elderly man wearing a *si'em's amhalait*. The *si'em*, the man of power, said something in Salish, and Archie replied, though he didn't understand the words, after which the meeting room disappeared.

He woke up alone on a long fog-shrouded beach covered with rounded stones, his browned hands grasping a kelp rope, the traditional kind the old ones once used. He had coiled one end of the line about his waist while the other sounded into a silver-shot sea. The thing below fought to break free of Archie's grasp, and the rope had tightened to the breaking point.

Instinctively, he adjusted his stance and pulled. He felt strong, though his muscles cracked with effort and his feet skidded on the stones. He was almost naked; a red cedar ring circled his neck; fat or oil greased his skin against the frigid air; cold rain pattered against the cedar bark cloak covering his shoulders and the woven hat on his head. The west wind blew strong, yet it failed to ruffle the surface of the ocean, imparting a magical, unworldly quality to the scene.

At first, Archie enjoyed the struggle, an ancient one repeated a thousand times over the centuries. To win was to secure a great treasure he had long sought, but losing would certainly mean his death. With the realization came fear, and to comfort himself, Archie began to sing, the chant coming from deep within him.

At first, chanting strengthened him, but soon he hit more and more off notes, and as he forgot important words, he lost ground. With each mistake, the power beneath dragged him closer to the water's edge and a new wind from the east chilled him, making the grease which once protected him useless. Nor was he alone in that strange place. Animals, real and mythical, wandered out of the forest and came down to the beach, drawn to the spectacle.

Off to his left, a klatch of heron-like birds stood hunch-shouldered discussing Archie and his task, watching as his heels furrowed the sand and the sea spirit drew him inexorably towards the tideline. The herons were kibitzing, advancing the proposition that if he did things correctly his fate would not be so horrible, but they were not optimistic. When Archie looked at his feet, the round beach stones moved to clear a runway so as to deny him purchase and tumbled over each other, clattering and heading for the forest. Everything, animate and once inanimate, now lived.

He heard a noise near his left ear, barely audible at first but increasing in volume. Within seconds it became a harsh drone trying to wear a hole into his eardrum; it would, in time, certainly drill through into his skull. The thought terrified him, but he resisted the urge to panic and to let go of the line and to clap a hand to his head. He reset his grip on the kelp line and dug in his heels, determined not to lose the battle with the thing in the water.

The chorus of noises from the creatures gathered at the forest edge to watch his struggle grew louder. Some urged him to release the rope; others counseled the opposite. The humming in his ear was now unbearable. Against his will, his fingers relaxed and the rope slipped a bit, but then the deadly noise faded, displaced by the strong baritone voice of his Uncle Tony chanting. Tony's words, repeated again and again, gave Archie strength and cleared his mind too, made him understand he must not resist the thing below. He kept hold of the line but relaxed the muscles in his legs, slid down the beach and followed the kelp rope with its stream of bubbles down and under the surface of the cold, green sea.

CHAPTER 29

Archie awakened to diffused light, the soft sounds of preoccupied voices somewhere in the distance and the occasional beeps of medical machines monitoring his vitals. His situation puzzled him. He remembered being in the briefing room talking to Thomas and Patsy, but then only disjointed fragments of a long dream. A middle-aged woman in a yellow patterned uniform, a nurse, checked his pulse.

"I think you're awake, darling, aren't you?" she said.

"Yes, I'm, awake, but I'm not sure what I'm doing here. Enlighten me."

The nurse ignored him and went about her business. She put the cuff on his arm and took his blood pressure before she shot him a smile.

"I don't know all the details except you're supposed to rest, but you've got visitors and I have other patients. I think it's okay I allow them in."

Soon after, Thomas Lee arrived. He lifted his hand in a wave.

"We thought we'd lost you, Arch," he said. "It was touch and go for a while, apparently."

"What happened?"

"You were poisoned, is what they figure, and it was lucky Ray Jameson came in when he did. He recognized the effects of poison and knew what to do, which is why you were in Emergency twenty minutes after you collapsed."

Patsy Kydd came into the room. She went to him and touched his hand.

"Feeling better?" she asked.

"What actually took place? Did I have a seizure or something?"

"Yes," she said. "Something like one, at least. You stared at the wall, turned kind of a green color and dropped like a stone. You scared me."

"I ate at Avril's this morning, so maybe I got something bad. Likely it was food poisoning."

"You didn't get it from Avril's. We think it was in a can of cola. I didn't discover any evidence of food poisoning in your 4Runner. I sniffed the soft drink container and I'm checking into it further."

"You were out cold," Lee said, "Ray worked hard to start you breathing."

"Ray did that for me—you got to be kidding."

"He's not so bad once you steer past the personality thing."

Archie's slightly out-of-body vibe abated somewhat and he felt stronger, but when he tried to pull himself upright, but his muscles refused to obey him. Patsy stared at him.

"You look like you're going to black out, Archie."

"I'm not."

The unpleasant sensation seemed to pass. He refocussed.

"What's happening with the case?" he asked.

"Not much. We need you."

"Then let's go."

He tried to rise and fell back. Then he rocked his body from side to side in an effort to roll off the bed. Patsy grabbed his shoulders and stopped him.

"Too much motion and you're going to set yourself back," she said. "The doctor said so."

"There's something else, Archie. Cal Fricke got sick," Lee said.

"Cal—damn. What happened?"

"I'm not sure, but possibly a heart attack. It came on suddenly."

"Will he be okay?"

"He seems to be fine, but they've made him stay home," Patsy said.

"I'd better go visit him. Give me a hand to start me, and then I'll be on my feet."

He raised his hand. She took it and pulled, but she could not raise Archie even with help from Lee. Archie cursed his situation, the hospital and his immobile legs. The nurse returned, saw him struggling, pursed her lips and tut-tutted.

"The doctor will be here soon," she said. "Why don't you wait and ask him what you can do? You don't seem injured physically, but in my experience, sometimes there's a simple, mental reason for this kind of thing."

Archie folded his arms across his chest and sulked. His colleagues, realizing he wanted to be left alone, made excuses, promised to return and quitted the ward. The nurse checked his pulse and his blood pressure again and made her escape. Archie fretted. The doctor, when she arrived to discharge him, had little to offer, other than to suggest he would recover better at home, after which an orderly brought him a wheel chair, since he could not get around otherwise.

CHAPTER 30

Back home in the condo, Archie tried to focus on his work. He spent hours online researching the university, its operations, its committees, and its finance and eventually got some of the information he needed. He would find the motive for murder there. The other thing that occurred to him was that if someone wanted to remove him from the case, they hadn't missed by much. He would still be suspended if Patsy hadn't gone searching for his pistol, and he'd be dead if Ray Jameson hadn't showed up. Thinking back, his fall from the *Cherish* in Jeremiah Strait seemed accidental, but he also remembered seeing a figure on deck just before the lifeline he was holding went slack. Even now, unable to walk, he could do little more than computer searches and pondering. The criminals had created plenty of Archie Stevens-free time to finish whatever time-sensitive project they might be completing.

Everything about the case seemed now to revolve around the university and its administrators, students, professors, research, buildings and basements. His mind went to Morris Denton; things usually went badly for Archie when he appeared. Yet, the extent of his involvement and his motivation remained a mystery, especially since he seemed far removed from university affairs. Somehow, Archie planned to bring the parts of the puzzle together.

Patsy dropped by to see him often, to check up on him and feed him and, as a result, he was eating and sleeping better. She also brought news from the station. Ray Jameson had taken over as acting chief until Cal Fricke's return, and Martin Demio was back at work too and covering some of Archie's duties, something which did not sit well with Archie.

One evening, his Uncle Tony arrived for a visit. When he saw the wheelchair, he scowled.

"It's worse than I thought."

"If you've got a solution to this, Uncle, I'll be happy to hear it."

Tony plunked down in a chrome and leather occasional chair opposite his nephew, leaned forward and peered into his eyes. Then he settled back, unwrapped a mint and popped it into his mouth.

"I quit smoking. Now I'm addicted to candy."

Archie crossed his arms and waited.

"The little beggar did a number on you, didn't he?"

"Who you talking about?"

Tony pulled off his cap, clapped it on his knee and sighed. Twenty years older, he appeared much younger, and some people took him for Archie's older brother, although they looked nothing like each other. Although Archie had been a troubled kid and a mischief-maker in his day, he knew he hadn't been in the same league as Tony. At some point, out of the blue, however, his uncle reversed direction and went into healing—shamanism, some said. Now, in late middle-age, he was a respected, sometimes feared, elder who carried a lot of weight when it came to settling disputes. Very private and never political, he had turned down the job of tribal chief at least three times. Tony made his living fishing and seemed to want little else. Now he scrutinized Archie like a doctor making a diagnosis.

"I'll bet you remember some parts of a dream," Tony said. "In fact, I'm sure you can, because this could only happen in the other world."

"I'm not a believer."

"It don't matter much what you believe, Archie. You got trapped anyway. Your own doctor couldn't find anything wrong with you, right?"

"It'll be something nobody has found yet. I've had tests. Somebody poisoned me and it affected my nerves, I guess. I've been trying to figure out what I ingested and what the antidote might be."

"Ingested—I like that word. Is that the same as 'you ate'?"

"Ha, ha."

"Cheer up, nephew. You're making things worse for yourself by being gloomy."

"Nothing to be cheery about, but I'm glad you came. I was wondering if you could confirm something for me?"

Tony lifted his shoulders.

"Sure."

"How come you sent Morris Denton to me?"

"Morris Denton?"

Tony seemed surprised. A moment before he seemed ready to make light of Archie's dilemma, but now he touched his zip-necked shirt at the place where a tiny doeskin medicine bag lay hidden. Tony never did that casually.

"You got the name wrong, I think. Describe this man to me."

"Low-slung kind of a guy, barrel chest, brush cut gray hair, mid-forties—you need more?"

Tony put up his hand, and waved off the description.

"Morris Denton may or may not be active now. Somebody by that name got into buying and selling and did well, maybe too well. I haven't heard much about him for years."

"Larry Aberle acted like he knew him."

"Larry Aberle," Tony said. "You can't believe anything he says, not anymore. He uses people, but never mind. The immediate thing is to try to fix you, and that ain't going to be easy. You contaminated yourself, and you got attacked while you were vulnerable."

"I told you before I don't buy any of that superstitious mumbo-jumbo, so you're wasting your time."

"Nothing will go well for you, Archie, unless you follow the right path, and that is not an easy way to go either. I wish you'd let me help. It's not all hocus-pocus, you know."

"I can solve this myself, Tony. I have to."

Tony rose from his chair and crossed to the kitchen counter.

"I got to go, nephew. I'll tell you this. Every minute you don't deal with this thing is bad. I can help you but not here. You know my number. You can't will this away, Archie, because it feeds on your will. Call it psychology if you want. It don't matter. You're making whoever is after you become stronger and soon he will get the upper hand. He just don't want to do the deed yet because he's enjoying itself too much. Before I go, I can do something to help."

Tony's next move surprised Archie. He stepped quickly to Archie's side and touched Archie's shoulders, heart and head with a charm he held in his hand. As he did so, Tony chanted and, for once, Archie understood Salish perfectly, although each word was gone from his mind the moment Tony uttered it, but he recognized Tony's song from the dream. Archie's eyes closed involuntarily and he saw again the beach and remembered his struggle. When he opened his eyes again, Tony was standing at the counter drinking a cup of tea as if he had never moved.

"You want tea?" he said.

"Sure."

Archie rose from his wheelchair and started to walk towards the kitchen. He was almost there before he realized he was walking. His spirit soared, but Tony watched him closely.

"I'd like to say you were halfway there," Tony said. "You ain't perfect, but you're mostly back into this world. You were right about the fact you got infected."

"I thought it was breakfast from Avril's Donut Shop, but the folks at the cop shop think I drank something, but the evidence is inconclusive."

"You were mostly attacked in the dream world, not this one, but perhaps somebody offered you food or liquid, or snuck something into a drink, and like an idiot you ate or drank. Do you recall anything like that?"

"Not in my dream, no," Archie said.

"Did anybody throw powder at you?"

He remembered Morris Denton scattering the powder in his condo.

"Possibly."

"You got a powerful dose of hallucinogenics somewhere is all I know. Anything else?"

"Other than what happened to me after I blacked out, not much."

"You wouldn't. You're still half in the dream world even now, but you won't truly understand your situation. All I can say is that you're also fighting within a dream right now, or part of you is. The fight is for control of your will, and you will lose if you're not careful."

Archie, thrilled to use his legs again, put the improvement down to hypnosis or some such trick of Tony's, but he still felt deeply grateful.

"I got to get you to someplace where I can make power to deal with this. I know where we can truly tackle this. We'll go there."

Archie shook his head.

"I feel much better, but I'll wait," he said. "Now that I'm walking thanks to you, I got lots to do, like my work, for example."

Tony got his jacket on, ready to go.

"You're not up for your job, but I'm not going to convince you of that—for sure I'm not. Call me when you want to get serious."

He started to go, but something occurred to him.

"You're investigating those anthropologists at the university, right?"

Archie said that he was.

"There something weird going on there, Archie. Watch yourself."

"What do you mean by weird?"

"I'm not sure myself. I don't trust Aberle. though, or Robertson Foley—none of those professors there, in fact."

After Tony left, Archie suddenly felt light-headed and queasy again. He imagined he saw bruises and blotches of discoloration appearing on the skin on his forearms and went into one of the bathrooms. His image in the mirror shocked him. His face seemed marked by some other terrible disease, and a wild panic threatened to engulf him, but he resisted the urge and slowly things returned to normal. He put the experience down to the lingering effects of the poison, the toxins still working on his psyche. On the positive side, the fact he could stand delighted him. He ran a shower, washed off the hospital smell, shaved, dressed in fresh clothes and combed his hair.

CHAPTER 31

At the police station, Archie had to plow through the congestion of shift change to get to his office, where a flashing light on his phone indicated he had more messages than he wanted to deal with. Delia John, the receptionist and sometime dispatcher, rang him almost as soon as he sat down.

"I made you an appointment this afternoon with Doctor Eliot on Schooner Drive about your seizure," she said. "Ray's orders."

"Jameson can't fire me if I don't go. He's just acting chief."

"True, but I think you ought to. People worry about you."

"Give me the address again."

The doctor asked the kind of questions Archie liked to evade, and he persisted until he got what he wanted. Since not to answer was also considered an answer, Archie decided to cooperate, if for no other reason than to set the story straight. After an examination, the doctor gave him a conditional okay to return to duty but insisted he do deskwork for a few days in case he experienced another episode.

Two hours later and back at the station, an intern brought him an armload of files that needed processing, a gift from Acting Chief Ray Jameson. Archie flipped through the pile and realized they came from Cal Fricke's desk, probably set aside before the chief's heart attack. As he spread out the folders, Patsy Kydd stuck her head in the door to say hello.

"Heard you're not getting out of this office for the foreseeable future," she said. "Staying put is for the best, I suppose."

"Come in and close the door."

She entered the room and sat down facing him. She was dressed for court— silk blouse, pencil skirt and heels and wearing more makeup too than she usually did. He was tempted to tell her she looked fantastic but did not.

"What's up, Archie?"

He blinked.

"What are you working on right now?"

"A million things. Why?"

"I've got multiple murders to solve, and I'm sitting here with Fricke's junk."

He gestured towards the cardboard and paper covering the surface of his desk.

"I don't envy you. Any recent thoughts on the other?"

She meant the twin cases they'd been investigating, and he realized he was waiting for an opportunity to outline his ideas to somebody he trusted. Being cooped up for a few days after his blackout had had its benefits.

"Yes and no," he said. "The key has always been to figure out how I fit in. The note was addressed to me, I've been attacked and screwed with, and my informants get killed before I can talk to them. So, somehow I'm an actor in this little drama or, to change the metaphor, a player in the game. It's been move and countermove from the beginning, and I keep making dumb moves. The stakes are high, clearly."

"And this understanding leads you to what?"

"I now think Helerstone's death is peripheral to something else, something larger. Perhaps the same is true for Stella. There's a major play going on here, and we're being constantly directed away from it—distracted."

"Distracted? Like in magic?"

"Just so," Archie said. "The trick is to identify the magician and the illusion."

"And the game part?"

"I got suspicious after Ron's killing because of its theatricality. After that, I kept thinking I was being gamed, and I still do. Gamed and distracted. I'm certain there must be a time element involved too. Once something's complete, the game ends. No need for distraction anymore."

"Why you, Archie? Why choose you and not some other detective?"

"You're right, there has to be a reason. I'm sure my finding Stella Picard kicked it off, but I'm not sure why, nor am I sure of the rules."

"Do you think you might be the target because of some desire for revenge on somebody's part?"

"I considered the possibility. In any case, I need to sort it out and soon."

She raised a hand, a gesture of denial.

"You personally don't have anything to sort according to the new boss, except for files. We've all been briefed. You're not supposed to do any-thing much until they figure out why you had the episode. You still aren't quite right, and I can see it in your face."

He came out from behind his desk and half sat on the edge of it facing her, trying to seem as fit and healthy as possible.

"Tell me again what happened when I blacked out. I assume I appeared the same as I always did?"

She straightened in her chair and peered at him.

"No, not the same, not quite anyway. The incident scared us. Everything seemed normal. We were talking about the case, when you stood up and went rigid, and you slurred your speech and I couldn't make sense of it. I think you spoke in Salish, but I'm not sure. Then you turned away as if you planned to walk out and toppled over like a tree."

"I fell?"

"People tried to catch you, but it was too late. I'm sure you landed square on your face, but when Thomas turned you over there was no blood or anything, no physical damage."

"I don't have any bruises or scrapes."

She shook her head. She lowered her head and raised it, her hand on her chin, a gesture of emotion, or fear.

"And?"

"You went into convulsions like you were having an epileptic seizure, except that you started kind of chanting and your hands made pulling motions. You went hand over hand for about, I'd say, five minutes before you let go. You screamed once and stopped moving, almost like you were dead. Ray came and did CPR and helped you to breathe again on your own, after which the paramedics arrived and took you to hospital. It scared the hell out of me; it still does. I was so worried for you."

He was touched and searched for the appropriate words to answer her but failed to find them — again. He had never known how to deal with her feelings towards him, or his for her. He was in unfamiliar territory.

"It's likely a drug somebody slipped me. Anyway, I can walk, and I'm going to keep working."

Her gaze went past him.

"You think so?" she said.

"I do. I'm going to continue with my investigations into two murders and maybe even Carpenter's too, with or without help."

"Ray won't like it."

"I'm not to worried about Ray. I plan to operate like normal, more or less, which means we're still a team, if you're agreeable?"

She sat down and linked her long fingers into a cat's cradle, studied it, tilted her head and considered him from under her eyebrows, as if she were weighing things over in her mind.

"I could get into Ray's bad books," she said. "Plus there's a good reason you're riding a desk right now. I'll think it over, but anyway, I've got to go to court, so I'll leave you to your files. Be happy in your work, ha, ha. Talk to you later."

"All right."

When she had gone, he went to the canteen and got a coffee from the machine before returning to his office to attend the task set for him. Then he turned on his desk lamp and began to go through the files, the third being a kind of confidential employee dossier with the name of the person in question blacked out. It made for interesting reading, being concerned with a former senior detective suspected of corruption and even murder. When Archie figured out the file came from Empire City and put two and two together, he realized the corrupt cop must be Martin Demio.

CHAPTER 32

The expression on Ray Jameson's usually mobile cadaverous face did not change. He set his jaw and leaned his head forward; his eyes went flat as he tried to intimidate Archie, who blocked his passage down the hallway.

"Move," Jameson growled.

Archie didn't move.

"I don't think so."

"Like I already told you, Stevens, the case is none of your goddam business, and I'm the ranking detective here, plus you're on desk duty. Did you finish those files?"

"I've done all of them I plan to do, and now I need information pertinent to the murder cases on my docket."

"No," Jameson said.

He was an old-time cop, tough and cynical—the kind who likely preferred to work a suspect over in a back alley or on a dark side road somewhere, the kind Archie loathed. The two men had never got along. Jameson made it abundantly clear he didn't like Archie, and Archie had reciprocated. But Jameson was a good detective in many ways. Plus the fact he recently saved Archie's life made him think he should revaluate his position. Right now, though, he wanted to know more about the Bobby Carpenter killing, and Jameson, the lead on the case, was the only one who could give him the information he wanted, something the other cop refused to do. Archie thought he might try diplomacy.

"I just want a few minutes of your time, Ray," he said. "I need information, and I don't have time to fart around. For sure you and me don't get along, but this is important."

"Yeah, and before I know it you'll be calling the shots, and fuck that noise."

"This is important, Ray."

"You don't need to do anything except to finish those files I sent you."

"Dammit, Ray. They killed Bobby Carpenter just before he could share important information with me, and I would appreciate your sharing what you found out at his compound."

"I haven't got time, dickhead. I have responsibility for the whole shop until Cal is back. I know none of us are as smart as you and as good at detective work, but that's the way it's got to be."

"Normally I don't give a goddam what you think of me, but this is ridiculous."

Jameson tried and failed to push Archie aside.

"Are you going to get out of my way, or do I got to kick the crap out of you?"

"You can certainly try, but maybe we should go outside and settle this."

Jameson paused to consider the proposition.

"All right, I'll be in the back parking lot behind the cedars. We don't want spectators."

They left the building by different doors. Jameson was waiting when Archie got there, shirt off, ready to fight. He stripped off his own shirt and threw it to one side.

"We don't need to do this, Ray."

"The hell we don't."

The fight was brief. The men were well matched, but Jameson was older and out of shape, and it soon became apparent neither had the heart for a scrap. At length they separated. Jameson put his hands on his knees and bent over, winded, while Archie went and picked up their shirts. He shrugged himself into his own and handed Jameson his. Jameson grunted his thanks.

Archie felt his lower jaw, running fingers along the jaw line, relieved when he discovered Jameson's last punch hadn't loosened any of his teeth. His jaw ached nevertheless. Jameson straightened, pointed at Archie's face and chuckled.

"I tagged you good. That cheekbone will probably swell up on you too unless you stick ice on the fucker pronto."

"You don't look so good yourself, buddy. I reckon I blacked both your eyes for you. Are we done now?"

"For the time being, I guess."

"Good," Archie said. "I never understood why you have such issues with me. I don't expect you to like me, but you've amped this to a point where I don't understand. I know it's not racism—I don't think it is, anyway."

Jameson wiped a knuckle across the underside of his nose and checked it for blood, seemingly happy with the result.

"Fucking nose stopped bleeding, at least. It's your family I got problems with, Stevens, mostly with your old man."

"You attended the crash when he died. I heard you let him die there."

"That's bullshit. I tried to save him is more like it—not that I should have. He deserved to die, and as far as I'm concerned the world is better without people like him in it. He was a criminal, and you know it."

Archie shook his head. He felt his shoulders, his whole body tense with anger, the sensation so familiar, the inevitable and immediate boyhood response to any slight or slander. He used all his self-control to master it.

"I don't believe you."

He knew his voice was barely audible. Jameson's face softened, became different, sympathetic—kindly even.

"I don't get it, kid. You really don't know your old man was a gangster?"

Archie felt light-headed. He wanted Jameson to be lying, but he'd always known Curtis Stevens raised hell sometimes. His mother's family and others skirted around certain topics, and there were many times Archie got the impression no one missed his father. And what did he know about him for sure? The old man joked with him, taught him how to fight, took him to the carnival once, took him to a tavern to hear him play in his band *once*, called him "Slick." Thinking back, he didn't really know his father at all.

"My father played guitar with his own band," he said. "He even ran a restaurant in Taggart Bay."

"Curtis had a band, that's right, and was even a good musician, they say, but his other side cancelled out anything positive. He ran the restaurant as a front for drug sales. Ask some of the old-timers, the retired guys, if you don't believe me. I'm sorry, Archie. I figured you knew. And then you become the star detective, and it made me want to puke."

"If you know so much, tell me more about my father, tell me the whole story."

"I don't think I will. It's not my place. Besides, I'm not no fucking therapist. There's an old cop named Eddie Froese who would maybe talk to you. I'll give you his number."

They parted, Jameson going back into the station. Archie lingered. Too many things started to make sense, and now he had to learn as much as he could about Curtis Stevens, no matter how painful the education process.

CHAPTER 33

Eddie Froese lived in a tiny townhouse in a senior's co-op near the Eagle Wing Casino. Like many older cops who couldn't give up the fast food habit after years of shift work, Archie heard Eddie had gone to fat and wasn't very mobile. This turned out to be true. After he unlatched and opened the door, Froese leaned forward, belly resting on the handles of his walker, breathing hard. He scanned Archie's face and nodded his recognition. Archie thought it was because he resembled his father, and he was partly right.

"I seen you in the papers and on TV," Froese said.

He wheezed rather than breathed, and his sentences came out in one-breath phrases, with a pause after each one.

"Plus you got the look of your old man about you," he said. "Anyway, I expected you. Ray Jameson called and said you had no clue about your father. Ray vouched for you. It's good, because otherwise I wouldn't give no son of Curtis's the time of day."

He motioned Archie inside past a table overflowing with mail and into a small living room dominated by a big-screen TV and the strong odor of cigarette smoke. Froese made no move to turn off the box or mute the game show he'd been watching. He indicated a side chair kitty-corner to the recliner into which Froese lowered himself.

"So what can I do you for?" he said, after catching his breath.

"I guess my father had a life I knew nothing about," Archie said.

Froese laughed, coughed, laughed again.

"It's true for more fathers than you'd suspect," he said. "Mothers too. Every family has its secrets. Usually everybody is in on them one way or another. I knew your ma, too, by the way. She was a sweet kid, and Curtis wrecked her. I was real sorry to hear about her and how that fucking serial killer Foster murdered her. But you're here to talk about your old man."

Archie's eyes wandered to the Froese family picture gallery on his wall. The Froeses all looked more or less alike, even the women.

"Yeah, I want to learn about my dad," Archie said. "Ray Jameson said my father was some kind of criminal."

"Damn right he was. Don't mean he ever served time—too smart for that. He was more the concept guy. He planned deals out for others and got things organized. He had his good side, son. He wasn't all bad."

Froese was half-watching the TV while he talked, but now he turned in his chair so he could focus on Archie, and his breathing got better and his speech less choppy.

"See here, kid, your father went wrong somewhere along the line," he said. "He never got out of the pattern. He got in with the bikers and took part in a lot of their crap. He had a black belt something or other in the oriental martial arts. Him and an American Indian guy used to do crimes, small stuff mostly at the start. I'm sure they hit a liquor store or two, but you could never prove it, which is what I mean about your old man being smart. They holed up on one of the islands out in the strait, organized a camp out there. One up coast too, I think. They had a falling out, pretty violent, apparently."

"Do you remember his partner's name?" Archie asked.

"I sure do—Robert Carpenter—Bobby Carpenter Senior."

"Bobby Carpenter the do-gooder? You're kidding."

"His old man. Young Bobby's been okay, I think, up to a point. I learned the hard way about his old man twenty-five years back. Basically, Carpenter's old man and your old man got the idea they would operate these martial arts camps to train muscle for gangs and get paid for it. They would bring in bad kids from other places and educate them in unarmed combat and other stuff. Bobby must have inherited the place when his old man got offed. Like I say, I think they had another place up coast too."

"Bob's father was murdered?" Archie asked.

"I heard bikers killed him, but why I don't know," Froese said. "It's ancient history now. It happened at their other camp and not in our jurisdiction."

"Where was that the other place?"

"North of Rochville, I think. I could find it for you."

Archie's mind was now on his own father—and his mother.

"You said you found out the hard way about my dad and Carpenter?" he said.

"Yeah. During my investigation of Carpenter Senior, my house got burned down."

"How come nobody got prosecuted?' Archie said. "Didn't anyone follow up?"

"No, nothing beyond the fact my house got torched. I got no support from the department, so I took the hint. The investigating officer was a young guy on secondment from Empire City. I can't remember much about him."

Archie wasn't listening. His mind was on his parents and the new information he was getting about their lives.

"You said you knew my mother and that my father wrecked her?" he said.

"Yes—I knew Celia—Darlene Celia Stevens," Froese said. "Most people called her Celia. She was a university kid who did volunteer work in the community, but then she fell for a rock musician with a band. Curtis had the looks too, like yourself, and the rest is history. I think when she found out what he did for a living, she just couldn't handle it. I don't think he ever beat her, but who knows. I doubt it. When I seen them, they were always lovey-dovey. Anyway, things went basically downhill, except when you were born. Word was he tried to change, to give up being a creep, but got himself killed in the car crash before he accomplished it."

Eddie didn't have much more to add, and after some small talk about policing and Cal Fricke and what a good guy he was, Archie thanked the old cop and took his leave.

At the turn before the highway, he pulled over and called Tony, asked him point-blank about Curtis Stevens. Archie ended the call before his uncle finished; he had heard enough.

He put the 4Runner in gear and drove aimlessly for an hour, ending up at the Point. Here he parked his old wreck above the surf line and stared out across the sea. There unthinking life went on, timeless. Gulls wheeled upwards on the thermals, auklets flew in line along the wave tips, eagles made great circles overhead. Beneath the surface life and death intermingled. Memories of his mother came to him and sadness too. A clear image of her came to him, and his eyes moistened. When a shudder, the kind that might become a sob, started deep within him, he stifled it, said, "Fuck this," angrily, and scraped away any incipient tears with the backs of his thumbs.

Back on the road, he plugged in his phone to the jack and punched *Emily* by San Fermin — *let the night take me, down the rabbit hole.* He downshifted, stomped down on the gas pedal and let anger crush his grief, as he always had.

CHAPTER 34

In no mood to go home, Archie felt the need to talk, to try to put his past into perspective. He drove to Patsy's street, hoping she might welcome him in and parked across from her house in time to see Tracy Gillot walking up to her door. She came out smiling, greeted Gillot with a hug and accepted the bottle of wine he brought. They went inside, leaving Archie sitting alone and feeling like an idiot. He didn't think she'd seen him, but his embarrassment burned him. He eased the 4Runner into gear and drove slowly out of the neighborhood.

Thursday nights were busy at the Eagle Wing Casino, forcing him to drive to the far end of the parking lot to find a spot. Now in a foul mood, he stalked across the asphalt, wet now from a light rain Archie hardly noticed, but near the front door, he met Susana Yip going the other way. Yip loan sharked gamblers, and she once advanced

Archie some money, but the small advance cost him ten times what he borrowed. If it hadn't been for a timely winning streak, he couldn't predict what might have happened—nothing good, in any case. She greeted him, ready, he expected, to exploit any weakness or any need she saw there.

"You don't come to me for money anymore, Archie?" she said. "You must be getting luckier."

"I'm not getting luckier," he said.

"No, nobody does, but folks think different, which is what makes the world go round. Doesn't hurt me either."

Her observation about how the bad luck of others didn't hurt her brought a smirk from Archie, and the exchange, so pedestrian and yet so grounded, even lifted his spirits a little.

"I plan never to borrow money from you again, Susana," he said. "Not in this lifetime."

She put a hand on his arm, a motherly touch. In fact, she acted the mother part well, what with her old lady-style hairdo and conservative, thrift store retro clothes, she seemed like the kind of person who would make you soup to help you feel better. He could envision her doing just that right before she sent her thugs to beat you up.

"Wise man," she said. "Maybe you make money in the stock market, or you could always sell drugs from the police impound like some others have done. One of your colleagues is a regular seller to bikers. You ever considered it?"

Archie ran through a mental catalogue of detectives, made a guess who she meant and came up with a short list of one—Martin Demio. He thought back to the shotgun attack outside the restaurant, which now seemed to him to be a lot like a screw-up in which the wrong person got hit. He remembered the dossier on Demio he'd read.

"Nope, I never have," he said.

"No marginal stuff for Archie Stevens, right?"

"No, but I always wondered how you keep out of jail, Susana. I thought somebody would have arrested you long ago."

She reached up and patted him on the cheek.

"Arrest me? Archie, sweetie, why would they? I'm a public service. I make it easier for folks to help keep the government afloat. Besides, I'm just trying to make a living like everyone else."

Archie shook his head but knew she was at least partly right. People went to Susana because she loaned money when they needed it, even though she set harsh terms and, on the plus side, she often cut them slack when other loan sharks would not. Archie wasn't quite sure how it worked; being a gangster with a bit of a heart, but Yip seemed to be able to carry it off. When he'd been down and desperate for money, trying to get his luck back, she'd steered him away from the Triad-sponsored sharks and given him a stake at twenty-five percent per month, reasonable terms in her world. He'd had to sell a collector Mustang his father left him to pay it off. Susanna Yip drove the vehicle now, which was okay considering what he learned about his old man.

"I can give you a stock tip, an investment opportunity," she said. "Could be you make your fortune that way, because you sure won't make it in the Eagle Wing. You can't be a gambler if you want to succeed there. You've got to know what you're doing, not like you. Figure out the math and how to put out money when the chance of a good return is greatest, but most people just go in there to lose."

"So you told me before. What's the tip?"

"The company hasn't been listed yet. A lot of offshore cash invested, billions maybe. This thing will happen quite soon. On second thought, I think it's better you save your money. You make good dough as a cop. Practice financial management—that's the key. I'd even sell you back your old man's Mustang at a good price when you got the cash."

"I don't need the car. What's the stock?"

She sighed, hesitated and then told him the symbol for a land development company Archie had never heard of.

"SKRL—is that it? You sure it's good?" he said.

She lifted her shoulders, an expression of possibility, but also doubt.

"It's supposed to be when it's up and running, but how would I know," she said. "My sources say it's got dibs on some major land holdings. Word is the company's lining up a huge pile of such assets, and it's got financial backing big time. As I said, the ticker symbol is SKRL, which stands for Skeleton Resources and Land. If you ask me, gangster money is involved, but that's true of a lot of legit companies. You never know who's laundering money these days. Personally, I wouldn't touch it with a ten-foot pole."

Susana seemed to think Archie wanted to invest in the stock.

"And no, I won't lend you the cash even if it is a sure thing," she said. "I like you too much. Do you need anything for the casino tonight—low interest for you?"

"I got money," he said. "I just hope the cards are good to me. I'm strictly short term."

"If I was your mother, I'd have lots to say to you."

He shrugged.

"I'll bet you would."

He waved a good-bye. He didn't want to think about mothers anymore. He watched Susana get into the Mustang, gun it for effect and peel out of the lot. As the casino doors slid aside to admit him, he felt once again like he entered the jangling, flashing machine-lined alleys of some Dantesque level of hell with the damned, the regular patrons, attached to their demons with coiling plastic cords.

Later, when he left the Eagle Wing, he had serious green in his pockets. The cards surprised him by running his way for once. He experienced a brief period of elation, followed by the realization his winnings made no more than a dent in his liabilities. Even so, he congratulated himself on leaving the place ahead rather than staying until he lost everything as he usually did. Perhaps he should think about investing in SKRL after all.

He passed through the lobby, which featured a large, bronze sculpture of a Salish spindle whorl. The faces on that disc reminded him of the stone bowl Helerstone used as a key catcher and took his thoughts back to the murder. Helerstone had obviously treated the artifact as a catchall, and yet it was as empty as the plastic container in his lab fridge, which likely meant that someone cleaned up after Helerstone was gone.

It was late, but he still couldn't contemplate the idea of spending the night alone in the condo in a desperate hope that sleep would come. He kept his phone on vibrate while he played black-jack. Now, he checked his missed calls, found and ignored three from Ray Jameson. His Uncle Tony said to call as soon as possible. And Tessa Simons wanted to talk to him no matter the hour. Reck-lessly, he punched in her number, and she came on line after three rings, apparently happy to hear from him.

When he apologized for calling late, she said she didn't sleep much and liked the night, so it was good he rang her. To meet her at such a time without witnesses was asking for trouble, but when she mentioned a local lounge, a more or less public place, he agreed.

She kept him waiting, entering through a side door in fashionably torn skinny jeans and a fur-trimmed leather jacket, obviously expensive. She smiled when she saw him. He stood up, and she kissed him on the cheek before sliding into the chair opposite him; the tight, dark-wash denim conformed exactly to the shape of her thighs.

She began with small talk but, almost immedi-ately, she suggested they go elsewhere. When he asked why, she said something about being watched, or being followed, but switched to a less urgent reason, saying the lounge wasn't set up for private chats.

"It might be better if we talked tomorrow anyway," he said, almost meaning it.

"Are you afraid of me?" she asked. "That thing at Ron's house with Ghent wasn't my idea."

He sipped his bourbon and water.

"No, but I don't usually meet people who are part of an ongoing investigation in circumstances like these. I've already forgotten about last time."

She shrugged and leaned forward, displaying too much décolletage for a lonely man in a bar to ignore.

"I guess this doesn't look good, right?" she said.

"Depends," he said.

"Naughty," she said.

Her smile seemed warm. She spoke softly, and the timbre of her voice made her words darkly intimate and sexually charged, or perhaps after seeing Patsy and Gillot together he was just more susceptible than normal. He ought to refuse her while he still had the presence of mind to half mean what he said.

"I'd rather we met at my office in the morning, and then we can talk, okay?" he said.

She raised her eyebrows and sat back, laughed, mocked him.

"You're perfectly safe with me, Detective," she said. "And I *do* want to share something important with you."

She was mocking him.

"Hey," she said. "Are you listening to me? You went somewhere just then."

"Yes, I'm listening."

She reached into her purse and retrieved a cigarette and gold lighter, lit up and blew smoke in his direction, not asking is it was okay with him or not if she smoked.

"I'd rather not talk here anyway," she said. "It's too public, more so than I thought. I have information on Ron Helerstone I think should be known. I'm nervous about confiding in you, but I would rather take a chance I can trust you than just try to forget about it."

He studied her, still wondering if she were telling the truth and what her purpose might be. He couldn't let her know how much he wanted that information.

"I'm ready to listen," he said. "We have a pretty good idea what went on, so I'm not sure you could add anything. Also, I'm puzzled why didn't you come forward before?"

"I didn't say anything before because I was too scared. You don't know everything, even if you think you do. I couldn't talk earlier without certain people knowing I betrayed them."

"What people do you mean?" he said.

She grinned, blew out a smoke ring, shrugged.

"I still can't say," she said. "I feel vulnerable here. Won't you come to my place? Don't say no. If you trust me, I'll tell you anything you want. You won't regret coming."

Archie knew he should use his head and insist she go through channels, but now her attempt to entangle him had further piqued his interest. Maybe, he thought, he liked gambling after all, but going with her would be just plain stupid no matter what the return on investment, and he was about to tell her so when she upped the ante. She stubbed out her cigarette in a crystal ashtray.

"Here's something," she said. "Are you familiar with the Cannibal Society?"

Archie set down his drink.

"What should I know and why?" he said.

She leaned in towards him so that their heads almost touched, and he could smell her perfume.

"Archie, they are very dangerous people," she said. "They eliminate anybody who gets in their way."

"As far as I know the Cannibals are extinct," Archie said. "And even when they were active hundreds of years ago, they weren't what most people think. There was a lot of stagecraft involved, particularly at the big winter ceremonials. They used props and pretended to kill people and eat their flesh. I've seen carved heads they substituted for those of alleged victims who were supposedly decapitated and later brought back to life."

Tessa focused her gaze beyond and behind him. He turned his head but saw no one. She grabbed his hand and squeezed hard.

"What is it?"

"I think I recognized a person I hate," she said. "Can we go? I don't trust any public place now."

"Not this again?"

She acted insulted.

"Please," she said. "I have to go even if you don't come with me. I'm definitely not staying here."

"You want to go to Ron's house in Falcon View? I don't think I'll follow you there."

"No. I can't live there anymore. My lawyer is lending me an old house he bought on spec."

Archie thought about this. He drummed his fingers on the arm of the chair.

"You must think I'm an idiot. The answer is no. I'm not taking you to Dave Ghent's house."

She stood up, fidgeted; she did seem worried.

"Please," she said. "He doesn't stay there. It's not like that. I'm in trouble, and you're a policeman, so protect me."

He let out his breath. She kept bringing up new cards and playing them well.

"I'll escort you home, but I'll expect you in my office in the morning."

"Okay," she said.

Outside, the street was deserted.

"Nobody dangerous out here," Archie said.

"You won't see them until it's too late."

Once they were in their separate vehicles, she sped along Whale Bay Avenue in her Porsche, going so fast Archie almost lost her. Her taillights became dots and soon disappeared entirely while he picked up one red light after another. He accelerated, forced the 4Runner to go faster than it ought to. The Porsche reappeared and turned off towards Promontory Street, which meant she was going to Harbottletown, a semi-slum of tiny turn-of-the-century miners' houses and a strange place to take a car like hers.

Ghent's spec house was a stucco bungalow with an overgrown and untidy yard. Tessa exited her car and waited for Archie to get out of his vehicle and join her. She unlocked the front door and he followed her inside.

"It's not much after Ron's place, is it?" she said. "Dave said I could stay here as long as necessary, and it's not as bad as it looks. Can I get you a glass of wine?"

He replied in the negative. Whatever was going on with her, it wasn't without its risks for him. She seemed to sense his caution, ran her hand down his arm and touched his fingers with hers.

"You don't mind if I get something?"

"It's your place."

She smiled at him, nodded and left the room. He heard the fridge door open and the sound of a bottle being breached. She returned with two glasses half-filled with clear brown liquid and ice cubes.

"You were drinking bourbon at Piccolo's Lounge with me," she said. "And right now I don't want to drink alone."

She handed him the condensation-wet glass, and he took it. She sat down on the couch at the same time, indicating he should take the seat beside her. When he remained standing, his drink in his hand, hesitant as a shy suitor, she laughed.

"You don't trust women, do you, Archie? You don't trust us at all."

"I hear that from time to time. And the last time you wanted to talk I got beaten up."

"I'm very attracted to you," she said. "I also feel safe with you. Come sit down."

Now he was sure she wanted something from him and was quite prepared to compromise him to get it. The thing was that he needed information from her, so he took the bait and sat down beside her. She moved closer to him, pulled her legs up under her, and leaned against the back of the couch facing him.

"Good," she said," "Now we can talk comfortably."

He nodded. Indeed, he had a keen interest in her, especially since his visit to Patsy's where he saw pictures of the Stella Picard facial reconstruction created by the sculptor. Tessa looked too much like Stella for it to be a coincidence.

"You can tell me your real name. That would be a good start."

She opened her mouth to speak, but something or someone behind Archie stopped her. He turned to look but saw nothing, and when he faced Tessa again, she smiled at him. She was a good actor; he was impressed.

"You already know my name."

He shook his head.

"I know it isn't Tessa Simons."

He expected that she would deny this, but she caved quite quickly.

"I'm surprised that I got away with it as long as I did, but you got me. My name is Tessa Picard."

"Same first name—Stella Picard's sister?" he said. "I thought so."

"They killed her, and now I have to do something to set things right. I already knew Ron, and he confided things to me. He liked to talk after sex, so before long I suspected he was up to his neck in some pretty shady stuff. I got the impression that once he started down that path, he couldn't get out. I had just started to work my way in when he got killed."

"So who was Tessa Simons?"

"I made up Tessa Simons and gradually created her ID with help from some friends."

Archie crossed to the sink, poured the bourbon away and rinsed and wiped the glass. He couldn't shake the feeling he had got himself neatly in a trap. The upside was that a few pieces of the larger puzzle were falling into place, and he'd confirmed some of what he already suspected.

"Which friends?" he asked.

"I can't tell you yet."

"This is way out of line for me. I can't stick around, sorry."

She rose from the couch and came to him and gazed imploringly into his face.

"Stay a bit longer. Those who helped me are not nice people. They think I owe them, and I'm afraid they'll try to kill me. That's why I've been hiding here and in other places. When you came to Ron's after he died, I was keeping the pistol close because of them."

He decided she could be quite convincing when she wanted to be, which was not the same thing as telling the truth.

"You should have told me this earlier. I'm the police, as you pointed out."

She actually put her hand up to her mouth, just like Mary Astor did in the *Maltese Falcon*.

"I couldn't. I thought if I kept my mouth shut I'd be safe, but it doesn't work like that apparently."

She went to the window and beckoned him to follow. As a precaution, he turned out the living room light and went to her.

"Come, look. You'll see why I'm afraid."

As he came up beside her, she took his hand, linking her fingers in his, squeezed tighter when he attempted to disengage them.

"See the car over there?"

She pointed to a low-rider gray Chevy Impala parked halfway down the block. She leaned in to him, putting her head close to his shoulder as if to get a better view.

"I see it," he said.

"It belongs to a guy who is spying on me."

"What does he want from you?"

She tilted her head away from him. He glanced at her reflection in the darkened window, thinking how much she seemed like an actor on a stage.

"He wants to know where I am at all times. It has something to do with Stella."

"Like what?"

She shook her head.

"I need time," she said. "Stay with me."

He separated his hands from hers and turned to go, but she moved to block him, taking both his hands and leaning into him, with the top of her head brushing his cheek. Somehow, his arms went around her. When he spoke, protesting, his voice was almost a whisper. She swayed a little, her body moving against his, and turned herself so that he was behind her. She put her hands on his hands and moved them so they cupped her breasts. She squeezed his hands, and when he took over, she pivoted. Her lips went to his, and her hot breath was in his mouth. He pushed her away.

"Why?" she said.

"I got to go. Now, what's all this about?"

She shrugged, looked away.

"Simple. I have to make sure you'll back me up and you won't treat me like a criminal. If that means seducing you, so be it."

So, it was a deal she wanted after all. He managed to manoeuver her away from him.

"I don't think I can promise anything."

"But why not?"

"In the first place, you keep lying to me," he said. "Have you told me anything close to the truth at any time?"

"I told you I was afraid, which is the truth."

Perhaps she truly was afraid, and some of what she was saying could be the truth. He never found it easy to resist cries for help, even when he knew he was being conned, which is what he was certain was going on. This time he wasn't buying it.

"I have to go," he said.

She crossed her arms over her chest, dismissed him with a lift of her chin.

"Go," she said. "Get out."

He nodded, walked to the door, opened it and went out into the early, early morning. He glanced back over his shoulder. She stood at the window, watching him, but then she dropped her head and pulled the curtains closed. He noted that the gray low-rider had gone.

CHAPTER 35

On his way to his vehicle, Archie reassessed the night's events, putting together what he had learned. The 4Runner was already dewing up. As he opened the door ready to climb in he caught a movement out of the corner of his eye. He turned as Brenda Volio stepped out of the closest hedge and pointed her shotgun at his chest. With her pinched face, schoolmarm glasses and blue hair, she seemed harmless, but he knew better. She motioned him to turn around. His SIG was under his jacket, and he had no chance of reaching it, a moot point because the twelve gauge could cut him in two at such a short distance. In any case, he doubted Volio came solo, the suspicion confirmed when Jeff Riggs came from behind to disarm him. His partner, the shotgun ported, ordered Archie to stick out his hands, and when he did, bound them with a police-issue plastic tie, and then made him get into the 4Runner, after which she went round the cab and slid into the driver's side.

Ten minutes later, sitting back in the passenger seat of his own vehicle, Archie focused on the road ahead, silently scolding himself for being so easy to kidnap. Volio informed him that they were going for a ride, said he should relax because Riggs would keep his Steyr auto pointed at the back of his head until they got where they were going. When he asked what it was all about, Brenda said somebody didn't like him and refused to elaborate.

The two killers seemed very relaxed. Soon, Archie heard the tinny sound of electronically transmitted music coming from the back, which meant Riggs had his earbuds in. Volio hummed a Nirvana tune as she drove.

"Where we headed?"

"You'll find out in a few minutes."

When Volio turned onto Chancel, he knew that the university was their destination. After taking the service road behind the Anthropology complex, Volio parked the 4Runner behind some dumpsters and cut the engine. The cacophony from Riggs's phones ceased, and he called someone to announce their arrival. Moments later they were on their way up the path. Archie glanced over at the security camera, the one he'd seen footage from with Lee and Fitter; however, the device now pointed up into the trees instead of at the door. Riggs, impatient with the slight pause, urged him on with a hard jab of the Steyr.

They took him to the back entrance, which Volio opened, and led the way through the familiar aisles of the *Cemetery* to Helerstone's secret office. The door stood open, waiting for them to enter.

"You two don't strike me as university types," Archie said.

"We're here on a scholarship," Brenda said and smirked.

They shoved him forward.

"The Varsity Felons Team?"

Riggs said, "Ha-ha," and dug the muzzle of his rifle deep into Archie's back. He half-turned and stretched out his bound hands.

"Cut me free and I'll do something nasty to you with that gun barrel, Jeff."

Riggs slashed the metal across Archie's shoulder. He turned halfway around, ready to take the hit man on, unarmed or not.

"Cut the crap and bring him in here."

A voice Archie recognized came from the office. Riggs and Volio shoved him inside where Dave Ghent waited.

"How are you doing, Detective Sergeant?" Ghent said.

Archie inclined his head slightly.

"As you see, Dave,"

"You know something, man. Everything in the world is tied together. You did some real damage to some friends of ours a year or so ago, and now it's payback time."

"This is Children of Eli stuff?"

"And other things. You're getting a bit too close to an important operation, and we can't allow it."

"Skeleton Resources, no doubt."

"He's clever. I told you."

It was a woman's voice. Archie turned at the sound. Andrea Dhillon stood in the doorway of the small kitchen holding a thermos bottle.

"You kept pursuing your case," she said. "Persistence is a commendable trait, but it is about to work against you. You could partner with us and get rich."

"No thanks. It's not my scene."

He wondered if he could turn around fast enough to take away Riggs's weapon but decided such a move would be plain stupid. As if to reinforce the point, Riggs shoved the gun barrel harder into his kidneys.

"I like things uncomplicated," Ghent said. "But knowing you were the son of Celia and Curtis makes this a problem for me. Your old man screwed me around big time, and I ended up in jail because he got a conscience. Lucky for him, he died in a road accident before I got to him, but with you here I still get my revenge."

"We'd better finish this," Dhillon said. "I don't like mixing a personal vendetta with business."

She picked up the stainless steel thermos. Riggs and Volio forced Archie to a nearby chair with Riggs reinforcing Ghent's command to sit by placing the barrel of the gun on Archie's shoulder and bearing down on it. Dhillon took the seat to his left. When he glanced at her, he saw resignation in her eyes, but she made the half-rotation motion with her hand that meant *what the hell*.

"I cut through university red tape for the business, if you must know, and I'm on display when necessary."

"It's a pattern with you. Is it what got you fired from the British institution?"

"One always needs money," she said. "I'd turn back the clock if possible, but I'm in way too deep to jump ship now. David will tell you I don't have a choice."

"You don't," Ghent said. "When Coyote gets hold of you, there's no escape."

"Coyote again. Who exactly are we talking about?"

"Coyote is just a name. We've learned a lot from Coyote. For one thing …"

Ghent shut her up with a slashing motion of his hand. Brenda Volio coughed impatiently.

"Can we do the damn thing?" she said. "This has taken too long already, and Riggs and I got other jobs to go to."

Ghent nodded, said, "Yeah."

He unscrewed the top on the thermos and poured steaming liquid into the plastic cup. Archie caught an odor of rotting vegetation and fungus and coughed against the acrid stink, but Ghent held the cup in both hands and breathed in the fumes. Riggs handed Ghent a pistol Archie recognized — his own SIG Sauer. Ghent placed the gun on the table and held out the liquid.

"I actually learned to like the smell of this stuff. Most people hate it, but not me. It doesn't taste bad either, but you'll find out for yourself."

Archie grimaced.

"You expect I'm going to drink that stuff? I don't think so."

"Like there's a choice."

"Is this what happened to Helerstone?"

"I have no idea what occurred with Ron," Dhillon said. "I'm not even sure why they brought you here. I didn't want it."

"Because we were told to."

"I don't like to be so directly involved."

"Me neither. but we do what we're told, Andrea."

He turned back to Archie.

"You'd better drink it. We have our orders. Nobody wants to hang out here any longer than necessary."

"Go to hell."

He wondered who gave the orders to this crew, not Ghent or Dhillon certainly. He needed time to think, but Volio leaned forward, drew a knife and set its point on his cheek just below his right eye.

"If you don't drink, I'll cut your eye out. I mean it. Drinking this shit, at least gives you a chance."

She turned the knifepoint like a corkscrew. Archie felt its bite where she drew blood. Ghent set the cup in his bound hands and raised it to his lips with his fingers. Archie sipped the bitter-tasting contents, holding onto the mouthful, hoping he'd be able to spit.

"Gulp her down, Stevens," Ghent said. "You might even like what this brew lets you see."

Archie drank. Moments later, a migraine-like headache forced him to clamp his eyes shut and vertigo swept through him. When he opened his eyes, the room had vanished and he stood alone once again on the beach of his former dream. A wolf-like creature appeared, laughed and called Archie by name, and shadows surrounded him, grasping at him. He kicked and fought, and they fell back. He heard a clap like thunder and another and another, looked down at his hand and realized he had his gun, yet he remained in the dream world. He staggered down the sand to what appeared to be a cliff, and found a passage at its base and stumbled into a narrow canyon that appeared to offer an escape route and ran for his life, tugging the towering walls in his flight. Behind him, mountains swayed and crashed down and thunder rolled, echoing through the blackness, and beings like angry bees clanged around him.

He kept running. A bee stung his leg hard and caused him to stumble, but soon he ran free of the things pursuing him and gained the outside world. Confused, with dream and reality mixing and shifting around him, he stumbled on into the night. And beside him, a bear loped.

CHAPTER 36

The sun had risen well above the horizon when Archie returned to consciousness. He opened his eyes, let a moment of confusion pass and tried to figure out his location. Beyond the fact that he'd parked his 4Runner fender deep in a clump of alders alongside a rutted gravel road, he had no idea where he was.

An early morning dog walker glanced at the vehicle, glared disapproval at Archie before hurrying on, so at least Archie knew he wasn't totally in the wilderness. If his headache indicated anything, the previous night had been a bad one, a suspicion strengthened by the sharp stinging in the area of his hip. When he touched the place, he immediately flashbacked to his headlong run through the *Cemetery* and groaned.

He wondered how severe his wound was. Although he didn't hurt overmuch, he also remembered that shock sometimes dulled one's pain. Gingerly, he undid his belt and peeled back the stiffening top of his jeans until he saw the red groove where the slug ripped the fabric, and the dried and thickened blood smearing the skin. He brushed the darkest area and swore when he probed the burning furrow left by a high-velocity round. He'd been lucky; the injury was superficial, which didn't stop it now stinging like the blazes. He reached around behind the passenger seat, retrieved one of the bottles of water he kept there, opened it and took a drink before he got his first aid kit from the glove compartment. Ten minutes later, he'd cleaned and sterilized the bullet graze and bandaged the wound.

The feeling of displacement he'd experienced upon wakening passed, but some mental fuzziness still lingered. For one thing, he could not recall the journey from the university to his present location, wherever that happened to be. It occurred to him that he had fired his gun during his escape, and the thought alarmed him. For confirmation, he searched for his pistol and recovered the weapon, still cocked and lying on the floor on the passenger side. He picked it up gingerly, eased the hammer down, and when he smelled the barrel he confirmed the piece had been indeed fired, likely by him. He checked the clip—only three rounds remained, which meant he used four of the seven in a full magazine, a worry for sure.

He found the box of bullets he kept in the glove compartment and reloaded. Now shivering in the early morning cold, he turned the ignition key, started the engine and tried to get the heat going. Gradually memories of the past night returned, or enough to let him mentally sketch out its events. He remembered some high-speed driving and reckoned he lost any pursuers, his being free and alive a proof of his supposition.

The vehicle heater took time to warm up, and he was anxious to be on his way. When he went to relieve himself, he realized he half recognized his surroundings. Then it dawned on him that, like a homing pigeon, he brought himself to a place he knew; he was not far from his old home at Kokishilah.

Relieved, he returned to the cab, backed the 4Runner out of the brush and made his way to the highway where he joined the early morning commuters and heavy traffic going to Harsley. He kept the scanner on low volume, but he could tell something was up by the level of activity. Normally, he'd tune in, but after the night he'd had, thoughts of food dominated his mind. When he got to Avril's Donut House, he swung into the lot, parked and entered the restaurant. Just inside the door, Tony intercepted him.

"This is a surprise," Archie said. "Come here often?"

"I've got coffee and breakfast here." Tony held up a takeout bag. "When I couldn't find you, I figured you might come here if you got hungry enough."

"Why the hell would you do that?"

"You are in deep doo-doo. Your buddies want to arrest you."

"What are you talking about?"

"I'll tell you outside," Tony said.

He pushed Archie towards the back door, down the stairs and out into the open area behind Avril's. Archie, irritated, rounded on him.

"What are you doing, man?" he said. "I just want my breakfast."

"Which can wait. You stay here and you'll be arrested. Plus, you called me to ask me to meet you here."

"I never called you."

"I know. Sounded like your voice though."

"What do they plan to arrest me for?"

"Murder."

"Damn."

"Yeah, you'd better follow me, Arch."

He led them out to where he had parked his pickup, a spot half-hidden by holly trees. When they reached it, he grabbed Archie by the shoulder, scanned his face and peered into his eyes.

"Did you go off the wagon, nephew?"

Archie shook his head.

"Don't think so, but I can't remember much about last night."

They were standing behind the pickup, out of sight of the front door and most of the building's windows. They could keep track of what was going on but remain unseen. Tony stood hipshot, hands in his back pockets, looking down at one of his truck wheels, his face obscured. At length, he raised his head and nodded.

"I also dreamt you needed me, by the way," he said.

Suddenly, he pulled Archie down. At that moment, police cruisers and a SWAT van sped into the parking lot and uniformed officers from his own department jumped out and took up positions behind their vehicles. The SWAT team covered the cafe's doors and windows with submachine guns.

"Slide into the back of the truck and get under the tarp," Tony whispered. "This place is a trap for you, Archie, and now we got to get you out of here."

Archie nodded. He followed Tony to the rear of the pickup, waited while Tony eased down the tailgate. As Archie slid beneath the plastic, Tony passed him the Avril's takeout bag. Archie was hungry, but too keyed up to eat.

For a long minute or more, nothing happened, although the sounds of police activity seemed perilously close, but when a large vehicle rumbled across the lot, Tony started his engine. Archie wondered how they could leave without being seen, but the pickup moved slowly forward. He figured out the drill—Tony was using the arrival of a garbage truck or some other behemoth to cover their retreat.

Soon they were speeding away. Archie guessed Tony would use back roads when he could and would avoid the main highway. He settled back into the pile of vegetation, the waste from his uncle's gardening, opened the takeaway bag, drank the coffee and ate the egg bun it contained before he stretched out and tried to get comfortable.

CHAPTER 37

Archie glanced repeatedly at the luminescent numbers on his watch as the journey continued. Even after he'd been under the tarp for three hours, Tony drove on. Twice he poked his head above the sheet and pounded on the cab window trying to get Tony to pull over, but both times Tony gestured him to stay down and kept driving. Occasionally, the lingering affects of the drug they had given him kicked in and he experienced mild hallucinations, but these passed. At last the pickup bumped up some rough road, came to a halt and the tailgate opened and the cover came off. Archie, battered and sore, slid out of the truck box and limped across the graveled logging landing to where his uncle had engaged a young woman in conversation. Archie recognized her, a member of Bobby Carpenter's delegation when he demanded Stella Picard's remains.

"We're going to need help on this, nephew," Tony said, as Archie came up them. "When I searched your eyes, I could see you still had drugs in your system. We have to perform some cleansing ceremonies, and then we can do the bigger stuff."

Archie snorted.

"I'm not getting involved with shamans and magic spells, if that's what you're thinking," he said.

"Roger that," Tony said. "Now, there's somebody I want you to meet."

Archie sighed. Hunger and the pain made him irritable.

"First, I have to make a call," he said.

He pulled out his phone and began keying in the station number when Tony knocked it to the ground and drove his boot heal into the device, shattering it into pieces.

"What the hell?" Archie said. Now he really was irritated.

"You want to get arrested? You make that call and they're here within the hour. Maybe they even shoot you on the spot."

"They're not after me. Why should they be?"

"Because they think you murdered somebody, idiot."

Archie hesitated.

"Did you hear me?" Tony said. "You killed a woman at the university, is what they're saying. Good God, man, you were even on the news first thing this morning."

"Why would you come get me if I did such a thing?"

"Because you didn't kill nobody. I know you, Archie, known you since you were born. You done a lot of stupid things in your life, but you didn't like to hurt nothing. Plus, I know something other than the cops is after you. If we work together we might be able to help you save your bacon."

Archie figured Tony meant shaman magic, but the first item of business for Archie was to find out whom they accused him of murdering. Tony seemed to read his mind.

"Some woman named Andrea Dhillon," Tony said. "The university president apparently."

Archie leaned back against the pickup. His head seemed unbearably heavy and he put a hand to his forehead to try to stop the pounding in his temples. It occurred to him that if he hadn't accidentally shot Dhillon, which was possible, then they killed her because she had outlived her usefulness, which was a significant development he needed to follow up on.

"I've got to go back and sort this out, Tony."

"You ready to go to jail? You haven't got a chance right now. They have witnesses who say they saw you do it. They say you're armed and dangerous, which is why all the fuss this morning."

"Who's in charge of the investigation, do you know?"

"Yeah, the lead guy's name is Demio, Detective Martin Demio. He broadcast a message saying that if you were watching, you should turn yourself in."

"I'll bet he did."

So Martin Demio had grabbed the case. It figured. Ray Jameson would have his hands full doing Cal Fricke's job and reluctant to take Patsy or Thomas Lee from their other work. Demio was the logical choice and probably volunteered for the job. Archie knew he couldn't stay in hiding, not for long, anyway. Demio would be relentless. On the other hand, turning himself in limited his ability to complete his investigation and prove his innocence at the same time.

"I've got two questions for you, Tony. First, how did you figure a garbage truck, or whatever the thing was, would drive through Avril's lot exactly when we needed to make our getaway?"

"Easy. Walter George brought the garbage truck. He arranged the diversion. What's your second question?"

"Walter, huh, I owe him—and you, but where are we at the moment?"

"In one way we're in the middle of nowhere, but in another we're at the center. Close to something like one, anyway."

"Right, some kind of power place. Okay, but where are we in real time and space?"

Tony grinned, slapped Archie on the shoulder.

"It's not that weird. We're not too far from where you grew up, but you probably didn't come up here because it was off-limits to juvenile delinquents like yourself, except when the juvie came here for fixing. We're close to Coffee Creek, just near Franklin Mountain."

The young woman now stood within five feet from Archie, but he hadn't noticed her move closer. She peered at him in the same birdlike way he remembered from the interview in his office, a lifetime ago now it seemed, with eyes so black they seemed to draw in the light, then and now.

"Hi, there," she said. "Long time no see."

"Hi—aren't you a friend of the late Bobby Carpenter?"

"Well, I came with Bobby Carpenter to the station, if that's what you're remembering. I was with my aunt when he came to enlist her, and I just tagged along. Besides, I've been after the Cannibals for years, and when Morris Denton showed up at Carpenter's, I came. Right now you need to take care of business."

"Lend me your phone so I can get on with it."

"My name is Sophie Anderson and, no, I won't lend you my phone."

Archie assumed Tony had his best interests at heart, but there were limits.

"We need to know what they did to you last night," Tony said. "And determine what drugs screwed you around."

"You're going to figure that out? Give me a break, Tony!"

"Relax," Tony said. "Sophie can do it."

"And how the hell could she do that up here?"

"The usual ways," Sophie said. "Hopefully, you got enough piss in you to do a urine test."

"I've been on the road since Avril's. Pissing in a jar shouldn't be a problem. What then—magic?"

"Kind of," Tony said. "You'll see. It won't happen here anyway."

Archie looked across the forested hills towards the sea. Whatever else, he realized he felt part of this landscape, and the knowledge gave him a profound sense of security.

"Okay. How long is all this going to take?"

Sophie handed Archie a clean lab specimen bottle.

"Not long for the first part. You'd better fill this."

Tony grinned.

"She's a medical doctor, by the way. So you don't fret about things not being done right, or done all spooky."

Archie took the bottle from her outstretched hand and stalked off with the container to the away side of Tony's pickup.

CHAPTER 38

"Just because real people are in on the attacks on you, don't mean things from the other world ain't involved, Archie," Tony said. "Besides which, you need to slay some of your inner demons if you want to stay strong. It's part of the process too."

Tony was squatting beside the cold-water pool where Archie sat, recovering from the nightlong ordeal he'd just undergone in the sweat lodge, exhausted now but better. During the night, he had been able to more or less reconstruct the evening when they said he killed Dhillon.

"Fine but I don't believe there are spirits out there out to screw people up."

"I know you don't. Want to know what we think anyway?"

"Tell me again when I'm dry."

He shivered, one effect of the icy water. He hauled himself out and stood while Tony slapped his shoulders with cedar branches. After he dressed, Tony led him to a mossy rock where he'd spread out some food. He reached for some of the salmon morsels lying on what appeared to be an oilskin and ate them, but when he stretched his hand to grab a bannock, his uncle stopped him.

"Let the salmon digest first," he said. "In a few minutes you can have the carbs. I don't know why breaking it down helps after you get drugged, but it seems to work with some folks."

Archie nodded, happy to get a meal but still felt ravenous. By his reckoning, he hadn't eaten much for almost forty-eight hours. The fish settled his stomach and seemed to strengthen him.

"What's the deal with Sophie?"

"Northern girl," Tony said. "Very smart. She helps out the cops up there."

"Analyzing piss?"

Tony laughed.

"And a lot more, but let's talk about other things. You asked about the dream world last night. You wouldn't get most of what I might tell you, so I won't bother."

"Big secret, I guess."

Tony shook his head.

"Not so much that. I could tell you all kinds of things, but it'd be like me telling you about something, sex, for example, if you'd never experienced that delightful pastime—not the case with you, I know. I could give you lots of information, but you'd understand a million times better than any lesson on the subject the first time you did it. I'm not saying you have never experienced the other side because you have, more than a majority of folks. You're kind of open to it in a way most aren't. You would have made a good shaman, a very powerful one, if you'd taken that path, but you didn't and that's just the way of it. For now, it's enough to know you broke down a door between our world and the other one, and you let somebody out who don't wish you no good, and who has found human allies who want to hurt you."

"When I visited the burial cave I stayed respectful. Anyway, I think the dead don't care much about the living one way or the other."

"I guess it depends on the dead person, but it ain't no ghost I'm talking about. Do you recall when you told me about your dream last night?"

"I remember."

Tony looked away into the trees as if thinking about what to say or how to say it. Archie recognized that out-in-the-distance stare, the set of Tony's broad face, had seen it many times on the fishboat when Tony strategized about the location of a school of fish and how best to set the net. After a minute or so, he shook his head and indicated the bannock.

"Forget it. Eat up, boy. You'll need your strength."

But Archie had lost his appetite and didn't eat, remembering too well his mother's role in his dream, and his father's too. During the night, Tony told him that this Coyote person would use anything he could to get to a person to go along with what he wanted. When Archie had problems with the concept, Tony said that Coyote was just a different name for the Trickster, and that on the other side, you took all bets off the table. Whoever carried a grudge against him in this world had no problem destroying him in the realm of dreams. In fact, a good sorcerer could more easily kill a victim in a dream.

The day promised to be warm, the beautiful May weather everyone loved, but Archie wouldn't spend much time enjoying it. He planned to turn himself in in order to sort things out, although first he had to figure out a way to stay out of jail. Cal Fricke might help if Archie created an opportunity to talk to him before Demio arrested him.

CHAPTER 39

Cal Fricke lived on a side street in Fairpark in an old Edwardian style house with a large porch and a partially concreted yard where Fricke stored a motor home, a boat, and his motorcycle. Archie expected he had but one chance and that he would likely get himself arrested if Fricke didn't buy into the plan. Sophie Anderson volunteered to drive Archie to Fricke's place, as Archie was now without a vehicle, and now, she waited with him in the darkened street, backed into the high hedges bordering the house next door.

Archie shifted position, about to make his move, when Sophie grabbed his arm and pulled him back. She put a finger to her lips as two men came out onto Fricke's porch and stood under its light, talking. Ice clinked in glasses as the conversation ebbed and flowed, a discussion about an ongoing investigation between Cal Fricke and Martin Demio. Although their voices rose and fell,

Archie got the gist of the conversation, which mostly concerned Jameson's leadership and how Jameson botched Demio's plans to arrest Archie. He wanted, it seemed, to replace Jameson, and soon. Apparently Demio didn't like his boss's response, which Archie didn't catch, because the detective tossed the remains of his drink in the shrubbery, said a loud good night, and clumped down the porch steps.

Archie eased them back behind the hedge alarmed, because Demio was heading in their direction. Sophie, seeing the problem, moved quickly. She put her arms around Archie, turned his back to the street, arched up and put her lips to his. He understood. He wrapped himself around her and they became, to other eyes, two lovers making out. Her lips were soft and hot and he almost began to kiss her for real. A door of a car opened and closed while they embraced, and it started up, revved and pulled away. Sophie, detaching herself from Archie, let her hands rest on his forearms a moment before she stepped back.

"I wasn't expecting this," Archie said.

At that moment, Fricke came out of his house, got into his car and drove away.

"He's gone, but now what are you going to do?"

"Something drastic, I guess. I need to get out to the university to check something out."

"Isn't that a kind of bad move, going back there? They might expect you."

"They're all bad moves right now, but I've got to do something, and fast. I'm not going anywhere near the Anthropology building or the museum, so it should be all right. The guy I want to talk to works at the other end of the campus. It's still risky."

"Sounds like, but I hope your enemy isn't laughing at your efforts, Archie."

"Perhaps he is, but not in the real world, where my career is in the toilet and I'm about to be arrested for murder."

"If you say so," Sophie said.

"Okay. Let's go."

The Department of Soils and Geology was located in the southwest corner of the campus. The buildings were leftovers from the war years long ago, evidence geology had lost out to high tech and hard science in the constant jockeying for resources. The overlord of the department was Frank Sanchez, a taciturn and abrasive expert on metamorphic rocks. Archie once called him on a minor police matter, a case involving a soil sample from a crime scene. This time, however, Archie was not interested in soils—or rocks; he wanted information about the university's huge land endowments, on which topic Sanchez was an expert.

Sophie parked near the largest of the Soils and Geology buildings. Archie led the way to a locked back door and rang the bell. When Frank Sanchez opened the door, he did not seem surprised to see Archie.

"You got here," he said. "I've been waiting. It's been weeks since I called you guys."

Once Archie got the professor talking, he became almost chatty. He had already contacted somebody in the department, he said, but got the brushoff. He produced a package of maps and other data and gave these to Archie.

"This takes in the Velasquez Island portion of the endowed properties. It's totally illegal, and I don't understand how they expect to get away with what they plan. I made the point to President Dhillon and she more or less blew me off, said nothing's happening, but anybody who believes that is an idiot. I've seen the surveyors' stakes myself. I think it's largely overseas money behind the project."

"We're investigating," Archie said. "We may still be able to do something if we find proof."

"I expect you will, with diligence and speed, son."

Archie used Sanchez's phone to call Lee who promised to give Patsy an update. He needed to go to the properties on Velasquez to see for himself as soon as possible. If he could confirm his suspicions on the ground, he figured he could prove motive and even get himself out of the jam he was in.

"Now where to?" Sophie said when they got back to her vehicle.

She put her key in the ignition and, aware that his eyes were on her, turned her head and smiled. He smiled back.

She repeated her question.

"For now, I'm not sure. Going anywhere near my place or the station would be stupid, but I need time to come up with a plan."

"I know somewhere where you'll be safe."

She waited until he nodded agreement and started the car, backed out, shifted gears and drove them out into the night.

"You have to be very careful now, Archie. The risks for you are high whichever way you go. Do you trust me?"

"Possibly," he said. "Are you one of the risks?"

"Don't be silly. As long as you're sure it *is* me you're dealing with, you're okay."

She laughed. Archie said, "Ha, ha." But she might be serious about shape shifting and the like. He knew Tony believed it happened, but Tony believed all sorts of crazy things.

She left the campus road and drove down Oceanic towards the city before backtracking through residential districts to get to an area of rundown houses along the river in a section of town Archie hardly recognized. Halfway down a deserted, poorly lit street, she pulled into a drive-way, killed the motor, got out of the car and beck-oned him to follow her inside the fifties-style ranch house to which the drive belonged. He re-laxed a little. At four in the morning, in this neighborhood, he ought to have very little to wor-ry about, and so far as he knew, no cop had any idea where he was. Once through the door, she turned on a table lamp, turned to him, put her hands in his and peered into his eyes.

"You don't recall me at all, do you, Archie?"

He studied her, searching his memory.

"I don't think so, no."

"There's no reason you should, but I sure re-member you. When I was fourteen, I visited my aunt at Kokishilah one summer, and you were at a party. You were so handsome you almost took my breath away. I never forgot you."

He half-remembered a social event long ago and a gaggle of young girls annoying him and some of his friends. He would have been about eighteen at the time.

"Maybe I do recognize you," he said.

"I've been waiting a long time."

"I can't do this."

His mind went to Patsy and the joy and struggle of being with *her*, but he remembered too the night scene with Tracy Gillot on her porch with a bottle of wine and her inviting Gillot in, and he pushed thoughts of her aside as Sophie pressed in close to him, her breathing quickening, kissing him on the lips and the corners of his mouth.

"Come on," she whispered. "Hurry."

She put her arms around his neck and he lifted her up. She said something he heard as *bedroom* and he carried her, her skin surprisingly cool against his cheek, in the direction she indicated.

CHAPTER 40

The sound of the wind rattling a window woke Archie from a troubled sleep in which he dreamed about betrayal and death. He glanced at the unset clock on the bedside table, fought the urge to try to doze some more, but when consciousness crept back, he checked for Sophie, even called out for her, and was not surprised to find himself alone. At first irritated, he now felt relief. She was a beautiful and exciting woman, but he did not want or need any more romantic entanglements.

He swung his legs over the edge of the bed, hauled himself to his feet and got dressed. When he went through to the kitchen to get a drink of water, he realized things were not, as she warned him, what they seemed, with appliances disconnected and water turned off. Had she said she lived in this abandoned house when she brought him to it? He didn't think so.

After he checked outside for vehicles, he made a quick tour of the place, trying to understand his situation better. She had furnished the living room and bedroom normally, but like a stage set, because otherwise the house was empty. He could tell no one occupied the surrounding structures either, most having been spray-painted with big fluorescent orange letters ready for demolition.

The sound of jets overhead gave him the clue to his location he needed. He'd ended up near the airport in a neighborhood soon to be cleared for runway expansion, its houses all to be razed. As he wandered through the building, some other sense kicked in alerting him to impending danger. He realized he must leave immediately, but without a vehicle and miles from any bus route, getting anywhere would be difficult.

As he pulled on his boots and prepared to walk out of the subdivision, he heard the sounds of vehicles in the street outside. He rose, ran to a window and peered out through a broken blind. Beyond the unmowed lawn, a half-dozen police patrol cars and a SWAT van had moved into position, which meant cops would be hammering on the door within moments. Archie knew the drill. They would crash through both doors simultaneously, brandishing their weapons, shouting. Not many people escaped such an assault. He needed a diversion, something big so he could escape. He racked his brain and decided on fire—ideal, if he could start one in time.

The basement was the obvious place to find flammables. He bounded down creaky wooden stairs into a low-ceiling cellar, picked up an old laundry hamper and filled it with crumpled newspapers, rags and scrap wood. He added some half-empty aerosol cans from under a workbench to the mix and drenched the lot with a half-quart of motor oil he found on the floor. The former tenants had been obliging. They'd even left matches. When he finished his preparation, he ran the hamper up, dumped the contents onto the living room couch, and when heavy cop feet sounded on the front and back steps to the house, he lit the pile.

The fire caught instantly and soon flames roared up to the ceiling. He had only a few seconds and, as the room filled with smoke, he dashed to the cellar door, closed and secured it before he half-jumped, half-fell down the stairs into the basement.

Above him, all doors crashed open and the floor shook under the thunder of boots as officers charged into the house. He jumped up on the workbench, unlatched the window and exited the house, rolling under a clump of dense and ratty cedar trees along one side of the building. Bent over, he sprinted to a neighboring house, knowing attention would be focussed on the blaze. Crouching in the evergreens amongst the tree litter, he waited.

His chance to escape came when the first fire truck appeared. With the house now fully engulfed and nobody looking in his direction, Archie tore out of his temporary hiding place, dashed to the parked police cruisers and picked one. As he'd hoped, the driver had left the keys in the ignition—a cop leaving a vehicle ready to go. The roar from the flames grew louder and more fire engines arrived with sirens blaring. Archie backed the patrol car out onto the road, flicked on the emergency lights, and sped away, just like any other police officer on a call might do.

Once clear, he accelerated, flashers still on. Whoever commanded the early assault would certainly order a roadblock when they missed the cruiser. If he knew the area better, he could have picked the spot they would set one up and not got caught. Instead he got lost and drove into the trap anyway. Ray Jameson, running the roadblock, grinned when Archie pulled up in the highjacked patrol car. Jameson strolled to the driver's side door and waited while Archie lowered the window.

"I always told Cal I never underestimate Archie Stevens," he said. "You'd better get out, Archie, and give me your weapon."

"No weapon, Ray."

"You're lucky it's me, Stevens. I think Martin planned for you to be shot. He's got a few of his buddies on in SWAT convinced you're a dangerous fugitive. His operation this morning, by the way."

Archie lifted his arms.

"And I think he would be happy to shoot me, so I guess I am lucky."

He levered himself out of the vehicle, put his hands behind him and waited as Jameson reached under his jacket for the cuffs.

CHAPTER 41

Archie hadn't been on the wrong side of the desk in an interview room since his teens, and he still didn't like the feeling. At least they'd fed him—after he insisted. Martin Demio prepared to start the procedure and was obviously enjoying the process. Ray Jameson attended as an observer. Demio started the recording.

"Archie," he said. "Tell us about your relationship to Andrea Dhillon?"

"I didn't have a relationship with her."

"That's not what her assistant says. She says you two met on more than one occasion, and that you stalked Andrea Dhillon."

"Her assistant? Come on—this is bullshit."

"You apparently made threats against her according to a sworn statement signed by Kari Fletcher, executive assistant to President Dhillon."

They had engineered a nice little setup, Archie thought. He wondered if Fletcher had been bought or threatened?

"Do you want to say anything?"

Archie shrugged.

"Not much point. Is this your whole case against me?"

"Martin is still digging," Jameson said. "Stay tuned."

Archie reclined, stuck his legs out and linked his fingers behind his head. He doubted they had enough evidence to hold him long, not really. The arson charge might be a throwaway since the houses were scheduled for destruction within weeks anyway, but Demio obviously figured they could pin a murder on him and would be hoping Archie's fatigue would bring on a confession, it being one of the first principles of interrogation to capitalize on such situations where the suspect grew tired, fed up, or otherwise weakened. The interrogator pressed on.

"Time to confess, Archie, and do the right thing. I think you're possibly innocent of anything but manslaughter, so if you give me a little to go on, I would be in a position to help."

"Martin, you've got to do better. Either charge me or release me. So, do you have a charge?"

Demio nodded, smiled.

"We've got two possibles — arson and resisting lawful arrest. And murder is obviously under consideration also, and who knows what else. You stole a cop car too, remember."

Archie reclined and linked his fingers behind his head.

"I borrowed one of our cruisers to go get coffee," he said. "I don't suppose you ever asked yourself why I would kill Dhillon. What's my motive? You must have constructed some little scenario to explain this fiasco."

"Gee whiz. How about this? You tried it on with the president. Fletcher seemed to think you were fixated on her boss. I don't know why you killed her, but I know you did."

"This is laughable. How did I kill her?"

Jameson, displaying mild disinterest, scratched his left shoulder.

"You strangled her, Archie, is the deal."

"This is my case, Ray."

"I'm still in charge, Martin," Jameson said.

Demio took a pull on his coffee. Archie eased his chair down so it stood on all four legs.

"I'd like to talk to Cal, Ray. This is a waste of my time."

"I wish I could oblige, Archie, but he's had a relapse and is now in intensive care."

"What? Is he going to be all right?"

"Hard to know."

Archie slumped in his seat, put a hand up to his forehead.

"So, we're going to hold on to you," Demio said. "For two days at least."

So that was the time parameter, Archie thought. Whatever criminal operation they planned would complete in forty-eight hours.

"I've got to discuss this with my lawyer. Until then, I'm not saying another word."

"She's around. Another old girlfriend perhaps?"

"This is tiresome, Martin. You're boring the hell out of me."

Demio smirked. He rattled his chair away from the table, got up and paced for several minutes more before he grunted something about stupid people and left the room.

"He's sure got a thing about you, Stevens," Jameson said. "You must have really pissed him off somehow."

Archie stood up and stretched.

"I assume we're finished here?"

Jameson scratched the side of his long nose and nodded.

"Your lawyer is working on bail for you, if that's any consolation," he said. "I don't know the why or the wherefore, and but right now, you stay in jail."

Archie settled into his chair. Everything had shifted. He got himself set up, and now he was paying for his stupidity.

"I figured as much. I need some sleep, Ray. Make them pick a quiet cell for me, will you?"

"I'll see what I can do. I think this is all bull-crap, Archie, so you'd better start thinking through everything that happened and who might be out to torpedo you. You've been screwed, but who did the deed and why? That's the question."

"I think I'm getting closer to the answer. This little charade takes me out of the play, but the charges won't stick, so that means it's all about timing. I figure the bad guys will be free and clear within forty-eight hours. That's why I've got to get out of here soon."

"I hope you do," Jameson said. "It's up to the judge, but I can't see bail being denied. I put in a good word for you. So, sit tight."

He lifted his hand in a half wave and departed just as a constable arrived to escort Archie to his cell.

CHAPTER 42

As it turned out, Ray Jameson, as Acting Chief of Police, decided that no charges would be laid, there being insufficient evidence to make a case against Archie. Archie was grateful to Jameson since somehow, Demio now had the mayor's ear. Archie thought gambling debts might play a role in this; he had seen the mayor at the Eagle Wing several times and, once, deep in conversation with Susanna Yip.

If Demio were successful, Archie's investigation would get held up just long enough—two days and Coyote and his associates would disappear. Since killing him was the easiest solution to their problem, Archie figured his best move was to throw any watchers off his track. As he left the jail, he called Thomas Lee to set things up and learned that the mayor was pressuring the new chief to shelve Archie's cases and assign his team to other duties. After he finished up with Lee,

Archie contacted John Robbie for some extralegal help. Lee arrived at the pickup an hour later in a nondescript gray Japanese sedan, a car exactly like a million others. Patsy Kydd was driving. Archie wasn't expecting her, and she grinned when he saw Archie's look of surprise.

"I was bored," she said.

Archie nodded and got in the back.

"Thank you," he said.

"We made sure we didn't pick up a tail," Patsy said. "Now we plan to do a starburst maneuver. Know what that is?"

"Not a bad idea," he said. A starburst maneuver was something spies used to lose a tail; it involved using multiple more or less identical vehicles to confuse pursuers.

"We'd better get going," Lee said. "If things are as tight timewise as you think they are."

"They are," Archie said.

When they were underway, Lee reached over the seat and dropped something wrapped in a towel in Archie's lap. He unwrapped the Glock 9mm, weighed the gun in his hand and then returned it to Lee.

"I appreciate this, Thomas but the pistol might make matters worse if Demio happens to pull me over."

Lee shrugged, nodded.

"Just thought I'd give you the option, amigo."

"Now where do you want to go?" Patsy asked. "You didn't give Thomas your ultimate destination."

"I need to take a quick boat trip to confirm a theory. John Robbie's meeting me on the island."

"I got the boat arranged like you wanted," Lee said. "It's at the Rochville Marina, which has the added advantage of being in another jurisdiction."

"You'd still better keep your head down," Patsy said. "Demio's got some of his buddies on the force keeping an eye out for you. There's a cap under the blanket on the seat. We picked up a blond wig."

"It's not Demio I'm worried overly about," Archie said. "The wig is a nice touch. They won't be thinking blond guy."

Patsy laughed when she saw him in disguise.

"Maybe we should all be blondes," Patsy said. She pulled on another pale wig. She looked good too, he told her. Then, to his surprise, Lee stuck a similar one on his own head. Archie noted that they both wore black jackets.

"Now we disappear," she said.

She motioned Archie down. He nodded, stretched out on the seat, and she drove them out onto the street. After a few minutes, the car slowed and stopped.

"Grab a quick peek if you can. We're okay here, but now we go out into traffic."

Archie glanced to the right and left. On either side of their vehicle, gray Japanese sedans paralleled them. The blond, black-jacketed occupants in the nearest vehicle waved. Archie chuckled.

"Pete Wilson and Delia John," Archie said. "I wish I could have taken a picture."

Patsy kept her eyes focussed on the road ahead.

"Pete arranged it when I told him what Thomas and I planned," she said. "Delia volunteered right away. Walter George is driving the other sedan, by the way. You need to get him on film. He's wearing a woman's wig and his passenger is a blow-up doll."

Archie chuckled at the thought.

"When we get farther along Ocean Park Avenue," Lee said, "we'll split up and the cars will go in three different directions."

"So there's no way for a tail to know which car you're in," Patsy said. "At least I hope so."

The image of Walter George in a blond wig flashed through Archie's mind again and made him laugh, loud enough for Patsy to tell him to shut up. At the same time, he felt deeply moved. He had no right to expect any of them to help, and he was anxious to send them on their way as soon as he could so they wouldn't run any more risks on his behalf.

After a time, when Patsy reported she was confident they hadn't picked up a tail, Archie sat up and looked out the rear window. She was right; no one was following. Before long, they reached the marina and she parked behind a row of Norfolk Pines while Lee described the boat, the berth where it he had moored it and the location of the key.

"You sure you don't want us to tag along?"

"Nope, this shouldn't take long. I'll need your help again later, but I'll call you when it's time."

Lee said Jameson expected him at the station, wished him luck and walked towards the sedan. Patsy stayed where she was.

"I'm coming with you," she said.

When he refused, she pressed the point until he gave in. They walked to the slip and the small runabout waiting there, boarded quickly so as not to attract attention, cast off, started the motor and were soon on their way to the rendezvous with John Robbie at a deserted farmstead at the east end of Velasquez Island.

When they reached the island, Robbie came out of the trees to meet them. He nodded a greeting, shot Patsy a sideways glance, flicked his cigarette butt away and helped them tie up.

"You were right, Archie," he said. "I did like you asked. There's some surveyors working the island, and I found stakes at the north end like you thought, but I didn't see any ground-breaking yet."

"I guess that will wait until the deal is finalized," Patsy said.

"It's never going to be finalized," Archie said. "They're going through the motions so their overseas investors think their money is well invested. This is all part of a show. Did you spot any boats in the area that might be doing something other than fishing or sightseeing?"

"As a matter of fact," Robbie said. "There's a big modified Bering Sea crab boat kind of a deal in November Harbour right now. If you like, I'll take you there."

They reboarded and motored along the rocky, surf-lined coastline to where the *Tiger* stood at anchor. She seemed a well-outfitted vessel, a cross between a luxury yacht and a state of the art workboat. Archie hailed her, and when he got no answer turned over the tiller to Robbie and slipped aboard.

He got the evidence he needed in the spacious main cabin where heavily marked-up maps, copies of those he'd got from Sanchez, lay spread out on the chart table along with architects' renderings of shoreside destination hotels and prestigious condos — more charade. Likely moneyed investors came aboard recently and were shown the extent of the property and had the concept outlined.

He worked quickly now, taking pictures and saving coordinates and other data to his phone before he searched the cabin further. In one overhead locker, he found several small, clear bags containing dried plant matter. He opened one and took first a sniff and touched some to his tongue. He recognized its taste and stink immediately, so reminiscent of the concoction they had forced him to drink. He spat, wrapped the sample in a handkerchief and tucked it into his pocket.

In less than fifteen minutes, he was in the boat again with Patsy and Robbie. They'd been lucky, motoring into the bay, so visible, a stupid move. It seemed like they'd gotten away with it, but Archie felt ill at ease nevertheless. He asked Robbie to take him to where the staking went on, and when they got close, they ran the boat ashore and stepped out.

"I'll take it from here," Archie said.

"I can stay, pal. You might need backup."

"My thoughts exactly," Patsy said.

"There's no need to take the risk. I'm going to make this quick, just get the information I need and scram. Do you need the boat, or can you leave it for me?"

"We can go overland to my place and meet you there no problem."

"I'm staying with you, Archie," Patsy said.

He shook his head and handed her his phone.

"Go," he said. "It's an order. Take my cell with you and upload the photos. I'd rather the evidence went back to the station. I'm not sure we weren't seen."

She nodded, took the phone.

"What will you use?"

He pulled a beat-up old phone from his back pocket and held it up.

"My old reliable. It will do the job if I need it. Now beat it."

She lingered.

"Damn it, Patsy. Will you go?"

She sissed through her teeth, the very sound of exasperation, shook her head to further make her point.

"All right, but only because you're still the team leader as far as I'm concerned."

"Thank you for that, Pat."

Robbie reached into his jacket and produced a folding knife, which he handed to Archie who turned it over in his hand and slid it into his own pocket.

"It's not a gun, Arch, but it's better than nothing."

"It might come in handy. My granny always told me not to go into the bush without a knife and some matches."

Robbie nodded.

"She was right — take these."

He tossed Archie a pack of matches, turned on his heel and legged it into the forest. Patsy lingered. For a moment her eyes lingered on him before she turned away and followed after Robbie.

CHAPTER 43

It didn't take Archie long to find a well-used path, which he followed inland to the first plot on the maps he'd seen. When he located the surveyors' stakes, he snapped pictures of them with his old phone. The way he figured it, the prospectus would indicate that half of the island was being purchased for development, something Andrea Dhillon would confirm. The deal would complete when the cash was in some numbered bank account somewhere. If concerns were raised over Tribal land claims, an unscrupulous professional archaeologist could put investors' minds at ease. Perhaps Bobby Carpenter was called in to help too. It was a neat magic trick—a kind of shell game in which the pea never existed. Many millions of dollars would disappear and the players who put up the money would get nothing. By the time the penny dropped, the con artists would have vanished.

Half an hour later, Archie was at his boat, anxious to return to the station and meet with Jameson, at which time he would reconvene his team, try to get a copy of the prospectus if possible and start making arrests. Time was of the essence. He pushed off, hit the starter button and got nothing. He cursed. The boat drifted to shore and he got out, checked the fuel, pumped the bulb and tried again—still nothing. The motor had worked well on his way to the island but not now, and he couldn't figure out why.

As he pondered the problem, a large inflatable boat swung round the headland and turned towards him. Archie recognized the passengers. Dave Ghent, Brenda Volio, and Jeff Riggs were coming his way at speed. There seemed to be no point in running, they were so close, so Archie sat on the gunwales and waited for them. The inflatable beached and crunched up the shingle. Ghent jumped out.

"Archie Stevens," he said. "I never know where I'm going to find you."

"I didn't know you were searching."

Ghent shrugged.

"Yeah, we've been looking. You've become kind of a problem, buddy."

The two killers pulled the craft up above the tideline and walked towards him. Riggs rolled a shoulder, winced and grinned.

"You put a bullet into me, Stevens, back there in the museum."

The news cheered Archie up.

"Would it help if I say I'm sorry?"

"Screw off."

Archie shrugged and turned his attention back to Ghent.

"I'm surprised to see you here, Dave. What's up?"

"We're just touring," Ghent said. "I'm thinking of applying to build a cabin, take advantage of the scenery. Get in before anybody else does. What do you think of the idea?"

Out of the corner of his eyes, Archie saw Volio and Riggs reposition themselves. Riggs put himself between Archie and the sea and Volio, on Archie's left, cut him off from the forest.

"How about you, Stevens. What are you doing here?"

"Same as you, Dave, standing on a beach on a pleasant day lying my ass off."

Ghent chuckled.

"Your boat not start?" he said. "Usually you got a spark problem when that happens."

"It could be a plug," Archie said.

"I've got one here," Riggs said. "It'll be the one you need."

He held up a spark plug for Archie to see and then tossed it down the beach.

"Damn, I dropped it, so now you're screwed."

Archie sighed.

"I guess I am."

"You sure are," Ghent said. "So let's cut the guff and get moving."

"Where are we going?"

"Shangri-La."

"I like it here and don't feel like going any-where."

Ghent opened his cruiser jacket so Archie could see the butt of the pistol peeking out from the shoulder holster.

"You convinced me."

"Are you carrying a gun?"

Archie shook his head.

"I didn't think it was smart to carry one under the circumstances."

"Always a good policy. Now let's get a move on."

Archie shrugged and got into the boat. He took a seat opposite Ghent and braced himself as Riggs throttled the Zodiac around and accelerated in the direction of November Harbor. Fifteen minutes later the *Tiger* came into view.

They ran up to the stern, boarded the craft and went below into the main cabin where an older man leant over a chart table examining maps and diagrams. As they entered, he straightened and turned towards them. Archie nodded a greeting.

"Robertson Foley," he said.

Foley leaned back against the map table, ran his fingers through his goatee and shrugged.

"Good for you. You figured it out."

"Should I call you Foley or King?"

"For this kind of deal, especially since the university lands are involved, I'm using Rafe King rather than Robertson Foley. You've heard the name before, I gather?"

"Yep."

Rafe King was the name of the mystery man behind some major land development projects. Working through subordinates, he made millions by bullying or buying politicians, land inspectors and town planners and ramrodding mega-projects into communities whether they wanted them or not. Most of what he did skirted the poorly charted area between the legal and the illegal. He also sold Ron Helerstone his mansion. Foley came out from behind the chart table.

"What happened to the original Rafe King?"

"He had an accident early in the process, and I took over," Foley said. "As ruthless as he was, Rafe was basically honest, which wasn't going to cut it here. By the way, I thought they arrested you for the murder of poor President Dhillon. You surprise me."

"No kidding?"

"Yeah. Now, tell me everything you know about me."

"I know enough, Foley," Archie said. "But why do you ask?"

"I seldom ask—usually, I tell. Plus I know most of the ins and outs of your life anyway. Since you became a nuisance, I've researched you."

"Big deal. There's not much to know."

"*Au contraire*. You're a complicated man, my friend. By the way, what did you expect to find on my boat?"

"A cup of coffee. I needed a pick-me-up."

Foley moved towards him and backhanded him across the side of the head. Archie righted himself and wiped his bleeding lip.

"Damn you," Archie said.

He saw Ghent pull his gun out and restrained his wish to retaliate.

"I don't like smart-asses, so be warned," Foley said.

"Don't worry. I won't forget anything about you."

Foley turned to Ghent, who seemed impatient and anxious to get on with whatever it as they planned.

"Call Demio and tell him to come here."

"Now?"

"Of course, now. In the meantime, Detective Sergeant, Brenda will get you a beverage and you can sit tight."

So here it was at last—proof of Demio's complicity. While Ghent made the call, Foley directed Archie to a seat and told him to wait. Volio brought him coffee, and when Archie hesitated to drink it, Foley laughed.

"It's not poisoned," he said. "We don't need it anymore. You don't have to be drugged now."

"Why before?"

"We hoped you'd kill Dhillon that night in Helerstone's lab," Ghent said. "It was a nice setup, drugs, a stalker, meaning you, and both you and her dead. Unfortunately, you got away, so I called on Brenda to get rid of Andrea. Even so, if Martin had caught you and shot you when he had the opportunity, everything would be better."

"And Kari Fletcher supports the stalker thing?"

"Money talks," Ghent said. "She didn't care for her boss anyway."

"Enough of this," Foley said. "Enjoy your coffee, Detective. It might be your last."

Archie settled back, took the drink and cradled it, but he kept his eyes on Foley and Ghent. Martin Demio arrived by speedboat a short time later and came aboard immediately and entered the cabin. He glanced at Archie and shrugged.

"I'd be sorry, Archie, if it'd help," he said.

"It's not a surprise, Martin."

"I got in over my head. Now I got no choice."

"We always have a choice, Martin."

"I think it's too late to make new choices."

He turned to face Foley.

"What do you want me to do exactly?"

"Your colleague has to go," Foley said. "But it has to be done right, which will be your job, Martin. We still need the better part of twenty-four hours for everything to go through and the cash transfers to happen."

"You expect me to murder him?"

"He's figured out too much about this project in spite of my efforts to misdirect him, and I don't see any other solution, so carry out your assignment."

"I can arrest him. We're searching for him anyway, and he'll likely go to jail. I can hold him on charges until the business completes and we're all out of here."

"Not going to work," Foley said. "Try not to avoid doing what the operation requires of you. We don't want get to the point where we don't need Martin Demio."

"He should get shot trying to escape.," Ghent suggested. "He's a fugitive, after all. It's quite convenient."

Foley, obviously impatient with the direction the conversation had taken, shifted position. Ghent dropped his head and avoided Foley's stare. Foley pointed at Demio.

"Stop screwing around, Martin," he said. "Figure out the details or you're toast."

Demio hesitated but then nodded.

"All right. We hang onto him until I can set it up and poof, he's gone."

"Just make sure he's not around tomorrow morning. I've got some work to do. I'll join you at the camp later."

Soon, Ghent, Demio and Archie were in the inflatable again, leaving the *Tiger* in their wake. Archie was quiet, trying to come up with a plan. The others seemed preoccupied, concerned with the business at hand, namely his murder.

"This has to look right, Ghent," Demio shouted over the roar of the motor. "I can't just shoot him. He has to be put in a spot where shooting him makes sense to a police review board."

"I get it," Ghent said. "We'll figure it out. We'll have to hold him until you work out what will seem right cop-wise."

Ghent made some phone calls. Archie tried and failed to pick up the gist of the conversation above the boat noise. They finally arrived at a familiar place, the dock servicing Bobby Carpenter's property on Velasquez Island, and hustled Archie up to the compound.

CHAPTER 44

In the interests, Archie supposed, of getting the timing of his murder right, they shut him up in a shed and left him there. When they were out of hearing, he felt for the folding knife Robbie gave him. They had not searched him beyond doing a quick check for a gun. He took the knife out, opened the blade, closed it and put it out of sight on a shelf in the shed. If they locked him up again, he'd do something with it. In the meantime, he did the only thing he could do—he slept.

At dusk, they released him, took him into the main house and into the kitchen. A stocky man with short gray hair, his back to them, was cooking. He turned as they came into the room. It was Morris Denton. He grinned at Archie and with the pasta spoon he was holding waved Volio, Riggs and Ghent away.

"You three can wait outside," he said.

Ghent grunted, grabbed a quart of rum from the counter and stalked out, followed by the two killers.

When they were gone, Denton indicated a chair while he concentrated on stirring his sauce.

"They didn't kill you right away," he said. "They should have offed you immediately. I keep telling them not to underestimate Curtis's kid, but none of these people get it. I thought of shooting you with my 30-06 after you almost caught up with me at the rifle range but that plan got nixed. Robertson had other ideas at the time."

He kept his eyes fixed on Archie.

"I gather you're going to educate him," Archie said.

Denton shrugged.

"Not needed anymore. The decision's been made. It's for the best for us, but not so great for you. Too bad. You've kind of grown on me."

He sampled the sauce and shook salt into it, sampled it again and let out an extenuated "ah."

"I'm a good cook," he said. "I think you'll enjoy your last meal. Want wine?"

He held up a bottle of Barolo wine, turned it so Archie could see the label.

"Professor Foley doesn't skimp when it comes to the better things in life. I'll bet this stuff costs about five hundred a pop. The perfect bevvy for the occasion, don't you think?"

"Sure, and what the hell," Archie said. "At least I get something out of all this bullshit."

He took the glass, sniffed the contents, tilted the glass and sipped.

"I'm not sure I'd pay five hundred bucks for it, but it will do."

Denton laughed and drained his glass, his expression now one of benign bemusement.

"It seems like you want to talk, Archie, and I say why not? Go for it."

Archie lifted his hand, an acknowledgement of Denton's gesture.

"I'm curious," Archie said. "I'm still trying to piece it all together. How the operation went from art and antiquities theft for Helerstone and old Professor Porteous to your involvement and to a big fake land deal that got the originals killed."

"No mystery. It started with Porteous who saw the potential for making money out of forgotten artifacts. He got Helerstone involved. Foley's a smart dude, and he forced his way into their operation. They were getting stuff from me, or I should say, having my people steal things for them. I already had the Cannibal Society up and running to make sure my young guys stayed loyal to me and kept their mouths shut—people are easy to scare under the right circumstances. Helerstone, in particular, wanted to believe, so I let him. One thing led to another. Foley saw the land part of it and put the whole thing together, and I guess Helerstone got greedy, or scared, or something."

"So you killed him?"

"Me? No."

He was about to say something more when the door opened and Foley entered the room.

"Enjoy your drink," Denton said. "It'll be kind of a last meal for you, I understand. You could do worse. I'm a hell of a cook, if I do say so myself."

"Where's my old friend Detective Demio?" Archie asked.

"He's where we want him to be," Foley said. "You'll see him again. You might wish you never met the guy."

"Right, my murder, I forgot."

After the exchange, Foley seemed to lose interest in Archie. He held a sotto voce discussion with Denton and then left the room.

"They tell me the plan is for your colleague to kill you tomorrow," Denton said. "Not here, of course. They've set it up. There'll be an attempted takedown in Harsley, plus a shootout, an insane charge, and you get shot. It's like a TV drama. Quite exciting. I think it's too complicated, but there you go."

"And what happens to Demio afterwards?"

"Robertson hasn't decided yet," Denton said. "The good detective seems to be getting cold feet, which makes him a liability. Anyway, let's not worry about tomorrows. Tonight we'll sit down and eat well. Life's short, Archie, particularly yours. But, look, here's Detective Demio now."

Dave Ghent entered, followed by Volio and Riggs and the Harsley detective. Denton motioned Archie to a chair while the others took seats. After a time, Foley returned to the room and took a chair across from Archie. Denton ladled out portions of food and they all began to eat. For a few minutes, no one spoke. Foley pointed at Archie with his fork.

"I'd ask you how you figured this out but it's plain good reasoning, isn't it, Archie? It's archaeological thinking. Asking what actually happened at a site and how. I like to think our university training made the difference."

"It's a well I keep returning to," Archie said. "Every time I ran a scenario, you popped up, and then Denton. I figured Morris played an important role too."

"Morris has been very helpful," Foley said. "We appreciate everything he's done for us."

Archie caught the bemused look on Denton's face, his expression saying that Foley didn't understand what was really happening.

"What I can't figure out is why you felt you needed to kill the girl?" Archie said this to Denton.

"What girl?"

"Stella Picard."

"I never heard of her."

"I thought not."

Archie glanced at Foley who sat with his head lowered as if he were deep in thought. Meanwhile, Denton swung the conversation around to world events. When they finished dinner, Volio and Riggs took Archie outside, half ran him down the steps and out to a utility shed. As Riggs closed and locked the door, Archie saw Martin Demio standing on the porch observing.

CHAPTER 45

Archie, secured in the shed, waited until all sounds of activity died down and retrieved his knife from its hiding place in the rafters. Through a crack in the door, he could see they had left a single person to guard him; Jeff Riggs sat about ten feet away, with his Steyr lying on his lap, a hand on the action. When he saw Archie peering through the space between boards, he made the throat-slashing sign, drawing his finger across his throat, and he took a long drink from the now half-empty rum bottle. Archie grinned and turned away, hoping he might get his chance to break out if the sentry fell asleep, but an hour later, the other man was still awake and playing games on his phone. Shortly after, a slender shadow passed behind Riggs and the lights of the house. Archie heard him grunt and when he checked, he lay stretched out on the ground. Sophie Anderson whispered Archie's name and her face appeared at the crack. She held up a metal bar for him to see.

"I caught him right under the ear with this. He'll come around soon, so we'd better go. I'll get the key out of his pocket."

Then she disappeared. Moments later the shed door opened and Archie grabbed his knife and slid it into his jeans and stepped out to meet her.

"Thanks, but I have to tell you that you are the last person I expected to see."

"It's just by chance. I was tailing Dave Ghent, hoping he'd lead me to Morris Denton. I saw what happened to you so I waited."

"You betrayed me back at the abandoned house," Archie said. "Why should I trust you now?"

"Well, because I just freed you, and also, didn't you read my note? I told you I had to do something important. I wasn't specific but I did say I'd be in touch."

"I didn't get anything. Where did you leave it?"

"I pinned it to the front door."

"I didn't go out that door."

"That's not my fault," she said.

"No, I guess not. Who sent you the text, by the way?"

"I'll tell you later," she said. "Right now, we'd better split out of here. Your pal on the ground there is making noises, and we don't have much time."

Archie no longer trusted her, but at least he was free.

"Okay, lead the way."

They skirted the main buildings and made their way over rugged terrain in the general direction of the beach. Archie pressed her to hurry. The glimmer of illumination from the rising quarter moon that made it possible for them to find the path would also make it easier for pursuers to track them. Indeed, moments after they left the compound, someone raised the alarm and lights came on. When she lost her way, Archie took over, leading them into the gloom of a gulley he thought should take them to the sea. A clamor of shouts from the forest behind them sped them on their way, half stumbling, half running. Finally, they came to a halt not far from the compound's now-empty service dock and its single stanchion light.

"Their tender is not there," Sophie said. "Now what do we do?"

"How did you get here?"

She pointed towards the south.

"By kayak," she said. "I left it at a poor excuse of a beach about a quarter of a mile away, but it's just a single-seater and we are two. What if we cut across to the other side?"

Archie considered her proposition in light of the fact that they had a few seconds at most, judging by the increasing sounds of pursuit.

"No time," he said. "Get back to your kayak while I try to divert them. I know this place reasonably well. Call my office when you can, because we'll need help here. I'll go towards the tip of the island. There's a little bay there where we could get picked up."

She put a hand on his arm, said, "Okay, I'll meet you," and then she was gone.

Judging from the noise, Archie's pursuers were closing on him, and he eased back into the shrubbery with Robbie's knife held ready. When Jeff Riggs and Brenda Volio came out of the trees and headed for the beach, Archie picked up a rock and heaved it as far as he could away from him, hoping to divert their attention away from Sophie. A burst from the Steyr shredded the foliage where the stone had landed, meaning the ploy worked. Riggs and Volio charged down the waterline, dark shadows against the light from the dock, while Archie reversed himself and crept away, heading north.

A setting gibbous moon illuminated his path and he walked faster. He had not gone more than a few hundred yards when Dave Ghent intercepted him and ordered him to stop. Archie waited for Ghent to call out for the others, but he didn't.

"You're too much bother, Stevens," he said.

Archie heard rather than saw him rack the slide on his pistol, but the shot never came. A dark mass appeared, followed by sounds of a scuffle, Ghent's call for help and a shout from Martin Demio.

"Get the fuck out of here, Archie. I can't hold him long."

"Martin!"

"Go, damn it. I can deal with these people. Remember me at my trial, will you?"

Ghent's call brought results, more people coming up the trail. Archie heard Volio's harsh bray.

"Get off him, Demio," she said.

Jeff Riggs's Steyr chuttered, its bullets spanging off some nearby rocks. Archie glimpsed its owner slamming a new clip into his weapon and threw Robbie's knife side arm, a desperate move, but the shooter cried out and dropped. The bush was now alive with dancing flashlight beams and shouting; Foley, Denton and the rest drawn by the shots. Trusting to his luck, Archie picked a direction and ran.

CHAPTER 46

With the commotion increasing behind him, Archie swung wide through the bush to avoid Bobby Carpenter's compound, which was so lit up it was easy to locate, and soon he picked up a clear trail, easy to follow and familiar. He felt certain the path linked up with the one he had taken to the burial cave where he'd found Stella Picard's remains. When he reached the place, he skirted the cave mouth and hurried on as the sounds of pursuit died away.

There was a glimmer of light in the sky when he caught up with Sophie, spotting her kayak drawn up on the beach and her sitting on a driftwood log, staring out to sea. She rose when she heard his footsteps on the gravel and came to greet him. She brushed a long strand of jet-black hair off her face and lifted her hands in the interrogative.

"What took you so long?" she said, half in jest.

"No wounds? I heard shooting."

Archie stopped and searched her face, now lit and flattered by the rising sun. He reminded himself she had her own agenda and likely harbored no qualms about sacrificing him in order to achieve her goals, just as she had back at the house.

"How much do you know about what happens up there at the compound?" he asked.

"What do you mean? You know everything I do."

"I don't think so."

She dipped her head as if he'd wounded her with his words, but when she lifted it again she was smiling.

"What gave me away?"

"To start with, you never saw me at a party years ago when you were a young starry-eyed girl, you never had a crush on me, nor any of that other bull crap. Are you even a doctor?"

"Yes, I'm a doctor and, yes, I did meet you before just like I said, and I thought you were hot. It's just a coincidence, I guess, we met again in these circumstances. I'm glad though, even if you're not."

She locked eyes with him, drawing him in, convincing him. After all, once you got past the flattery, he thought, the rest seemed possible. The incident at that party long ago party rang true.

"So what's this all about?"

"I'm after Morris Denton," she said. "I told you so."

"You're not a cop. I checked. So what are you?"

She turned her body away and faced the north. She seemed to be considering her options.

"I was in the military," she said. "In a way. I spent a lot of time overseas. My younger sister disappeared while I was gone. I traced her to a camp run by Morris Denton, but he pulled up stakes by the time I got there. He initiated his followers into this fake Cannibal Society he established and controlled them through fear. I found no trace of my sister until I searched the camp property. I'm good at that kind of thing, finding things others want to hide. When I found a bracelet I'd given her, I knew Denton or one of his thugs had killed her, although I never found her body. I've been on his trail ever since."

"Doesn't he recognize you?"

"It's hard to say, but I don't think so. We never met, and Stephanie and I didn't resemble each other. She was an innocent, which, by the way, I'm definitely not."

"I'm truly sorry for your loss."

"Thanks."

"What do you think of the shamanism he's supposed to be into?"

"He is a shaman, and he knows all their tricks. He can use your own mind against you. But he learned from somebody else. He has a master."

"And he makes business deals too?" Archie said. "Seems incongruous."

"Morris doesn't limit himself. I learned of this new setup when I got down to this part of the coast. I don't much care about it either. I want my sister's murderer—end of story."

"I want him too."

"We'll see who gets to him first. I'm not planning on going through courts and police and all that garbage, so back off, Archie."

"Not going to happen, Sophie."

"Your opinion, but now I've got to go. Unfortunately, there's only room in my boat for one."

"Did you call in for me?"

"I knew I forgot something. No, your cop friends aren't coming to find you."

She shoved her kayak out into the water and climbed in, grabbed the paddle and backstroked away from the beach.

"Sorry, Archie, but I figured you'd go all legal on me, and I've got stuff to do."

"Sophie …"

But she was soon out of range, paddling strongly into the sunrise. He watched her go, said, "Damn," and then headed inland in the direction of John Robbie's cabin.

CHAPTER 47

R obbie's place seemed deserted. He and Patsy should be there, but no one answered Archie's call. Alarmed, he picked up a section of two by four from a scrap pile and, holding it like a club, crossed the cleared area Robbie used as a kind of lawn to the open door and glanced inside.

A struggle had taken place there—that much was obvious from the broken or overturned furniture scattered about the interior. Archie's foot hit something metallic; a spent cartridge jingled across the floor. He reached down and retrieved the two-twenty-three Remington brass case—two-twenty-three, the ammunition used by the Steyr carbine Jeff Riggs carried.

A trail of blood led out the back door and into the forest. Archie started to follow it, half expecting to find Patsy dead; the thought froze his heart. He hurried, stopping when the trail vanished and circling until he picked it up again, a spatter of bright red here, a dark scarlet gobbet there.

But it wasn't Patsy he found. John Robbie was sitting upright in a jumble of large boulders, his blood soaking the once white tee shirt he wore. Archie jumped down into the rocks and went to his side. As he did so, Patsy came out of the brush behind him and hurried to them. When he saw her, Archie let out his breath, his relief palpable. She knelt down beside him.

"I went down to the shore where the reception's better to call the station," she said. "I was talking to Jameson when I heard firing and came running."

At the sound of her voice, Robbie opened his eyes.

"I'm glad you're here, Arch," he said. He paused to rebuild his strength.

"What happened?" Archie said.

"It was crazy," Robbie said. "We come here. Patsy went to call in like you wanted, but then Brenda Volio and Jeff Riggs come up on me."

He coughed, caught his breath. Patsy gave him a drink from the water bottle she'd been carrying.

"Anyway," he continued. "I got out the back and headed into the bush, hoping to draw them off, but Riggs caught up and shot me. I know this place pretty good, so I got away and hid."

"We'll get help for you," Patsy said "It's on its way as soon as Ray can get it here. In the meantime, I'll send off texts to Pete Wilson and Walter George in case they're out fishing near here."

She stood up, dispatched her messages and then knelt back down. Robbie coughed, grinned and grimaced in pain.

"Such attention" he said. "I could get into this."

"I'm sorry, John. I didn't mean for you to get so mixed up in this," Archie said.

Robbie laughed, a series of breathless grunts.

"Forget it. I feel pretty good right now."

Patsy brought the bottle to his lips and he took another sip, dribbling it down the corners of his mouth. In spite of his bravado, it was obvious Robbie needed medical assistance soon. Luckily help was on its way. Archie heard voices, among them Walter George's loud bray. He went to intercept them so he could lead them to Robbie.

When they met, Pete nodded a greeting to Archie.

"He's still alive," Archie said. "Down in the rocks, over there. I'll take you."

"We've got more help coming. We'll do what we can for now. Walter's first aid certified, and he was an army medic."

Walter held up the large marine medical kit he brought with him.

"I can do a fair amount, but I'm not a doctor," Walter said. "Hopefully he hasn't lost too much blood. Where is he?"

Archie led the way through the trees with Pete and Walter loping along behind him. When they got to Robbie, he had his eyes open. His gaze went from Patsy to the new arrivals. He shook his head weakly.

"God," he said, his teeth gritted. "Don't tell me Walter's the doctor."

"I'm all you can afford," Walter said. "Now shut up."

He knelt down beside Robbie, opened his kit and set to work. Archie leaned in.

"One more question, John—if you're up to it?"

"Yeah?"

"How come they didn't finish you off? The blood trail was easy enough to follow."

"They would have, I think, but somebody called them back. That prick Riggs was talking to someone on his phone, something about getting organized and preparing to leave."

"Stay with him," Archie said to Patsy. "I have to go."

She nodded, glanced at him from under her brows.

"Be careful," she said softly.

Her phone dinged as a message came in. She read it and turned to Archie.

"Jameson says he's rounding up a squad and figures he'll be on the island within the hour. Medical help will come here, but he'll hook up with you at Carpenter's compound. That good for you? He wants to know."

"Perfect. Tell him I'll meet him there."

"I will."

"My skiff's in the bay," Pete said. "With gas in the tank. Take it and good luck."

"Thanks. I could use the transport."

He took one more look at Robbie, nodded to Patsy, turned on his heel and loped away.

CHAPTER 48

Archie left the skiff a mile or so from Carpenter's and then jogged up the path to his rendezvous with Jameson and Thomas Lee, which was to be five hundred yards south of the compound's perimeter. They met and moved in closer and found cover, where Archie asked for details of the plan. Jameson explained that a SWAT team from Rochville would set up just north of the compound, ready on Jameson's signal to move in and close the trap.

"What about the *Tiger*?" Archie asked. "Some of these folks might slip out and get to the boat."

Jameson shook his head.

"I haven't got the manpower for it. Anyway, nobody's getting out of here without us seeing them."

"I hope you're right. I'm not convinced."

Jameson's phone binged and he answered it, said "fine" a couple of times and ended the call.

"The team's ready," he said to Archie. "Let's go."

As they left their hiding place, they heard the pop, pop, pop of an assault rifle firing and then, suddenly, a huge explosion sent showers of debris into the air over the compound, followed by a concussion wave that knocked Archie off his feet.

As the shock subsided, he picked himself up and saw the carnage, the haze of smoke blurring the air and the fierce fire burning in what remained of the longhouse. Several bodies lay about the clearing. A few helmeted SWAT team members wandered about. Archie's ears rang. Thomas Lee stumbled towards him, wide-eyed, disheveled.

"Are you okay?" Archie asked, his words sounding distant, although he was the one who had spoken them.

Lee nodded.

"I think so," he said, his voice shaky. "Where's Ray?"

Archie nodded to where Jameson was lying on his back, half-covered in wood fragments. He was cursing and trying to free himself of the debris. They walked over to him and pulled him up. Jameson grunted his thanks. He rotated his head like an angular weathervane so as to take in the scene.

"What the hell?" he exclaimed. "The place is gone."

"We'd better see who's still alive in there."

They found Robertson Foley first, his back against a tree, shirt gone, blood streaming down his powder-burned face and chest. Archie bent down, checked the vacant eyes, called Foley by name, but Foley could no longer answer. Jeff Riggs was dead also, his body jammed into fork of a shattered cedar. A team member discovered Martin Demio's body in the shed where they had incarcerated Archie, shot to death.

"Demio was a bad cop," Jameson said.

"He saved my life tonight," Archie said. He remembered how the son had looked after his father in the hospital and resolved to see what he could do for Demio's family.

"Well, that's something."

"Redemption might be everything," Archie said.

Jameson grunted and continued on. Archie lingered near the shattered porch of the long-house, wondering who might still be inside. Dave Ghent appeared with his clothing in ribbons and one shoe missing. He limped past Archie heading for the forest, but Archie grabbed his arm and stopped him.

"Dave," he said. "What happened?"

Ghent stared at Archie as if trying to place his face and shook his head.

"We didn't have a chance," he said. "We were all inside, trying to decide what to do afterwards, and I don't know, but the whole damn place blew up, Stevens. I got lots to tell you. ..."

A helmeted and still masked member of the SWAT team came out from the main house and joined them. He carried a medical kit.

"Your acting chief wants you," he said, and guided Ghent away. "You can talk to him later after I give him medical treatment."

Archie watched them go. The medic's voice was familiar, but he couldn't place it. Still thinking about it, he walked over to where Jameson was talking to the SWAT leader.

"What is it, Ray?" Archie asked. "What do you want?"

"What's what?"

"You wanted to see me."

"Not me."

Archie turned to the SWAT leader, a man Archie had met before named Bogart.

"The stocky guy on your team," Archie said. "Is he a trained medic?"

"No," Bogart said. "My medic's a woman and she's over there putting out fires."

He pointed to a short and sturdy woman, trying to put out a small flare-up near the main house and Robertson Foley's body. Everyone was staying back from the still burning longhouse as occasionally tanks and aerosols continued to explode.

Archie swore and charged back to the place where he'd left Ghent and the phony medic, picked up their tracks and followed them. He spotted Ghent's feet sticking out from under an Ocean Spray bush beside the trail and knelt down to get a better look, briefly entertaining the possibility that the man still lived, but the lawyer was dead, killed by the combat dagger driven into the base of his neck.

CHAPTER 49

Archie followed the man's tracks down through the trees to a tiny inlet and out onto a narrow and constricted beach between two steep bluffs where a deep keel groove in the sand marked the place a small boat had been waiting. Archie had a good idea where the killer had gone. He sent a text to Ray Jameson informing him of Dave Ghent's murder. Jameson gave Archie a list of casualties at the longhouse—Jeff Riggs, Brenda Volio, Robertson Foley and Martin Demio—and said he would add Ghent to the roster. Archie started to walk back up to the compound, not surprised to learn that Morris Denton was not among the dead.

After the Carpenter site had been secured, Archie made calls. The first was to Pete Wilson, who gave him the welcome news that John Robbie was alive and evacuated to Rochville hospital and that the prognosis was good. Archie also organized activities for his team—Lee to arrange to freeze the assets of Skeleton Resources, at least temporarily, and Patsy to visit the offices of the company. Then he contacted Pete again and asked him for a ride to Harsley.

He was aboard the *Cherish* and on his way when Patsy called to say that the offices in question were now vacant and that she had failed to turn up any other address for Denton. Archie wasn't surprised. Soon after, Lee sent a message saying that a warrant was in the works, but the firm's assets could be frozen only temporarily. It was a setback. Time was of the essence now. If Archie did not catch the shaman soon, he would transfer his money out of the country, leave the area and disappear. He gave Lee and Patsy instructions. Pete put more power to the screw.

Back in Harsley, he picked up a vehicle, a modern SUV, at the police station, and headed for the Eagle Wing Casino and the senior's co-op behind it. He needed to talk to Eddie Froese, the old cop who had known his parents. He seemed surprised to see Archie again, but when Archie showed him a picture of Denton, he recognized the man right away.

"His real name is Lambert," Froese said. "Kyle Lambert. He was the smartest of the junior thugs your old man and Carpenter Senior trained, a real creep too, older than the others too. I'm pretty sure he's the guy who put a match to my house. I thought he was dead."

"No. He's still alive."

"God help you then."

"What else can you tell me about him?"

Froese limped across the room and opened a drawer in an old metal filing cabinet. He pulled out a tattered folder and handed it to Archie.

"You'll find a lot in there," he said. "He did nasty enough stuff that your old man and old Bob Carpenter tried to put him down at one time."

"Tried?"

"Oh, yeah. They couldn't catch him."

"Too bad," Archie said. "One other thing, Eddie. I was wondering if you would point me to that training camp they maintained over here on the mainland?"

"That's easy. It's up behind a place you probably know quite well. Do you recall your dad's bogus restaurant at Taggart Bay?"

The old place in Taggart Bay was shut up and apparently abandoned. It had never been much, and Curtis only took Archie there once when it was operating as a café. As young as he was then, Archie wondered how it stayed afloat since it seemed to do almost no business. As a front for gang activity, however, it probably served the purpose, and now Archie figured it was a good place to start searching for Denton. He sent out a series of texts, checked the battery level on his phone and carried on.

Archie glanced at the rundown building and turned the 4Runner onto the access road behind it and followed that up into the hills. Five miles in, he came across a rustic camp consisting of a bunkhouse, a clubhouse and kitchen, an outdoor training ring and a firing range. The open gravelled yards were overgrown and empty of vehicles. Archie found a parking spot he liked and backed in the SUV, putting it more or less out of sight of the entrance road.

His mind was racing now, his thoughts moving quickly from past to present, from old to new memories to lingering psychological wounds, to what he had known and not known about his father and to his mother too. But he calmed himself, cleared his mind, got out of his vehicle, checked his weapon and crossed to the old clubhouse.

Once inside, he made a quick search, not sure what he expected to find. He was finishing up when another vehicle pulled into the lot. Archie peered through the window, watched as the driver got out. He recognized the figure. It was Sophie Anderson. She scanned the area of the camp, located his vehicle, walked to it and looked inside, even standing on tiptoes to check behind the seats. Archie's first impression was of nervousness, or fear. He waited a few minutes before he called out to her.

She turned at the sound of his voice and walked towards him, a hand raised in greeting. She smiled at him when she came up.

"You found this place," she said. "I thought you might."

"I'm surprised to see you here. What's the deal?"

"I was following Morris Denton, but he doesn't seem to be here anymore."

Archie shrugged.

"If this is the hideout or whatever we want to call it, it's missing some important features."

"He must be somewhere else. It's not the first time I've got it wrong. No sense hanging around."

She had just arrived and now she wanted to leave, and he found that curious.

"No," he said. "This is the place."

His sharp eyes caught a subtle change in color in the patch of trees and vegetation behind the kitchen. He shifted position and a curving line of gray-green revealed itself, an indication of a concealed path or roadway. He pointed it out to Sophie.

"I think we've got a trail leading up the hill. I'm going to check it out."

"I can't see it," she said, frowning. "This is probably a deer run and we're wasting our time here."

"You're not involved, so no worries."

"What do you mean?"

"I'm conducting a police investigation. Your vendetta isn't part of it. In fact, if you continue I might end up having to arrest you."

"Bullshit."

"Is it?"

He started to walk away, towards the hillside and the faint green trace. Before he went a hundred yards, she called after him, asking him to wait for her.

"Your call," she said. "I keep forgetting the police business bit. I know you have a job to do. Mind if I tag along anyway?"

He paused, considered the proposition. He owed her something for getting him out of the shed, but he didn't trust her. He was sure there was no note on the front door of the abandoned house he'd torched on the airport properties, and he couldn't shake the notion she'd betrayed him. In the end, certain she'd just trail him anyway, he relented.

"All right, but you have to do whatever I tell you."

"Aye, aye, Captain."

He led the way across the graveled lot and around to the back of the bunkhouse to a place where a latticework screen concealed a row of garbage cans. He tugged the screen back, and after scrutinizing the line of containers, he walked along it and pushed each aside. The trailhead began behind the fourth and fifth cans.

"You were right," Sophie said, lagging behind him. "You're a hard man to fool."

They continued upwards through a short stretch of jumbled rock and onto a narrow but well-maintained track that led away from the main camp. This stopped in front of a kind of line shack, painted to seem tumbledown and abandoned, a status belied by the camouflaged satellite dish built into one corner.

They were twenty feet away when the door of the shed opened and Morris Denton stepped out. He smiled when he saw Archie and shook his head ruefully.

"Dammit, Slick," he said. "You're too smart for your own good. You know that? Mind you, you come from smart parents, so I shouldn't be surprised, but now I got to figure out what to do with you."

Archie pulled his pistol from its holster and pointed it at Denton. As he did so, he felt the jab of a pistol's muzzle in the area of his right kidney. Sophie reached around and took the gun from his hand.

"Move over, Archie," she said.

When he stayed where he was, she moved out from behind him, ready for a shot.

"Sophie!"

"Payback at last, Morris," she said.

Denton smiled.

The shot came from within the cabin. Archie caught Sophie as she slumped down and lowered her to the ground. Larry Aberle stepped out and waved him back with his gunhand. When he checked Sophie's pulse with his fingertips, they came away bloody. Denton pointed at Archie.

"Kill him," he said.

"Hold off," Aberle said. "I still need him. There are millions at stake. If I'm right, he's put a temporary hold on our assets and we'll want him to release the funds."

"Is that so, Archie?"

"I'm afraid it is."

"I guess you stay alive a few minutes longer then."

The two men discussed the situation. Denton glanced at Sophie's recumbent form.

"I'm sorry about this one," he said. "Her persistence got her killed."

Archie thought he detected a slight movement from her. He needed to keep their attention on him.

"Not much in the way of mourning for a daughter."

Denton shrugged.

"You figured that out. No, I won't mourn too much. She had no love for me. I'm still a little sorry though."

"Crazy little Kyle Lambert, former juvenile delinquent."

Archie used Denton's real name. The other man flushed with anger, took a step towards him, his fist raised.

"Stop," Aberle said. "We have a very small window of time. Take the Detective Sergeant inside. You'll get your cut once the transfer is complete, and then you can kill him. After that, we part company."

Archie, with Sophie's blood soaking his shirt, faced Aberle.

"Quite the operation you've got here, Larry."

Aberle shrugged.

"I'm doing okay."

"Murder is okay too?"

"It's not a big deal."

"You're a genuine prick, aren't you?"

Aberle lifted a shoulder in agreement, or resignation. He pointed his finger at Archie, said "Bang," and smiled.

"Are you ready, Morris, to go inside your so-called communications center and run your algorithms?"

Denton turned away from Sophie's body and said, "Yeah."

"Let's go, then."

Within the outwardly derelict cabin, they had created a compact electronics hub. The establishment also contained a small kitchen and bathroom, a single bed and a couple of easy chairs and a *Ts'onaqua* mask hung above the bed. Aberle noticed Archie looking and clicked his teeth.

"Yes, my friend, the Cannibal Woman is here."

"It's quite the deal you've got going here, Larry. Complicated."

"Complicated? I guess it's become that way. Started out straightforward with the art thefts, but when a golden opportunity opened up, I had to take it."

"The land deal, you mean?" Archie said. "Is that the gold?"

"Yeah. Now sit down over there while Morris does his thing with the computer, and we can figure out what to do with you."

He motioned Archie to the easy chair and ordered him to sit down. He picked up an automatic pistol from the table, took a seat opposite and pointed the gun at Archie's head. Meanwhile, Denton returned to his computers, sat down and went to work with mouse and keyboard.

"This shouldn't take too long," Aberle said. "You might as well relax."

For several minutes, Morris Denton occupied himself, but, suddenly, he cursed, stood, shook his fist, stalked across the room and glared down at Archie.

"This bastard has screwed us around," he said. "The Skeleton Resources accounts are locked down. We can't do anything without a code word from him. He's his fucking old man all over again. We don't need this complication."

He swung a balled fist towards the side of Archie's head, but Archie sprang up from the chair, slammed a shoulder into him, knocked him over and stood waiting, fists cocked. Aberle rose from his seat and put the muzzle of his pistol against Archie's neck.

"Take it easy, Detective Sergeant," he said softly.

Meanwhile, Denton was stabbing a finger at Archie. Aberle waved him back.

"The problem is, policeman," he said. "The money is mostly mine, and I want it. I'm prepared to trade your life for cash. I hope you're worth a half-billion dollars."

"On our budget—I don't see it."

Denton's outburst meant Lee had been able to stop the electronic transfer and freeze the Skeleton Resources accounts, so, at least, part of the plan was working.

"Besides, I've left instructions that no such deal is to be made."

"You don't make those kinds of decisions," Aberle said. "Your chief, or somebody higher, does that. You're too full of yourself, son."

"I guess, so but we do have a policy to refuse to negotiate in these situations; otherwise, we have to deal with lunatics like you all the time demanding money."

Denton had been studying Archie. Something must have occurred to him because he went back to his computers, smiling. After a few minutes of work, he beckoned Archie over. Aberle kept his pistol levelled at Archie. When he hesitated to move, he tapped Archie's shoulder with the barrel of his gun.

"Don't be stubborn, Archie," he said. "It's best you do what you're told—less painful for you."

Archie shrugged and crossed the floor to the desk to where Denton was seated.

"Seems like I all I need is an electronic okay from you to release the funds," the shaman said over his shoulder. "It needs a five letter code. How about giving it up?"

"You must be joking."

"He doesn't joke," Aberle said. "He doesn't have much of a sense of humor. But what if I shoot you right now, maybe in the knee first and them moving up?"

"Here's another idea," Archie said. "Why don't you two surrender? I'm not sure I have enough of a case to charge you with murder. You might be lucky. They don't punish folks much for stealing millions of dollars. A hundred dollars, yes, but not a five hundred million."

"That's not going to happen," Aberle said. "I know another way to get you to agree."

His hand darted out and only Archie's quick reaction saved him from taking the cloud of fine powder full in the face, yet a portion still entered his eyes and nostrils. He sneezed hard, a migraine started, and he wanted to vomit. A whispering *Ts'onaqua* appeared in front of him, grinning, commanding him to obey its wishes, and the need to surrender himself and become mindless became overpowering. Even drugged, though, the thought terrified him. All his life he had fought against control, and he was not about to give up his free will now. He felt the presence of the Bear and drew strength from his ally. He coughed out the powder, the hallucination dissipated, and he was once again in the cabin, facing Aberle. He shook his head to clear it.

"Enough of this crap," he said. "How many people have you killed this way?"

Aberle grinned.

"How does it go? You can't make an omelet and so on. If you're thinking of Ron Helerstone, he wasn't supposed to die, so what happened to him wasn't my fault. Anyway, this is useless talk. I want my money."

Denton continued to tap in codes until, suddenly, he whooped.

"We've got it, Larry," he said. "Your people got our accounts unfrozen pending your approval. Once you contact them, sign in and authorize the transfers, we're clear."

To Archie, Aberle said, "I have lawyers other than the late Dave Ghent, and better ones too."

Just then, noises outside indicated that somebody was moving in, taking up positions around the cabin, which meant Patsy and Thomas had homed in on his signal after all. Denton rushed to a window.

"They're here. How?" he said.

Archie tapped his side, at the level of his belt.

"Tracking device and recorder," he said. "You should have checked."

"Sit down or I'll kill you."

Archie lifted his shoulders in mock agreement and dropped down again into the easy chair. Meanwhile, Denton darted from window to window checking out what was happening outside. He beckoned to Aberle, and they held an animated disputatious conversation, the upshot of which was that the shaman would keep Archie covered while his partner took the laptop, already set up ready for communications, out through a hidden exit and would play for time before surrendering.

"The assets of Skeleton Resources will be unfrozen within an hour," Aberle said. "And the money will be in our Swiss bank accounts. I just need time to make it happen. They have almost nothing to hold you on, Morris, plus you've got the best lawyers on the coast to back you."

He raised a trapdoor in the floor and disappeared through it.

Archie glanced at Denton and laughed.

"You idiot, Kyle. He's left you holding the bag."

Denton trained his pistol on Archie, but Archie could see doubt in his eyes.

"He's gone, Kyle."

"Shut up. I gotta think."

"I'm not wrong, and we both know it. We'll have evidence that you blew up Bobby Carpenter's place. You're screwed."

Denton, agitated, kept Archie covered, but he edged to a window and peered out.

"They're out there, waiting," Archie said. "Give up, Morris."

"No. I can't do that. We're going outside, and you'll be my shield, my hostage."

He set the muzzle at the base of Archie's jaw and tried to force him to the door. Archie pressed the signal clicker on his side, clamped his eyes shut and put his hands over his ears. Seconds later, flash bang grenades crashed through the windows and exploded. When he opened his eyes, Denton was on the floor, hands grasping his head, writhing. The door flew open and Patsy stood there, weapon raised, while Thomas and other officers charged in through the rear.

"Right on time, Patsy," Archie said. "Perfect."

"We aim to please."

They grabbed and handcuffed Denton, ready to take him away.

"Back in a sec," Archie said.

He walked quickly to where to Sophie lay. She opened her eyes as he knelt down beside her.

"I thought you were dead," Archie said.

She put out a hand, shook her head, tapped her chest.

"Kevlar. My head hurts though. I knocked myself out when I fell. Help me up."

Carefully, he pulled her up to a sitting position. The back of her head was matted with blood, which also glazed the surface of the large rock that had done the damage.

"What happened?"

As he described the action to her, she tried to stand.

"I feel woozy. I'd better sit."

"You got Aberle, I hope," she said.

He shook his head.

"No."

"Denton?"

"Yes."

She said, "Good," and closed her eyes. Archie was aware that Patsy, now behind him, was watching. He stood, drew her aside and avoided the question in her eyes. Luckily, Thomas Lee joined them.

"How are you feeling, Arch?" he asked.

"I'm fine. I have to go after Aberle right now. He's gone up into the forest. He's got a computer with him, and I'm quite sure he's capable of completing the transfer of funds. Make sure she's okay."

"We're coming up with you."

She waved her hand, indicating the officers she'd brought with her.

"No time," Archie said.

He retrieved his gun, took a bottle of water and searched around the back of the building until he picked up Larry Aberle's trail.

CHAPTER 50

Broken stone littered the track, which became steep and treacherous. Aberle did not seem to be good at bush craft, and his trail, once Archie isolated it, was distinct, a pattern of disturbed twigs and overturned rocks that led up the hill and deeper into the forest. Archie kept to the sides of the path, walking on moss and solid ground whenever he could and avoiding loose gravel, which was impossible to cross without noise. As he approached the top of the climb, he slowed his pace. He heard a familiar low hum and stopped to listen, ready. The hum grew louder and he tensed, knowing what the sound signified. The first rock almost hit him, whizzing by his head just as he leaned away out of its path. He ran crouched towards the timber. A second stone struck him a blow between the shoulders and he stumbled, drawing his pistol and firing where he thought

Aberle must be. Then he scrambled part way up, ready to dive into the brush.

Aberle's sling droned again, this time from a different place. Archie almost did not react in time. He twisted to one side as the stone grazed his head, crashed through some willows and fell heavily onto the rocks, his gun flying from his grasp and landing in the scrub. He dragged himself behind a boulder and checked for damage. So far as he could tell, he'd only been slightly concussed, but the missile had drawn a little blood. He needed to locate his SIG, retrieve it and then figure out where Aberle was concealed.

The forest became very still, and after a few minutes, birds were calling. Nothing was spooking *them*, but what could he infer from that? Not much, likely. He wasn't in the clear yet.

While he wondered if Aberle had moved off, someone began chanting a traditional-sounding tune from a thicket fifty yards away, a low mumble barely perceptible a first, but growing louder, clearer, more emphatic. The hypnotic cadence and the half-recognized words seemed to confuse him, and he lost focus. Some suggestion buried deep within his subconscious now ruled him; he stood up and faced not Aberle, but Coyote, motionless and terrifying, a shadowed monster standing in the heart of a grove of maples thirty feet away.

Coyote began to dance, spinning his cloak, the chant louder and more forceful. The garment flashed in the flickering sunlight as he dipped and turned, producing mesmerizing patterns of light shade and color with each rotation. Archie stumbled forward, captivated, towards the black spear in the shaman's hand, but at the edge of the dancer's striking distance, he halted. His mind rebelled against the other's insistent commands, and instinctively he brought his hand up to his chest where the bear had marked it back at Jeremiah Strait. As he touched the now raised striations, his thoughts cleared a little and the sorcerer's song grew weak, discordant, powerless. He stopped shuffling and repositioned himself, his movements now purposeful and strong. The dancer halted and screamed out a frantic, strident command to submit. From within Archie a mighty laugh bubbled up and broke the spell. Coyote disappeared and Aberle stood in his place, a pathetic figure in a motley of woven cedar, wool and canvas, his power dissipated and his magic shattered.

"It's done, Larry," Archie said. "Enough."

Aberle removed his leering coyote mask and tossed it aside, but he kept the spear and hefted it, ready to throw.

"I can still kill you. Magic or no."

He charged at Archie and slashed at him. Archie stepped aside and easily caught the shaft as it passed by him and held it. Aberle put all his strength into keeping possession. And because he was a strong man and he almost broke Archie's grasp once or twice, but soon the older man began to tire, his breathing labored. Archie tore the weapon from his hands and threw Aberle down.

"You're under arrest on suspicion of murder and conspiracy to commit murder, Professor Aberle," he said. "I'm sure the prosecutor will add money laundering and fraud charges."

Aberle sat on the path, his arms around his knees, catching his breath. He glanced up at Archie.

"I can't figure you out, Stevens. I used drugs and post-hypnotic suggestion on you, real magic too, but I couldn't finish the job on you."

"I'm not going to try to puzzle it out for you, Larry. On your feet."

He secured Aberle's hands, retrieved his pistol and ordered Aberle to gather up his regalia and then had him lead him to where he had stowed the laptop, a small lean-to built into the maples near the trail. Archie tucked the computer under his arm.

"Down the hill, Larry," he said. "I haven't got all day."

Aberle shrugged and started picking his way through the broken rock, but after a few minutes, he glanced back at Archie over his shoulder.

"You're probably feeling pretty cocky right now, aren't you, Slick?" he said.

"I'm feeling all right," he said. "Having you in custody at last. And stop calling me Slick."

Aberle laughed.

"I got that from Morris," Aberle said. "He sure hated your old man and wanted to revenge himself on you as a result. Anyway, there's no way you'll get me to trial, which you must realize."

"I've heard this before from killers and thieves. It means nothing."

Aberle chuckled and continued down. He seemed willing to answer Archie's questions about how Skeleton Resources operated and how he became involved with Denton, Helerstone and Foley, although he always prefaced his answers with qualifiers like "I heard this" or "So I'm told," so, legally, he never came close to anything like an admission of guilt. Only on the subject of the Cannibal Society was he reticent, refusing to say anything beyond giving a summary of the old, traditional ceremonials and a short bemused retelling of the *Ts'onaqua* myth to the point where Archie felt like smacking him on the back of the head.

Patsy and Lee were waiting at the cabin, along with uniformed officers ready to take the prisoners into custody. Sophie Anderson had disappeared. When Archie asked Patsy about her, she shot him a puzzling look but said nothing. Lee told Archie the site was secure for forensics, but he seemed unhappy, and Archie wondered about the reason.

"The why of it is I just got word my attempt at a court order locking the Skeleton Resources accounts was blocked," Lee said. "I just checked. The money had already been moved offshore. It's all in shell companies, I guess, and we have no idea where it is now."

Archie let this sink in and turned away. Behind him, Aberle snickered.

"Got you, Slick," he said.

After Aberle was taken away, Archie told his team about his capture of Aberle and how he had tried to kill him.

"So, that's how he manipulated people?" Patsy said.

"That plus hallucinogenics and using peoples' greed and their general willingness to believe."

"We've got him," Lee said.

"I don't know," Patsy said. "So far we don't have much that would hold up in court. Assaulting a police officer perhaps, but even there a good lawyer would have a field day."

"You're right," Lee said. "We can't link him directly to a single murder, for example."

Archie started to walk, and they walked along with him.

"What now?" Patsy said.

"Wait here until the forensics team arrives. We may get something from this place and his little hideaway up the trail that we can use. You can join me later here."

He wrote out an address on a page from his notebook, tore it out and passed it across. Lee read it and passed it on to Patsy. She nodded.

"You think?"

"I do, and I intend to arrest the persons who killed Ron Helerstone, and this is where they'll be, one of them at least."

"What about Stella Picard's killer?" Lee said.

"Helerstone killed Stella Picard, which was why he had to die."

CHAPTER 51

With summer session underway at the University, Archie found nowhere to park near the Anthropology department. He had to put the 4Runner onto a patch of manicured lawn, a delayed act of rebellion he found embarrassingly satisfying. Lee and Patsy, in Lee's BMW, followed him onto the grass, as did a squad car with its complement of two constables. An officious parking attendant appeared immediately, a voluminous pad of tickets in hand. She waved away the badge Lee produced and Archie had to lay down the law before, grumbling, she went on her way.

Inside the building, Archie stopped to speak with the receptionist and told her not to hold all communications until told otherwise. He didn't want his quarry to escape him.

"Give me fifteen minutes with her, and then come down if we don't come up first," he said to the other detectives. "I want to talk to her alone.

Keep your eyes open and be ready. I expect we'll have another visitor shortly."

He beckoned to the two uniformed officers. They accompanied him down the stairs to the lower floor and he posted them at either end of the hallway before he went on to Emily Frizzell's office.

She was at her desk in her office, her back to him, working on a paper or some other project, just like before. When he knocked on her doorframe, she turned to face him, her face set, grim, expecting him.

"How's my policeman?" she said.

He shrugged, entered the room and indicated the chair opposite her.

"Mind if I sit, Emily?"

"Why not?"

"Still investigating the death of poor Ron, or is it some other scandal this time? Are you still baffled, policeman?"

He took a seat and shook his head.

"No, I'm not baffled. By the way, whatever happened to that old tabby you used to have?"

"Old Margaret Mead," she said. "Thanks for asking. She died about a year ago, aged nineteen."

"Wow—a long life. She was a real fixture around here, wasn't she?"

"Yes, she was."

"You'll still have cat hair around your place," he said. "It gets on blankets and things and even vacuuming doesn't seem to pick it all up. I once had a cat so I'm sympathetic."

She stared straight ahead, but her eyes were unfocussed.

"What are you getting at, Archie?"

"I think we should stop pretending, Emily," he said. "We found cat hair on the blanket Stella Picard's remains were in, and I'll bet they'll match hairs we'll find in your house. We both know who killed Ron Helerstone. What I want from you is Ron's Walther pistol."

She closed her eyes for a few seconds. He waited, called her name. She blinked and her gaze wandered back to him.

"What makes you think I have it? Why would I have his gun?"

"C'mon. Emily—please. I know what happened on the night he died, and more or less how it went down. So—the Walther?"

"And if I don't feel like cooperating with you?"

"I have two constables waiting outside, and as soon as I give the word, they'll arrest you for being an accessory to murder, interfering with a body and whatever other charges the prosecutor can come up with. My detectives are upstairs waiting for us."

"If I hand over the Walther and go with you, is that the end of it?"

"No, sorry, I'll be arresting someone else too."

She slumped in her chair. He saw that her eyes were wet.

"Leave her alone, Archie," Emily said. "She doesn't deserve to be punished for what she did."

"It doesn't work that way."

"What way does it work?"

"You know how, Emily. The law decides, not me."

"I see," she said. "No compassion from Archie Stevens."

She turned back to her desk, lifted a folder and then swiveled back to face him, Helerstone's prized Walther thirty-two caliber pistol in her hand, pointed at him.

"I'm a good shot, Archie."

"I know you are, Emily. I'm not sure what you think pointing a gun at me will do for her case other than complicate it."

"I could shoot you and stall the rest of your lone rangers."

"That's the point," he said. "We're not *lone* rangers. I just told you five minutes ago I have two constables outside and my detectives are up-stairs. What are you thinking?"

"Some of us will do almost anything for the person we love."

She raised the pistol so that he could almost see down its barrel. Her eyes narrowed.

"She'll be gone soon, Archie," she said. "I wish it wasn't you. But I know you—you would want to finish this alone, to talk to me alone. Once you're dead, I can go out the lab door. No one will find her."

Archie opened his hands in an expression of regret.

"All the doors are being watched. There's no way out."

"Unless you have to deal with a suicide."

She swung the muzzle of the pistol under her chin. Archie leapt up, pushed her back, jammed his forefinger between the trigger and its guard and prevented her from shooting. She looked up him, eyes tearing.

"Please, Archie."

He held her eyes until she released the gun, after which she slumped down onto the floor. He held the Walther away from her and gently lifted her head.

"Tell me where she is, Emily, so we can end this terrible thing."

A noise behind him made him turn. Tessa Simons stood in the doorway, with Patsy and Thomas immediately behind her.

"Is this the visitor you were expecting?" Patsy said.

"She is."

"Leave Emily alone," Tessa said. "She's a gentle person and doesn't deserve this. I'm the person you want. Ron Helerstone killed my sister and I shot... ."

Archie stopped her, said, "Detective Kydd."

Patsy nodded, handcuffed Tessa and read her rights.

Tessa laughed.

"By the book, right, Archie," she said. "You wanted to make sure I didn't confess before I was cautioned. But I have a problem. What am I going to do for counsel now that that slimeball Dave Ghent is dead?"

CHAPTER 52

Archie watched Thomas Lee make his way to the table in the Weather Glass Lounge where he and Patsy Kydd were sitting. He was glad to see Lee arriving; a third person might diffuse the awkward two-party conversation in which he was presently engaged, the one in which she probed unabashedly for information on Sophie Anderson and, he guessed, any feelings he might have for the other woman. Cal Fricke, now recovered, was occupying a seat at the bar focussed on a ball game—no help there. Lee picked a chair and sat down, after which he smoothed the creases in his trousers and straightened his cuffs. Patsy watching this ritual with interest, sipped from her gin and tonic.

"Have you ordered yet?" Lee asked.

"We were waiting for you," Patsy said.

Archie had just returned from the prosecutor's office where he'd spent hours endeavoring to explain and separate the threads of all the cases he and his team were still clearing up. The feelings of frustration he had carried around all afternoon had begun to dissipate. He watched as Patsy amused herself by trying to bait her fellow detective, now picking minute flecks of dust off the sleeve of what appeared to be a very expensive chestnut-colored sports jacket.

"Do you ever dress down, Thomas?" she asked.

Lee shrugged, but he was obviously pleased someone noticed how he dressed. "Not if I can help it. Archie's the one who could use some tips in that regard."

He picked up a menu and began to read. Archie sipped his beer, rubbed an eye socket with a fingertip. When the server came, they ordered.

"Just for the record," Archie said. "I thought I dressed fine."

"You're dressed for the Eagle Wing, which is your go-to place, so I guess you do."

"Leave me alone. Besides, I've decided to cut out the casino. I'm no longer a regular there."

She nodded, got serious.

"Tell us what happened with the prosecutor today. How's our evidence holding up?"

Archie's face clouded. He shook his head.

"That depends on whether we're talking about the two women, or Morris Denton. For the present, Tessa is a Murder One, and Emily, so far, an accomplice to the fact. The prosecutor thinks we should dial the first back to Murder Two for Tessa, and I agree, given the circumstances."

Cal Fricke wandered over from the bar and sat down. He'd lost weight, but he still carried considerable poundage. The legs on his chair screamed as he plunked down, the ball game he'd been watching over now.

"Explain," he said.

"This is as near as I can figure out," Archie said. "She planned to kill Helerstone that night, and he obliged by showing up at the rendezvous drugged. For her, revenge was the motive."

"Helerstone shot Stella Picard who was Tessa's sister," Patsy continued. "This is a theme. Wasn't Sophie's story that Denton killed *her* sister?"

"So she said, but Sophie's backstory gets more and more shaky all the time. She wanted Denton, all right, but I'm not sure why."

"Let's get back to Helerstone," Frick said. "Do we know why he murdered this young woman?"

"The three anthropology professors worked as a team. She threatened to expose them, probably as part of a scheme to get money, to blackmail them. The profs were in pretty deep. They started with grand theft and forgery, but they wanted to expand their operations. From their point of view, Stella was a risk and they murdered her. Helerstone did the deed, maybe directed by Aberle as Coyote. I think they did some weird ritual stuff afterwards, that's how messed up they were."

"And Denton?"

Archie's food arrived, and he set to work on his salmon dinner. After a day of meetings, he was tired of talking anyway. Plus, he needed to eat. Fricke gulped a mouthful of beer, waiting. Finally, Patsy continued the story.

"Archie's theory is this," she said. "The academics needed reach and muscle since the things they planned to steal, duplicate and replace were in various places around the world. Denton filled that role. He attended the gangster training school Bobby Carpenter's father and Archie's father ran in his youth. They kicked him out because he tried to take over, so he went out on his own. He built up his Cannibal Society with fake freaky ceremonies to keep his thugs in line, but the professors fell for it too, liking the theatrics and the rituals, and the drugs, of course. Aberle has already experimented with shamanism and, being the guy with the ideas, he soon took over. Denton and Foley became his lieutenants, I suppose. Then Helerstone wanted out and seemed to be cracking, especially after he visited him. They planned to scare the wits out of him with shaman magic and drugs, but that scheme miscarried. Ron somehow got away from them that night."

"And his death," Fricke said.

"Tessa told Helerstone to meet her," Archie said. "Don't ask me how he slipped free of his two colleagues, but when he did, she met him in a pre-arranged location, put him in his vehicle and guided him to a place at the bluffs where Emily was waiting. By that time, Helerstone was unconscious and the two women saw their chance and sent the SUV over the bluff. When Tessa went down to the vehicle to check, she discovered that Ron was still alive and shot him with his own gun."

"Archie zeroed in on Emily Frizzell right away," Lee said. "Because of the note."

"I remembered her using a fountain pen. She always used a fountain pen. It was an affectation of hers, but when I interviewed her, I saw no such pen and asked myself why that might be. The cat hairs on the blanket sealed the deal."

"And the land scam was mostly Helerstone and Foley, right?"

"Aberle mostly. He started Skeleton Resources, bought President Dhillon, bought Martin Demio too. Almost all his investors were offshore, so it made it easier to fudge legality. He put on a performance, just like he planned to do with Helerstone to scare the crap out of him. He brought in money people, sequestered them, showed them the property and the plans, introduced them to Dhillon and so on."

The conversation ebbed. The Pickled Walnuts, a local blues band, was preparing to rehearse for an evening show. Members of the ensemble filed past the police table with instruments and electronic equipment and made considerable commotion doing so. String Johannsen, the leader, stopped by to say hello, and that took a while. When he left them, they ordered more food and drinks and talked of other things. After a time, Fricke brought them back to police business.

"So, how did the remains of the young woman get in the burial cave?" Fricke asked. "Did you figure that out?"

Now wishing he were somewhere else, Archie tried to put him off. Talk of the cave and the part Emily played in it made him sad.

"I'll brief you on it later."

"I'd rather you told me now. This is all going to fall in my lap once I'm back at work."

"You're the boss, boss. Tessa and Emily first wanted to get Helerstone arrested, because he was the one who had pulled the trigger on Stella.

Emily already knew of the murder, but she was too afraid to do anything about it, even though the thought of it tormented her. When Tessa came along searching for her sister, they got to know one another. Emily fell in love with her. Somehow she found out that Stella's remains were hidden in the second burial cave, the one John Robbie showed me. The two women retrieved the bones, wrapped them in the Chilkat blanket and put them in the Edenshaw box. I'm still trying to figure out how she came to have these items. Anyway, the big cave was more accessible, so that's where they put her. When I thought Tessa was putting one over on me by acting scared, now I think she wasn't pretending because, by that time, Dave Ghent was watching her closely. He was another one of Carpenter Senior's protégés, by the way."

"I'm still not clear on how the original note fits in," Fricke said. "Or who attacked you when I sent you to Velasquez Island."

"Well, Stella had to be found. Emily knew me, so she addressed it to me. I think Bobby was my attacker, but we'll probably never know for sure."

Fricke grunted.

"Word is Larry Aberle is not going to be quite so easy to convict. The prosecutor is worried. Our evidence there is not too strong."

"Can we not just eat?" Archie said. "I'm tired of talking right now."

"Yeah. I'm out of here anyway. It'll all be in your report, right?"

"That it will."

Fricke grunted his way to his feet and left. Thomas Lee had another appointment and he departed soon after, leaving Patsy and Archie, once again, alone and awkwardly silent.

"The hospital says John Robbie's doing better," Patsy said.

"I visited him, and he's on the mend. It's good."

"Sophie Anderson is okay too, isn't she? Did you visit her?"

He didn't answer, wasn't sure why, except he didn't want to be interrogated.

"It's okay to tell me," she said. "There's no romantic relationship, commitment or anything with us. I'm just curious."

He hesitated, wasn't going to tell her that he couldn't get *her* out of his mind. He had been attracted to Sophie, but not like he'd fallen for Patsy. And why, he thought, shouldn't he be interested in other women? She'd just made it clear to him *again* that there was nothing between them and, after all, she'd been dating Stacy Gillot. He crossed his arms over his chest and leaned back in his chair.

"I'll get the bill," he said.

"So you won't tell me?"

"No, I won't. I will share one thing with you, though."

"And what would that be?"

"Sophie Anderson wants Morris Denton for some reason. She told me she planned to kill him if she gets a chance."

"And you believe her?"

"Maybe. She's a woman without a past, except she's Denton's daughter. I asked Thomas to research her, and he thinks she was CIA, or something like it. Anyway, I'm just as happy Denton's in a cell in Rochville where they've got better security than we have here."

He called for the bill and prepared to leave. She tilted her head, peered up at him from under her brows, a fetching look, hard to resist.

"Can you sit down for a minute? I have something to say to you."

He hesitated, but, really, he knew he had no choice but to hear her out. He eased back into the chair he'd just vacated.

"If you're going to scold me for something, I won't be sticking around."

She brushed a curl back from her forehead, sighed.

"I'm not going to criticize you. Far from it. I just wanted to say I think we ought to give it another try. What do you think?"

"Patsy," he said. "I don't know …"

Before he could finish, his phone chimed to alert him to a text. He shrugged and shot her an apologetic look. She nodded. He read the message through—not good news. When she asked, he read the message to her, the upshot of which was that Morris Denton had been released from custody in Rochville that afternoon. Although he was supposed to be under house arrest, he had disappeared almost immediately, driven away in a car from a rental agency. Patsy stared at her feet, obviously deep in thought. Her face was set when she lifted her head, tension tugging the corners of her mouth.

"Do you believe what Sophie Anderson said about killing Denton?" she asked.

"I sure do. She will hunt him down."

She swore.

"Then I have to tell you that Sophie called me yesterday afternoon, and I helped her rent a car."

"Why the hell …?"

Patsy drummed her fingernails nervously on the tabletop.

"Because she said she didn't want to call you because she had feelings for you but it would never work and she needed to get away. She asked me if I understood, and I said I did. She said she didn't want you to try to make her stay. She appealed to me woman to woman, and I fell for it. She played me like a fool."

Archie leaned forward.

"Call them up and find out what kind and color car she got. We need the plate number too."

She did as he asked. He waited until she finished.

"A black Honda," she said. "I've got the numbers."

"Call in the details and put out an APB. We have to stop her. Let's get out of here. I have an idea where she might have taken him."

CHAPTER 53

Archie guided his reclaimed 4Runner into the empty streets of the university housing development where he'd spent a night with Sophie. Patsy sat beside him, occasionally chewing her lip. Lee rode in the backseat.

They passed the burnt foundation of the house from which Archie had escaped and continued along the riverfront where the larger houses were situated. At first, when they turned up nothing, Archie began to doubt his reasoning, but Patsy spotted the tailend of a dark Honda in the tumbledown garage of a once-luxurious rancher. Archie signalled the squad cars following them to stop and wait, and then he parked the 4Runner a hundred yards from the house. The three of them got out, pistols ready, and walked across the weedpatch lawn.

They went cautiously; Archie and Patsy creeping up to the front door and taking positions on either side of it, Lee circling round to the rear. When Lee signaled he was in position, Archie reached across the jamb and rapped on the door. When he got no answer, he knocked again. This time, the unlatched door swung inward. The two of them ducked inside, carried on though the darkened vestibule and into the living room with its expansive picture window. A silhouetted figure stood framed there.

As Patsy brushed past, pistol ready, two loud shots rang out, accompanied by muzzle flashes. Archie dropped to one knee and fired. Beside him, Patsy unloaded a clip, a deafening rattle of gunfire. Their bullets struck home. The shape swayed and fell over sideways. Archie reloaded and rushed to the fallen form and stopped. Patsy hit a light switch.

Archie laughed, reached down and picked up the hat stand that had formed the body of the dummy and stood the thing back up. The *Ts'onaqua* mask, which had surmounted it, rolled to one side. Patsy reached down for it and held it to the light, showed Archie the two bullet holes through its cheek. Slugs had also torn through the cedar bark cape that had covered and completed the dummy. Lee, who entered through the back, pointed to an electronic relay taped to the wall.

"Fires off bangers," he said. "Set off by a motion sensor. Cute."

Archie slid his pistol back into its holster.

"Check out the other rooms and the basement. I'm pretty sure we've been had and she's not here."

They left him to search, and uniformed officers arrived to help. Archie, a familiar exhausted feeling returning, slumped down in a decrepit easy chair and rubbed his face with his hands. Moments later, Lee and Patsy came back. She handed him an envelope with his name written on it.

"This was pinned to the back side of the door."

He released his breath in a loud puff and opened the note.

Patsy said. "What does it say?"

He handed it back to her and she read it aloud.

"Dear Archie,

I wish we could have met under different circumstances. I really like you, but I have a job to do. Sorry about the gag with the dummy and the bangers. I couldn't resist — this note on the front door either. I hope you get a chuckle out of it.

I'll be gone when you read this. So will Morris Denton. Don't bother searching for him.

Take care, Archie,
Love, or something like it,
Sophie."

Lee put his gun away, shrugged his sports jacket into a perfect lie.

"I'll be darned," he said. "Now what do we do?"

Archie laughed.

"We go to work. We got people coming up for trial, we have a fugitive to chase down, and an abduction to investigate."

"What you should do is take a holiday," Patsy said. "You look like hell."

"Gee, thanks," Archie said. "You're joking?"

"I agree with her," Lee said. "We've got several weeks of grunt work ahead before you need get involved. Think about it."

"Sure, and what would I do with myself. If I'm not working, I got nothing."

"Then work. Go fishing with your Uncle Tony for a week or two," Patsy said. "Just stay away from the Eagle Wing."

"It's good advice. I'll call my uncle. Now, let's get out of here."

They stood outside a moment, enjoying the evening calm. Patsy came up beside Archie and linked her arm in his, elbow to elbow. Lee crossed to his other side and did the same. Together they walked towards their vehicle.

The End